LISTENING TO VOICES

LISTENING TO VOICES

Sara MacDonald

HEADLINE

First published in 1998
by HEADLINE BOOK PUBLISHING

10 9 8 7 6 5 4 3 2 1

British Library Cataloguing in Publication Data

MacDonald, Sara
    Listening to voices
    1. Mentally ill women – Fiction 2. Suspense fiction
    I. Title
    823.9'14 [F]
    ISBN 0 7472 2218 5

Printed and bound in Great Britain by
Mackays of Chatham plc, Chatham, Kent

HEADLINE BOOK PUBLISHING
A division of Hodder Headline PLC
338 Euston Road
LONDON NW1 3BH

In memory of my friend Julie,
and my mother Margaret.
For summers when it never rained.

for love is strong as death; jealousy is as cruel as
  the grave;
the coals thereof are coals of fire, which hath a most
  vehement flame.

The Song of Solomon viii, 6

Chapter 1
Hester

I lie curled on my bed facing the open window. The curtains are blowing in the wind and the sun shines on to a bowl of flowers on the window-sill and makes an arc of light on the polished floor.

I lie very still hoping they will forget me, that they will not shout up the stairs for me to go down to breakfast. The curtains have big fat pink roses all over them. Wendy and I were allowed to choose the material. Wendy has gone down to breakfast. She is excited to be leaving. She is going back to live with her parents in Putney.

She says she will miss me but she will have her parents to talk to now. I close my eyes and shut out the sunlight and the fat pink roses. Behind my shut eyelids I see the flat I am going to. It is on the ground floor and it is brand new, much nicer than my old flat. I never liked the high rise, never got used to the smell in the lifts.

Melanie says it is a new beginning, a chance to put the past behind me. To concentrate on my future. She says I am not alone, that I will still see her and the psychiatric social worker regularly.

But I will be alone. There will be no one else in the flat. Wendy won't be there to have a laugh with. I can feel the tears start at the corner of my eyes, then my body starts to shake and I can't stop. I am afraid. I am afraid of being alone. I am afraid of thinking about them

1

together. I am afraid of those voices whispering on and on inside me.

I don't understand. Why do I have to leave? I'm all right here and I haven't finished my pottery yet. Melanie says it is called 'Community Care'. She says it will be much better for me to have my own place, my own independence. She says if people are here too long they become dependent and institutionalized and that is not a good thing. I only know I like it here. I feel safe.

Something will get me out there, I know it. It is dark and horrible and it is waiting. Here, I don't have to fight it, it goes away and leaves me alone. I try to tell them, I try to explain to Melanie that this dark thing will get back inside me, but all she says is, 'Hester, of course you are afraid, that is perfectly natural. You have been here on and off for nearly three years. Of course you are afraid about how you will feel living on your own again.'

She fiddles with the pencils on her desk. 'It will take time for you to adjust and we are here to help you. But you have proved yourself perfectly capable. You have coped well at your halfway house, Hester, in fact you have been able to help Wendy and some of the others. You should be very proud of yourself.'

Suddenly, I know it doesn't matter what I say or what I do. A door is closing in my face and I am on the other side. I thought Melanie was my friend. 'You are not inadequate, Hester, you have been ill. You have suffered from severe post-natal psychosis which went untreated and while it is hard to diagnose exactly what your illness is, we have discovered that it is most likely hormonal or chemical and can be treated successfully with antipsychotic drugs. As long as you take your medication there is absolutely no reason why you can't lead a normal life in your own surroundings. You won't regress, Hester, unless you stop taking the drugs. You do understand that?'

'Why won't the drugs take my memory away?' I ask.

2

Melanie sighs. 'We have been all through this in therapy, Hester. You have to put the past and its memories behind you. Accept them. Stop apportioning all the blame to your ex-husband and accept that your illness, which has been treated and something you could not help, was to blame for the breakdown of your marriage. Not you, Hester. Your illness.'

I never ever got her to understand that my husband made me into what I am now.

I make myself unroll from the bed and go to the window. In the sunlight I feel warmer and less afraid. I realize suddenly no one cares what happens to me. Not once I've left. Not even Melanie and her tired face.

From tomorrow I can do as I like. From tomorrow I don't have to do anything I don't want to do. I shake my head which always feels muzzy. If I want my head to be clear I won't take the pills. Who will know? I can just take more the following day and stay in bed and sleep.

Below me is the garden where I grow nasturtiums and sweet peas. Someone else will pick them now.

Chapter 2
Anna

Amaranthus caudatus. Love lies
Bleeding. A plant with pale green
leaves and crimson hanging flowers
in summer and winter. Amaranthine.
Imaginary unfading flower.

The letter lies on my desk. The words on the lined paper are as sloped and misshapen as the content. I stare at the incoherent, unfinished sentences full of a chilling confusion and bitterness and I have a glimpse of the glittering madness of Hester's make-believe world.

Fascination fills me, as if I have glimpsed amid those illiterate rantings something immensely hypnotic. The feeling is as frightening as her words on the cheap paper. The moment in the dusty room leaps out and I know that a relentless campaign against Ian, Jessie and me is about to begin.

My office is the summerhouse at the bottom of the garden and faces out on to the greenhouses and tunnels. Beyond the greenhouses lies the creek. I stare at the cobwebs round the window and the silver trail of a snail across the dusty wooden floor. Outside, a blackbird sings his heart out. I go to the door and look out on to the garden I am creating in stages like rooms. It is private and isolated and randomly beautiful, as important to me as the inside of my house.

As I stand there looking out, a seagull swoops and dives

5

into my pond and comes up with Jaws, the biggest of the golden carp. I shout in horror and run flapping my hands and the bird drops the beautiful fish on to the lawn, bloody and heaving, a gaping hole in his side. I run to the outside tap, fill a bucket, run back and lift the bleeding slippery fish and drop it into the water. Pointless. Jaws lies dead.

Shaken, I go back into the summerhouse. Hester's letter has blown to the floor. I pick it up and push it into a drawer and make my way to the greenhouses. Nowhere is ever safe.

I watch Jessie, my stepdaughter, walk up the drive from school. She has that sexless gait of an awkward teenager, emphasised by the huge Doc Martens on the end of long skinny legs. Her shirt hangs outside her school skirt and her wild, wiry hair springs out around her hot sulky little face as she approaches the house. I pour hot water into the teapot and put a large white loaf on the kitchen table with jam and peanut butter. Jessie might have tea or she might go straight to her room until Ian gets home.

'Hi,' I call as she comes in the back door. 'What sort of day?'

She sniffs and looks at me. 'Awful. Double games.'

Jessie hates games or anything which requires being upright for too long. She throws her bag into a corner where it folds into itself in a heap and she collapses at the table.

'This for me?'

'Of course. Tea or a cold drink?'

'Tea please.' She begins to cheer up. 'This bread is still squishy. Mm.'

I have given up trying to serve wholemeal. Life is hard enough with GCSEs and a stepmother, without imposing my dietary disapproval. There is silence as she munches. I am learning not to try to fill these silences, not to rabbit on or try too hard and she volunteers after

6

a while, 'You know Lily from school who lives on a farm? She's asked me for the weekend. They have cousins coming from up-country and they are going to have a big barbecue.'

'Sounds fun. Are you going?'

Jessie licks her fingers and looks straight at me with Ian's pale blue eyes. 'I'll talk to Dad about it when he gets home.' I am thus dismissed and she leaves the table, picks up her bundle and goes banging up the stairs to her room. I push some chicken into the Rayburn and go back to the tunnels. Monday is always exhausting as two flowershops collect early on Tuesday mornings.

When I married Ian I had this silly little fantasy of Jessie and me companionably pricking out after school. Friends, as she helped me repot for pocket money. I did not realize then that every stepmother has to be a wicked one to assuage the pains of the past. Like blotting paper, a stepmother is useful for soaking up all the blame and bitterness a real mother leaves behind her.

Suddenly, with my hands in moist soil, I miss the twins very much. Looking back on my other life it seems that boys were less complicated. I put Radio Three on. Behind the trees the creek glistens on a high tide and a strange, sad feeling of dislocation fills me.

I yearn suddenly for the past when the boys were small and filled my world. I was so often on my own it seems as if I did all my growing up with them. Lonely, an eighteen-year-old naval wife in foreign places, too timid to explore, I would get up and go to bed with them. They filled my young life and the loss of those familiar, part-of-me human beings will startle me with its pain.

Sometimes, when I am sitting with Ian and Jessie having a meal, I will look up and see two strangers and I will wonder who I am. I am in another life now, with another man and child and I will feel for a moment bewildered.

What on earth am I doing here? Listening to Mozart

among the familiar smell of foliage, I am not sure of the answer.

Ian is coming home. I can hear the old Saab on the creek road long before he reaches the house. I should have gone back up to the house long ago and peeled potatoes, yet I go on standing in the greenhouse watching the sun setting the water behind the trees alight.

After a while Ian weaves his way through the trees down the garden to me carrying two glasses. 'Hello there!' He calls, 'I thought you could probably do with a drink. I stopped off and bought some gin.'

I laugh and we kiss. 'Wonderful!'

'How are you doing?'

'Nearly finished. Quite a big order tomorrow, which is good.'

Ian looks at my grimy hands. 'Did Alice turn up today?'

'Yes, thank goodness, but she had to leave early for one of her demos.'

We both know I could do with help every day but we cannot afford it and have to make do with unreliable Alice twice a week.

'Jessie is doing the vegetables for you,' Ian says, as if I should be grateful. I am irritated. For me? We are all eating, aren't we?

I take a large gulp of gin and tonic. We both know that he had to go and winkle Jessie out of her bedroom and that she is at the sink with bad grace.

Suddenly I feel deathly tired and tearful. The feeling swoops like a shadow, like the sun going in. Something must show on my face because Ian puts his drink down among the seedlings and reaches for me. Pulls me to him and folds me in in one neat movement. He is a big man and I relax against the largeness of him for a moment with relief. Close my eyes against the tears. I feel all the things he cannot say to me. I feel his past in his hands clasping the small of my back and in his fingers between my shoulder blades.

8

I feel his fears for the future in his head bent sideways on mine beneath him as he gently rocks me and I try to reassure him in the stillness of my body against his. The moment is precious and silently acknowledged between us for we are rarely alone or we are too tired and busy for words.

The moment is broken by Jessie running down the garden calling, 'Where is everyone? The potatoes are boiling and I've stirred the chicken. I'm starving . . .'

Ian jumps away from me as if we are illicit lovers. 'We're just coming.' He moves quickly towards her and out into the evening. I check the temperature of the greenhouse and follow him, shutting the door behind me.

Before I follow them I check all the greenhouses and tunnels, then go to lock up the summerhouse. Something makes me take the letter out of the drawer and read it again.

Whore. No money and sick. Left with nothing after bad. No help to be alive in hands as I have. My husband should feed me. Jessie hates you not happy needs good food lots of liver. Jessie mine you a thief. I'm alone men come drunk and I've no money taking my husband and child. Hate you whore you took I'm left nothing.

Poor Hester. I push the letter back into its cheap white envelope, back into the larger brown DSS envelope from where it has been forwarded. Social Services have been warned by Ian never to let Hester have our address. Then I shut the drawer firmly on it.

The lights from the house stream down the garden. Looking in on lighted windows from the trees I see two heads bent laying the table. Two people Hester lost. I am on the outside. I am the stranger. They are all bound by flesh and blood.

Chapter 3
Ian

My new office faces the cathedral. I glimpse the bulk of it out of a tiny arched mullion window, casting a shadow of mellow honeyed stone and faceless gargoyles over the room. The white paint is still drying and the only things in the room at the moment are my black swivel chair from college days and an old oak architect's drawing board I found in a sale.

It pleases me, this room, the space and light is cool and still.

Another small square window looks down on to the street and a central wrought-iron staircase connects all three floors. I am on the second floor. Nick has the first and two secretaries and a fat YTS girl, who types rather badly, have the ground floor which doubles as an entrance and waiting-room.

We have been lucky to get such a prestigious and central position, especially with our finances. It was previously a teashop, but Nick knew the owners, who were happy to negotiate a short lease while they took three years out in New Zealand, travelling and visiting their family. Part of the deal was Nick and his wife fostering their two black Labradors.

The cathedral clock strikes six. I told Anna I would be home early and I am not going to be. There is no real excuse either. Why have I begun to be reluctant to go home? Things are good. I'm happy.

Perhaps it's a throwback to my life with Hester. The daily horror of not knowing what on earth I was going to return to.

I take a last look round and visualize exactly where I am going to put things. I'll get Anna to organize me a large green plant for between the windows, some sort of palm thing.

Excitement flares for a second, I'd almost forgotten how much I enjoyed setting things up, getting them running.

I think back to my previous large modern open-plan offices, buzzing with people and noise. So many of them. I remember with a shudder the possibility of Hester striding in, eyes wild, shrieking accusations at some poor little typist or secretary. My skin crawls with embarrassment even now, after all these years. Giving up jobs I loved and was good at because my position in a firm became untenable. Always moving on.

The poor sod with the mad wife, that's how I was known. Yet I have met other men with unbalanced wives who ruined their careers. I'm not unique.

One more look before I go down and lock up. The miracle of being safe, able to become established, at last, at bloody last. A normal life for Jessie and me. And yet . . . I feel disappointment. Unfairly.

I had such hopes of Anna for Jess. Anna cannot seem to find the time for Jess. A bit of mothering and time is all Jess needs.

I suppose I want things to be normal, as in normal two-parent families, and of course they can't be. Anna is not Jessie's mother. It is just I had such hopes. I knew Jess was desperate for female company, for a substitute mother, I knew puberty was coming and I just couldn't cope.

Jess has retreated, like she always does, to the safety of her room, making a little rat's nest up there, doing God knows what. Anna does not try hard enough. I do know that. The boys are away, there are no children to compete or be jealous. Jess is so needy, I can't understand it, I thought it would be instinctive in a woman to reach out, and yet I believe somehow she thinks it is up to me to cater for Jess's needs and of course I can't. I'm a man and I have my work.

I catch myself out with a sudden lurch of guilt. Anna is keeping us all at the moment. She is working every hour God made so I can buy into this partnership.

I stop off at the off-licence and buy a rare bottle of gin. A peace offering, a treat. A celebration of hope. Sometimes I am unsure why Anna married me.

As I get back into the car I suddenly see on the passenger seat the bundle of office mail I haven't yet opened. Sticking out of the elastic band is a brown DSS envelope.

I sit still for a moment staring at it, quite unable to reach out and open it. The traffic noise is all around me and yet in the hot airless car I feel the familiar sense of silent desperate isolation.

Hester. It has to be about Hester. How on earth did I think for a moment I could be free of the suffocating endlessness of her?

With her unerring sense of timing, mad but instinctive, she will fuck me up again.

Chapter 4
Hester

The flat still smells of paint. The walls are sort of yellow and the paintwork white. It looks nice. I was allowed to choose some of the curtains, I was given some money and Wendy and I and one of the occupational therapists, called Linda, went and got them in British Home Stores. Pink check for the kitchen and a sort of gold for the lounge. The bedroom already has flowery curtains so I couldn't choose those.

Linda left us having a British Home Stores' breakfast while she went off somewhere. It was very good, sausages, bacon, the lot. Wendy say I'm lucky having a new flat all to myself.

'I don't want it all to myself,' I tell her. 'Why don't you come and live with me?'

'They wouldn't let me. They told you, Hester, it's a one bedroom flat. I like my own bedroom.'

'Well, I could get a sofa-bed thing. You could have the bedroom.'

'They wouldn't allow it, Hester. I've got to go home, my parents are expecting me.'

Wendy always says, 'They' all the time, it makes me cross.

We go back to my new flat and we all have a cup of tea. My social worker is waiting on the doorstep. She is new. I think her name is Jane or Janet. She is tall and thin with frizzy hair.

'We'll have to organize some more cups and things, Hester,' she says. 'Here's to you and your new flat and lots of good things.' She raises her white cup and I see small chips like little teeth round the edges.

'I wish it was gin,' I say and they all laugh. Then we put up the curtains and they look lovely. Linda and this Jane, Janet, keep saying how great everything looks and how it will look like home and cosy, once I have got my things around me, pictures and photos and stuff.

'I haven't got any things,' I say. 'I don't know what happened to all my things.'

Suddenly they all have to go. Wendy is going home today too, but they have to go back to the hospital first to fetch her things. Linda takes Wendy and I wave to her until she turns the corner. My chest feels tight like I can't breathe. I want to run after them, I want to shout, 'Come back. Don't go. Come back, come back here.'

The social worker is watching me. I don't think I like her. She goes to the sink and pours some water in a glass and opens my bottle of pills.

'I've stuck a little note on a cupboard door, just to remind you to take them, Hester. It is so important. You know that, don't you?'

I don't answer. I take the pill.

'I will be round tomorrow to see how you are doing.'

But she does not go. She stands looking at me in the way people always do.

'Hester, it is going to feel strange at first, being out of hospital and on your own again, but you are going to have lots of support. I've left you contact numbers, so you can ring us.'

I am looking at her, she is turning for the door. 'I could make you another cup of tea.'

She smiles at me. 'Thank you, Hester, but I really have to go.'

Suddenly she comes back into the room and puts her bag down again.

'Tell you what, let's make sure your television is working. This one is only for the time being, we'll get you a better one later on.'

It comes on straight away. *Emmerdale* is on. I like that. Me and Wendy always used to watch it while we had our tea. I pull a chair round. This is quite good, I can choose any channel I like without getting shouted at. I don't have to take turns choosing.

Jane, Janet is saying something. 'I realize it is hard . . . New flat . . . New psychiatric social worker . . . But I am here to help . . .'

I put the volume up. I can't hear what's going on. 'See you tomorrow. Goodbye, Hester.'

I hear her feet go clop, clop, clop down the path. I can hear them even over *Emmerdale Farm*.

Chapter 5
Anna

Chamaemelum nobile. Chamomile. The
leaves have a spicy fragrance when
touched or trodden on. Good for paths
or small lawns. Flowers are small and
white. Infuse at night to induce sleep.

In bed Ian suddenly says, 'Hester is out of hospital. The
social services have re-housed her. Part of Community Care.
I had a letter from a DSS solicitor. Hester says she cannot
manage on the money she has coming in and they are taking
me to court for more maintenance.'

I digest this for a while but do not say anything. There
is nothing to say.

Ian suddenly thumps the pillow. 'My God, Anna, when
will it end? She has had everything I have. It just goes on
and on down the years, like a never-ending nightmare.'

There is a break in his voice and I turn and touch his arm.
'I had a letter from Hester today. Her envelope was inside
a DSS one. It was incoherent.'

Ian sits up, looking horrified. 'I rang and warned them
about keeping our address and telephone number from her.
I will not be hounded again, Anna. I will not move or change
my telephone number again.'

He runs a hand through his fair greying hair and turns
on one elbow and looks at me. 'She is going to be much

worse this time, now that I have you.' He lies back with a sigh. 'Hester's psychriatic social worker believes that, with the new drugs she's taking, Hester is capable of leading an almost normal life. What it probably means is, left to her own devices, she will forget to take them.'

He looks at me. 'I expect the social services want to recoup some of the money spent on her treatment. I'm seeing Anthony, my solicitor, in the morning. I've been divorced for so long I don't think the courts could make me pay more.'

But fear fills me. My house and garden, my small business could be at stake. My sister wept when I married Ian. 'Oh, Annie, you are just getting it together. You are taking on damaged goods. You could lose everything. Why? Why?' Who can say?

Ian reaches out for me now and we make love with a passion and an intensity that is somehow isolating. He falls asleep almost immediately but I cannot. I gently move his arm from over me and get up. I pull on his faded blue towelling robe which is like a comforter and go into the small dressing room adjoining the bedroom.

It has a tiny single bed, a chest of drawers and a huge window overlooking the garden. Quietly I shut the door and turn on the lamp, a china lamp with two Victorian figures entwined. Ben found it in a junk shop. I love it.

My mother's old square mahogany mirror sits on the mantelpiece above the small black fireplace. Around the wide edges of this mirror are photos of people I love most. They are all dead, but here I feel near to them, here the ache of losing them seems less.

Photos of my mother holding a grandchild, sitting in her garden. My father, long dead, in RAF uniform, mowing a lawn. June, smiling, holding a glass in every picture. If I bend towards the photos of her I sometimes catch the echo of her laugh.

There is Ben, looking young. Ben in naval uniform. Ben

receiving his wings. Ben with his helicopter crew. Ben in the garden of another house of another life.

At the top of the mirror the twins at university, very much alive, thank God, grinning out at me with their father's smile. Photos of them backpacking through India, in the garden of that other house in that other life that was so suddenly taken from me.

I touch my sons' faces with my finger and smile. Then I get into the narrow schoolgirl bed and turn the lamp out and lie in the dark on my back. Peace comes as it always does. Beyond the wall I hear Ian gently snoring. It is a comforting sound and I feel sudden affection for him well up inside me. Outside an owl hoots on the granite gateposts beyond the window under the huge cedars.

How I love this old lodge house set among the trees and, beyond the trees, my secret gardens down by the creek.

The house creaks and settles around me like a familiar and favourite shawl and I feel myself drifting into sleep.

Chapter 6
Ian

I turn on my back. The owl woke me up. I'd like to get out of bed to watch him on that granite gatepost but I'm too lazy. The house creaks like old houses do and the silence is measurable.

Why does Anna do this when she thinks I am asleep? Slide off into that bloody little room, a shrine to her past perfect little life?

The door is firmly shut. Does she cry in there for her dead husband? Does she long for her boys to be home? Those arrogant twins, who, as far as I can see, have wanted for fuck all. Am I jealous? Perhaps. I feel defeated tonight.

I'm middle aged, starting a firm up when I should be established and comfortable. Starting another marriage when I should probably have known better. And worried about my daughter. Is she still wetting her bed? I dare not find out. I suppose it must be all right because Anna has not said anything.

What if it is genetic and Jessie becomes like Hester as she develops?

I would have loved a son.

Women are so powerful in their neediness, their femaleness, their need for constant love and attention. Their disappointments. Their disappointment in me. That fucking look in their eyes like a kicked spaniel. It makes me cruel. It makes me withdraw. It turns me totally off.

I bang the bloody pillow trying to get comfortable. Why? Why do women always, always want more and more than one can give them? Suck you dry with their terrible neediness.

A son wouldn't bleed. Wouldn't have hormones that dictated his life.

Is this why I resent Anna's twins and their cocky happiness? Full of confidence and lust for life. Freedom and privilege, security and love. A life I will never have with a son.

I turn over and try to shut out my familiar demons but they remain on the edge of my mind. It's extraordinary how grim life can be at four in the morning.

Marrying Anna has made me realize how life could have been and I ache for the possibility of, the total loss of, a normal family life.

And yet. And yet at this time of the night when honesty faces only me in the dark, I have to acknowledge myself in all this. The truth of myself and the dictates of my life.

I remember my father. How cold he was with my mother. I don't know whether he was always like it, or the war left him like it. I remember him looking long at her with an unfathomable expression which one could have taken for dislike, except he was never rude, they never had rows.

I can still see so clearly her nervousness of him, her anxious clearing of the throat when he was around. I despised her for trying to please him all the time, avoid all individuality in an effort to be loved.

I colluded with him in many little cruelties. I was his son, the important one. Even her beauty seemed an irritation to him, for with it came her needs, her femaleness, which he found impossible to fulfil.

He died when I was sixteen and it was only then I began to love and admire all that my mother was. Without him she blossomed, and thrived and grew in confidence and stature.

24

'Your father was one of those men,' she told me once, 'who loved women but did not like them.' An odd thing to say. I did not understand it.

Do I love Anna? Yes . . . I do.

Did I marry her for the right reasons?

I don't know. I don't know.

I thought we could make it work.

But she is needy. Jess is needy. I am tired of women's needs. I want to concentrate on my architecture, my own life. I thought I could hand Jess over, that Anna would make it all all right. Let me get on with my life.

But I don't think Anna is going to let me.

Or Hester.

Chapter 7
Anna

Nigella damascena. Love-in-a-mist.
Wispy deep green foliage and pink,
white or blue flowers. Persian Jewels
are mixed. Miss Jekyll is sky blue.

I am up at six and, when the van for the shops in Truro
has collected my plants, I call Hebe, a small rescued Jack
Russell, and walk up the drive to the woods. Trevillian
Lodge which Ian and I bought when we married was part
of the Trevillian estate. The manor house at the top of the
drive is derelict, burnt out in suspicious circumstances in
the early 1900s.

The house is Palladian and strange and beautiful. I love
standing at the gates and looking up the drive, full of vast
rhododendron trees, where squirrels rush up and down and
birds scuttle into the undergrowth.

The windows gaze back with unseen faces. The stone lintels
are full of growing invidious creeper and purple wild flowers
caught on a breeze and flourishing. White crumbling stone
pillars give the house a dignified air, but it stands wistfully
as if it is waiting, holding its breath, to be reclaimed.

I squint up at it, imagining the rolling stretches of lawns
and formal flowerbeds and often, as I stand, a fleeting
intangible scent will reach me on the wind and a shadow
will pass over the overgrown lawns as if someone passing

is wearing a strong perfume. The mystery of the burnt-out house always rises like a form of excitement inside me, stills something dark in me.

Years ago when I drove over here to see friends in the village, the boys used to get spooked, or pretend to. Once, as teenagers, they came up here for the night and camped in a nearby field with schoolfriends but had returned hastily, hushing each other at midnight, apparently insisting they had seen a ghost.

I have no doubt the house is haunted but its atmosphere is not threatening, just achingly sad.

The woods behind the manor house are a different matter. They run down the side of the creek, bend round an overgrown lake full of herons and along the bottom of our garden. These woods do not feel benign. There is something crouched and malignant about them. Walking here with Hebe my flesh will sometimes creep and I will turn, heart thumping, at the sound of breaking twigs behind me. The rabbiting dog will come rushing back to me, the hair on the back of her neck like a ruffle.

Yet I cannot resist these woods because they are full of wildlife, full of self-seeded shrubs which I take cuttings of. If I am quiet in late afternoon or early evening I can come across foxes and badgers. Rare birds over-winter by the lake or stop off on their flights south. Anyone can be frightened in dark shadowy places. These woods are so ancient they are bound to hold time and atmosphere in a restless, rustling grip.

I skirt the lake and today Hebe happily dips in and out of the undergrowth. Ian is seeing his solicitor today. I push my unease away. I know, deep in my heart, that even if Hester does not win this round there will be another advance from another quarter we won't have thought of. Ian has convinced me that the unbalanced have innate cunning.

As I walk, unable to be unhappy because the day is so beautiful, I think how predominant Hester has been for an unseen presence in our marriage. How powerfully she has affected the two people I now live with. Their lives are like a jigsaw I piece together over the years. They want to forget. I want to understand.

As I round the lake I see a cormorant sitting on a dead tree trunk holding his wings out for the sun to dry. There is only the soft scuffling sound of birds in the undergrowth, the faint sound of falling twigs and the movement of the wind over new green leaves, translucent in shafts of slanting sunlight. Underfoot I am careful not to crush wild violets and the last of the fat creamy primroses.

When I first married Ian, Jessie wanted to talk and talk about Hester. She seemed unable to stop, it was like an incessant flow. She would wait for me outside the lavatory, outside my bedroom door when Ian had gone to work. For weeks and weeks I listened until I thought my head would burst with her bizarre tales.

Tales of being left forgotten in shops and bus shelters. Tales of Hester placing quantities of frozen pork chops in patterns on a sofa. Of her sudden rages and obsessions. Of Jessie and Ian waking and finding her asleep in the garage or curled under a tree. And later, much later, when Hester and Ian were separated, she would loom suddenly out of the night, face pressed against a window, frightening Jessie half to death.

I comforted, I tried to give reasons, to rationalize what I didn't understand. I gave sympathy and hugs in abundance. I showed horror and admiration for her endurance. Jessie, not Ian, was my priority. It was like a honeymoon with my stepdaughter.

Then, all of a sudden, I realized Jessie was looking to me to provide an answer she could live with, one that would take her forward. I understood the underlying truth that a bad mother is better than no mother at all. Jessie began to cite incidences of Ian's anger and frustration with Hester. Jessie wanted me, Anna, the stepmother, to say out loud, that maybe Ian had contributed to her mother's behaviour. For her mental deterioration, her bad mothering.

This is what Jess needed to believe as time went on. As she grew and realized her father did not tolerate fools gladly and could be cold and indifferent, unable to cater for her insatiable emotional needs.

Hester suddenly disappeared out of their lives one afternoon, leaving Jessie on her own at a railway station, surrounded by a sea of shopping. Ian had been called out of a meeting by the police to take a huddled and frightened Jessie home. Hester had walked away without a second glance or a word to her six-year-old daughter.

She had waltzed in again nine months later, in at the back door announcing she had sausages for tea as if no time had elapsed at all, and perhaps for Hester it hadn't.

Ian was never able to get Hester formally diagnosed during his marriage to her. He said that, like so many people suffering from mental illness, she became adept at appearing perfectly normal at assessments. He was told that she had a personality disorder and he would just have to live with it.

I couldn't bear to listen any more. I was beginning to feel traumatized myself. I was in unknown territory, an alien landscape. I hadn't bargained for this. I began to shut myself off. I cut Jessie off, hid from her. Once, desperate for peace, I hid under a bed. Anywhere I could not hear that insistent little voice calling, 'Anna, Anna. Where are you?'

Thus, in one fell swoop I forfeited Jessie's friendship and let her down by denying her her voice in the wilderness. I hid from her and from my feelings. I tried to breathe in space and fresh air to face the sudden reality of my marriage to Ian. There is no excuse for how I behaved. Jessie is just a child and I am a grown-up.

I suddenly felt as if I had married Jessie not Ian. Ian let me take the brunt in those early days. Relief made him selfish. 'Thank God, I've got someone to take Jess over,' he breathed. Anger at his sacrifice of me hardened my heart. To survive those early weeks of marriage I closed my heart to Jess.

Some hope in her for validity must have flickered like the frail flame it was and died. I woke one morning and she had retreated. We were no longer friends. All I felt was relief. Ian had sacrificed me. I had sacrificed Jessie. Now, I feel aghast at my coldness, at my irresponsibility in extinguishing that burning hope she had in me that I might be able to expunge the past by some magic explanation, and of course, by loving her, Jessie, above all else.

I can never live up to Jessie's expectations of me or of this marriage. She viewed her father's remarriage as purely for her, another chance of being mothered. I do not have the resources to cope with the problems Hester has left. I have my own nightmares. I was and still am out of my depth where she is concerned.

I knew Jessie needed counselling but Ian violently opposed any outside interference, refused point blank. If you don't admit there is any damage it is not necessary to take action.

I had a choice. I could try and make this tricky marriage to Ian work, or all my energies could be concentrated on a damaged child. I couldn't do both. I chose Ian who I had married with hope. Ian, who I thought would take the shadows of Ben's sudden death away and who has brought me shadows of his own.

As I reach the house the phone is ringing. I run to catch it but when I pick it up and say 'Hello,' breathlessly, there is silence. I wait in case it is one of the boys in a tricky foreign call box and, as I wait, the receiver on the other end is replaced with a click.

Chapter 8
Hester

Janice is the name of my social worker. Janice something Brown. Hardy-Brown, that's it. She looks even taller today, her hair is down and she has had a very bad perm. She won't give me my husband's address. She says she has to trust me not to be disruptive first. For Jessie's sake. Silly cow.

She says she has a date for the court hearing. It is 17 July and I have to travel to Truro with the solicitor they have appointed for me. Janice says she can't be there because she is in court in Birmingham.

She looks at me. 'Would you like me to write to your ex-husband, Hester, and suggest that a meeting be arranged for you to see your daughter while you are in Cornwall.'

'*She* won't let me see her,' I tell Janice.

'You don't know that, Hester, now do you?'

I look at her. I hate her with her frizzy hair and that silly little girl voice.

'Did you post that letter I gave you?' I ask.

'Yes I did, Hester. Is that what you asked? If you could meet Jessie while you were in Cornwall?'

'No.'

Janice gets up to leave. At the door she says; 'Do you want to see your daughter, Hester, or not?'

'What do you think?' I ask angrily. She is a silly, silly, patronizing cow.

She is staring at me. 'I want to be sure that it really is

your daughter you want to see and not an opportunity to get at your ex-husband.'

I am so angry I can't speak. I can't look at her. She comes back into the room a little way. 'Hester. You progressed so well in hospital. I'm anxious you don't slip back. You are taking your pills, aren't you? Only if it's a problem remembering, you can come in once a month and have an injection, it might be easier for you.'

I get up and smile at her. 'Of course I'm taking them, I know it's important.'

Janice smiles back at me. 'Good. I know it must seem like interference. As if we are infringing your rights, checking up on you. It is only while you settle into the routine of living on your own again, Hester. But you must take your medication exactly as prescribed. You do understand that, don't you?'

I understand all right. They want to control me. Leave me on my own but control me.

She turns for the door again. 'I'll get in touch with your ex-husband and suggest a meeting with your daughter. See you at the day centre on Thursday.'

She trips out and climbs into a cherry red Fiesta, pulling in her long skirt around her so it doesn't get caught. She looks just like a hippie.

I don't want to stay inside. I hate the silence. There is no one to talk to. I see my pills by the teapot. They are bright yellow and green. They dry up my throat and I can't wake up in the mornings. I'm sure they are not the same as the ones they gave me at the unit, I felt all right there. I am certainly not going to take them every day.

I open the bottle and take the one I am supposed to take at teatime and wash it down the sink, in case Janice counts the next time she is here. I may take two lots tomorrow and sleep all day if it's raining. Now I want to go out.

I go to the bus stop and wait for a number 7 bus. I wait ages and when it comes I forget where I am going. I have to think and the driver sighs and goes on to someone else, telling me to stand aside. The sweat starts to trickle down the inside of my arms. When everyone else has got on and paid he turns back to me. 'Where to, then, lovey?' he asks and I suddenly remember and smile at him.

'Shrub Road,' I say.

When I get to the house she is out. At bingo, I expect. She doesn't know I still have a key, hidden safely. I go inside and put the kettle on. I look around. It is all exactly the same. How funny it's the same when I've been away so long. I open drawers to see if I can find out what she is up to. What I can find.

She is clever, that one. I find what I want. It is taped to the inside of a drawer, at the top, right at the back where no one would think of looking if they didn't know. A small folded piece of paper. When I have copied what it says on the back of an envelope I replace it carefully where it was before.

I know her hiding places. When I was a child I saw her put a letter there. It was from an army man stationed near by. It was a love letter. I took it to my father. He was a good man, he deserved better. He told me never ever to spy on people or read their private letters. He said every person in this world had a right to privacy. He made me put the letter back exactly where I had found it.

He never said anything to my mother. He never shouted at her or punished her. That was wrong. She never knew he knew. He just became gentler and sadder. Bit by bit. I got very angry.

One day he committed suicide. It was all her fault. It was my mother's fault. I will never forgive her, ever. But I paid her back. The kettle boils and I go and make some tea. Then I put the cup exactly where it was before.

Up in the bathroom I find a small bottle of 4711 lavender water. It was my father's favourite. I put some behind my ears and then drop the bottle into my bag. I go back downstairs and let myself out. My mother will never know I have been here.

Chapter 9

Anna

Myosotis. Royal Blue. Forget-me-not.
Likes sun or partial shade. Clusters
of small blue flowers which seed
themselves.

I set off for Truro along the creek road. It is a high tide and
the day is going to be hot. The mist hangs over the water
like a dramatic theatre curtain.

It still feels odd not to be meeting June for coffee, for
lunch, for haunting the shops like country cousins on a day
out. Missing her does not get any easier. Why do I think it
should? As if she can be replaced, or the hole she leaves in
my life filled in.

Suddenly I find I am turning, leaving the creek behind me
and heading cross country in the opposite direction to Truro.
The thread of our friendship remained as tight as ever even
when I was living in some naval quarter the other end of
England or we were abroad. We swapped beautiful cards
every week of our lives no matter where we were. I have
thousands and thousands of them. They tell a story of our
unfolding lives together over the years.

Many of them now line my summerhouse or are in little
glass frames on the walls. We had been friends since the
boys were five years old and we moved into her village and
bought the house backing on to her garden.

37

The sun climbs higher as I drive along these familiar tiny roads and I have that poignant, sad feeling of wishing I had known how much I had then. I know these lanes well because I used to help June deliver her plants. She specialized in rare exotics and I have seen some wonderful gardens behind seemingly derelict cottages.

I turn and take the old Helston road to Penzance, realizing that I must have intended to come this way all along.

Ben had been posted to RNAS Culdrose and the cottage we bought behind June was our first and only house. Up until then we had always lived in naval quarters. I wanted roots. I needed to know that whatever quarter I was in I had somewhere to return to.

As I come near to the village I cross the dual carriageway and there is the sea glinting on my right. The tide is in and the estuary filled and my heart rises with the old joy of returning. For a moment I can feel that I am still that other woman of long ago, hovering in some timeless zone. The past hasn't happened. If I will it enough I can be there again. Anna again. As I was when the children were small. When Ben was alive. When June was part of my life. When my mother was on the end of a phone. When my life was small and narrow and safe.

I drive through the village, glad of my shorter hair and sunglasses, glad of my thinner frame. I don't want to meet anyone I knew, although the only people likely to remember me are Isobel and Bill at the Post Office.

I park by the church and walk down the narrow path to the beach. Red flags are out by the steps that lead on to the beach and a stiff breeze is coming from the sea whipping the waves in a full tide. I cannot get round the point so I take the coastal path over the dunes and down on to the long stretch of white sand.

How many walks have I done with boys and golden retriever on this beach? In the shadows the clouds make on the sand I see the ghosts of two small boys and a fussing dog running along towards the waves, disappearing in the shimmering light from the sea. Vanishing into the shadow of the cliff with the pink haze of St Ives above them. Vanishing into the youths they are now.

Tall, confident young men travelling in a group some-where in India, taking a year out after university. They might at this moment be lying on some island beach. Or maybe they are still in Nepal teaching English at the Tibetan school. Perhaps they are sitting in some cafe writing me a postcard. I laugh at myself, wishful thinking.

Just lately I keep thinking back more and more to the past. To things we did as a family, places we went. Remembering the joy we had in discovering Cornwall and being able to think of it as home.

June was always here, keeping an eye on things when we arrived back from a posting, so happy to have us home. She had never married or had children of her own so my children became hers and they loved her unconditionally.

When Ben was killed and our cosy world ended abruptly, the boys and I huddled together behind closed doors and curtains for days. I wouldn't let my mother or sister come. I wouldn't let anyone take the boys, I couldn't bear them out of my sight. They were fifteen but we all slept together, shell-shocked, for a week in the huge king-size bed Ben had loved after endless nights in sleeping bags. We lay numb and unbelieving, crying and clutching each other in the hopeless dark.

June let herself in with her key one morning, quiet and firm. She opened all the curtains and threw the windows open to the sun. She made the boys shower and dress, took them next door with her and cooked them a huge breakfast. Then she sent them off to the beach with her dogs. She came back and ran me a bath and brought me strong coffee and buttery croissants. She sat on the stool beside the bath and gently told me to get a grip, for the boys' sake, if not for my own.

I heard her downstairs throwing all the drink in the house

into the dustbin. That made me smile as I knew it would hurt her like hell. She came back upstairs and grinned at my face. 'We'll be dry together for a while, until we get the arrangements sorted, Anna. We'll do it together.'

Then her face wobbled and collapsed and her whole body shook and I held out my wet arms and we clutched each other sobbing our hearts out. She too had lost the love of her life. Ben had adored her, calling her his number one girlfriend, bringing her presents and scent from abroad, playing the endless games of Scrabble with her that I hated. June was a part of us all and I loved her almost as much as my mother, more than any other human being apart from Ben and the boys.

I walk towards St Ives, the wind whipping my hair. A fishing boat comes out of Hayle and sets out to sea, brightly coloured, the fishermen in yellow sou'westers. It looks like a child's fat little painting.

Four weeks after Ben's funeral my mother was rushed to hospital. She had had a massive haemorrhage. They removed a tumour and sent her home. She was amazingly brave and stoic confronted by a sudden death sentence.

I brought her down to Cornwall for three months and, after some initial reserve on her part, for she was a little jealous of June's place in our lives, she and June became firm friends. When she returned home they wrote religiously to each other. 'Oh, I wish I had a June,' she would say wistfully. I wished she had too.

When Ben died I began to spend hours in the greenhouses and tunnels in June's field adjoining her house. I have always had green fingers but I was a haphazard gardener. June taught me the Latin names for things and how to grow plants properly not randomly.

She taught me to propagate and graft, to nourish and fertilize. She taught me everything I know, encouraged me month by month to do more and more until I was more or less running her business. Much later I realized how unwell she must have been. Caught up in my own selfish pain I did not notice hers until too late.

Three years later, when my mother was in the hospice June cared for the boys and my house and got help for my fledgling business. She rang me every night I was away and sent her beautiful cards for the ten weeks it took my mother to die.

When it was all over, after the funeral and the house had finally been cleared and put on the market, I returned over the Tamar haunted with the memory of my mother's tiny body disappearing, sinking into the bed, hardly an imprint on the laundered pillow case. And the sun on those cheerily crocheted counterpanes casting her ghost-like into shadow.

There was such relief and longing to be home that the tears poured down my cheeks as I drove over the bridge back into Cornwall.

June was watching out for me and rushed out taking my face in her hands. 'Now, my darling, you must heal and have peace. We will both do special things together. I've missed you so very much.' And she hurried me indoors where a gin stood waiting.

It was then I noticed her weight loss. 'Oh, don't fuss, my darling, I've just had a bug.' But as she poured a second gin I noticed her hands were shaking.

She refused to go to see her doctor, so one day I rang him. Well used to June he sighed. 'I'll call in socially as I pass to go home. But I can't demand she come and see me, Anna.'

When he came he took one look at her and told her to eat more and drink less and to go into his surgery for some blood tests. She told him to sod off.

She rang me suddenly in the middle of one night sounding frightened and wavery. Rushing round I found her disorientated and strange. I rang an ambulance immediately. I went in it to the hospital with her and on the way she began to scream with pain. They rushed her straight into intensive care while I waited in a corridor. When they finally let me in she was wired to tubes and a mask was over her face. She was slipping in and out of consciousness.

Utter selfish panic seized me. Frantically, I whispered, 'June, you can't do this to me, you can't. You can't leave me, you can't die. Do you hear me? Fight . . . Fight. We need you, please, June. Please, I'm begging you.'

Her eyes opened for a second and she saw me. I leant towards her. 'I love you. I love you, June.' Her hand came up and moved her mask a fraction. She smiled at me, mouthed, 'Love you too.' And died, her colour draining away so fast my mouth fell open in disbelief.

I heard someone making terrible little moaning noises and nurses clustered around touching me. 'Is it your mother, dear? I'm so sorry . . . It was very quick wasn't it?' I stared at them blankly, realizing the noises were coming from me.

I turned and ran out to where the boys had come for me in their battered old Volkswagen. The noises had stopped. I didn't say anything to them, just asked them to drive me here to this beach. Then I ran and ran away from them because I couldn't hold the scream in any longer.

I screamed and screamed and sobbed and yelled at the sea and emerging morning. I ran and shrieked like a madwoman and when the boys tried to catch me I kicked out at them. 'I hate you, God,' I screamed. 'I hate you, hate you. Who are you going to take next? Come on then. Take everything I love. Take bloody everything.'

I punched the air and swirled around, getting my feet wet, anger filling me. 'How dare you, June? How bloody well dare you die and leave me? You had no right, you had no right to die. Do you hear me? Do you bloody well hear me? You had no right to die.'

Then I turned and saw my sons at the water's edge in torn jeans and ponytails, two lanky bookends, crying silently, not knowing what to do and I stopped crying and walked up the beach to them, ashamed.

My hands are sweating. I grow cold as I remember. I sit in the shelter of the sand dunes and I feel strange not knowing why images of death are surfacing faster than I can quell them.

Coming here feels like I do before I leave my house to go away. I go around touching all my precious things in case I might not see them again. Am I touching my sons in the same way? Here is my past where I was happy before death touched our lives. Am I touching these moments in case they disappear?

Is it Hester? Is she casting a shadow that chills me?

I sigh. This is silly. I start to walk back to the car. I make myself drive past our cottage where someone else's washing hangs and there is a different coloured rose around the door. I turn past June's large house and stop in the drive and look up to the house. It needs a coat of paint. It looks just the same, but I see the greenhouses and tunnels have disappeared and a pony stands in the field.

I conjure up the tiny figure of June in the inevitable wellingtons she always wore. I conjure her smoky laugh and the image of her passing me a gin and tonic through the hedge. I drive quickly on down the saltings, turn and head back for Truro.

I met Ian when June's house finally went on the market. He was a large sad-eyed architect. An interesting man. He looked at June's house but, like me, could not afford it. Both boys had just gone to university. The house was very empty and he filled a huge void.

But I know, deep in my heart, I know I would never have married Ian if June had not died. She was such a huge, important part of my life. I could not accommodate, could not accept, the loss of all the main people in my life.

June had meant to leave the house to the boys. She left the land to me for my lifetime, but she somehow forgot to file a codicil about the house and a distant relative in Australia inherited the house which now had no land to go with it. The estate offered me a good price and I sold.

Now, I wonder why I did not throw myself into my gardening, build up my business, work until I dropped. Expunge the pain with my hands in the earth. Paused. Instead I leapt into the middle of lives that disturb me deeply.

I pull myself up. Cull my thoughts firmly. Whoever said second marriages were easy? I knew about Hester before I married Ian. I suppose I just thought in my vague way she would remain in a place of safety for ever. That I would not be affected.

I turn left and suddenly in front of me is an anemone field, a mass of red and blue stretching uphill to the sky. My spirit soars. I leave the glittering green sea behind me and excitedly make plans. This time next year if I can buy the two fields the other side of the creek, I too could have anemone fields.

Chapter 10

Ian

I have not told Nick yet about Hester. I know I should, he's a good friend of such old standing. I just know how I would feel if it was the other way round. I would be terrified Hester would find out where we worked.

It's also a question of professional integrity. I do not want Nick regretting offering me a partnership or believing that having a court case coming up might affect my ability to get things up and running.

There is a huge Sainsbury's going up near the by-pass and we have put in a tender. Of course there is a lot of competition, but if we got it, we would establish ourselves.

There are four of us: Nick and I, as partners, and two younger architects we took on and have left at the old premises. Nick has worked for this particular firm of architects for nearly fifteen years and, when one of the senior partners died and the other wanted to retire, he asked me if I wanted to buy them out, go into partnership with him.

The two old boys ran a highly uncompetitive practice so Nick and I have spent two years virtually building the business up, changing the name, style and getting in young blood. Nick has organized a working lunch for the four of us but I am having difficulty concentrating today.

'How's that delightful wife of yours?' Nick asks as we eat. To Nick, everyone is delightful. 'What a delightful man, client, child, dog,' he will declare at intervals.

Ever since we were at architectural college in Oxford together, I have envied his totally sunny disposition.

'Extremely busy. She hopes to expand next year, buy two more fields and perhaps put Alice in a little shop a couple of days a week, sell our own plants. But it all depends on how well she does this year.'

Nick grins. 'Delightful girl, that Alice. I met her when I went to pick up Pud's plants.'

Pud is his wife, and I cannot for the life of me remember her real name any more. They have a chaotic, happy lifestyle of relative poverty as, a) they choose to live in Cornwall and b) they choose to send two sons to public school.

Nick asks suddenly, 'Everything all right, Ian?'

I look at him startled. 'Of course, why shouldn't it be?'

'Just you seem edgy today, a bit preoccupied.'

'Sorry.' I have to tell him, I see that.

'I'm told second marriages can be tricky . . .'

'Nick,' I say quietly, making sure the other two are deep in conversation. 'It isn't that. It's Hester, she's out . . .'

'Oh, for Christ's sake, Ian, after what happened?'

'She is on medication and supposedly cured. You know Care in the Community, all that . . .'

'Crap! The community doesn't care. Does she know you and Jess are down here?'

'No! But the DSS are taking me to court on her behalf for more maintenance, so she will know eventually. But I have insisted she never has our address or telephone number. She won't find out where we are, Nick.'

He stares at me. 'She always has before, Ian.'

'I know. But she is supposed to be stable, Nick. She has been on drugs and had counselling and therapy. Also, the DSS are duty bound to make sure she does not know where we are.'

Nick is angry. 'They should keep her where she fucking well belongs, in an institution.'

Nick has never been politically correct. I feel sad all of a sudden. 'That is hard, Nick, people do get cured.'

Nick leans forward and lowers his voice. 'Look, don't get me wrong, I'm not being self motivated in this, Ian. You are not in a big organization now and we are all capable of dealing with any embarrassment Hester might cause. I am just fucking anxious about you. God knows how you stuck your marriage for as long as you did. You are just getting established again. You've got a new marriage to think about. Just make sure she doesn't fuck things up for you again, for God's sake.'

'I've no intention of letting her anywhere near us, Nick. Unfortunately, we have a child and I cannot prevent her wanting to see Jess, which she will . . .'

'Just to get near you?'

'Yes.'

'Does Jess know she is out?'

'No, not yet, I'm about to tell her.'

We have to leave the conversation and get back to general topics. I am conscious of the other two listening now. 'Just keep me informed, Ian. I know you. You will withdraw and cope on your own. Just remember Pud and I have known you a hell of a long time . . .'

It's true. A hell of a long time and how the friendship survived Hester I will never know. Hester could not bear me to be fond of anyone else and was extremely rude on the few occasions we met up.

Hester also knew that Nick had been totally against the marriage. Hester was one person Nick never found delightful. When I met her she had been waitressing in Oxford at night and working for the tourist board during the day. She was very, very pretty. Skin so peach-like and thin you could see the veins underneath. Irish colouring. Somehow vulnerable in a way I could not fathom.

I only knew she touched me deeply and I felt an almost immediate love and instinct to protect her. She wept bitterly when she spoke about her father's death and her impossible relationship with her mother who disliked her. When I met her mother I believed all she told me because I felt her mother's antipathy to Hester immediately.

Hester seemed to have so few friends and I could not understand it, for she was so attractive and vivacious.

Nick could not seem to tell me why he disliked her. 'I don't trust her,' was all he would say. Or, 'Ian, have you not noticed how possessive Hester is? You've only known her a few weeks, she seems to have taken you over.'

I thought it was a bit of male jealousy. Nick was between women at the time and I had less time to go to the pub or cricket with him.

Just before I married Hester he tried to get me drunk. It is the only time we have had an argument. 'Please, Ian, wait. There is something wrong. Haven't you noticed the mood swings? Surely you must have.'

'It's living at home. She can't bear it, and I don't blame her . . .'

'No! Ian, for fuck's sake, listen for once in your sodding life.'

'Listen to what?' I knew my friends were not keen on Hester. I thought it was a class thing, she did not fit in with my group and it made me feel even more protective.

'Please don't get mad. Please try to believe what we have all been trying to tell you for weeks. Hester has slept with half the university and most of the college.'

I remember clearly it was all I could do not to hit him. 'You are just fucking jealous! Sod you all. You can all stay away from the wedding, I will find another best man.'

And I did. And they stayed away.

I asked Hester outright. Tears had welled up in her eyes, she had been astounded and hurt.

'I suppose,' she told me gently, 'it's about the worst thing you can say about someone if you want to put your mate off.'

Within months of our marriage, I learnt later, long before the baby and post-natal depression brought out her inherent

48

insanity, Hester slept with neighbours, builders, plumbers, anyone. She even tried the doctor once and had to be transferred.

We pay our bill and leave. I say goodbye and walk across the square as the cathedral clock strikes two o'clock. I have an hour before I meet my solicitor.

I smile wryly to myself. Once, I got her to a psychiatrist. A woman.

'She's got what is called a personality disorder,' she told me coldly. 'Like other people in your situation, you will just have to learn to live with it, I'm afraid.'

And so I did.

Chapter 11
Hester

Yesterday they brought me a new television. 'I'm afraid it hasn't got a zapper,' the man says. 'You have to get out of your chair to change channels.' He laughs, he has big yellow teeth. 'OK, then?'

'Have a cup of tea?' I say.

'No thanks, love, I have another couple of calls to make.'

When he has gone I wonder who he reminds me of. Then I think of my father. He's a bit like my father. He has set the aerial up for me and everything, and I switch it back on. There is a black and white film on about a little girl who is deaf and dumb and to get her to speak they make her press her mouth to balloons and make sounds and she cries.

It is very sad and it makes me think of Jessie and suddenly I realize it is a message. The television came today so I could watch this film. It is a signal. I must go and ring Jessie. I go to the nearest phone box but I have to wait ages until someone is finished, then I put a pound coin in and dial the number from my bit of paper.

The woman answers, not Jessie. I listen to see what she sounds like. 'Hello?' she says. She sounds as if she has been running. 'Hello? Hello?'

I listen to her waiting. I hear her breathing down the phone, then I put the phone down very carefully. 'We'll see, Mrs Posh Voice, we'll see.'

I go out of the smelly telephone box and I feel sick because it was so hot in there with the door shut. There is no green anywhere. I think of the hospital and the garden and how I planted seeds with Wendy and the ache starts inside me. If I was still there Wendy and me would be having tea together. I think about the park but it's too hot to walk there.

I look in my purse and I've got ten pounds so I go to the Spar on the corner. I buy mince and ice-cream, then I remember the Oxo and I have to go back to get it, then I remember potatoes and veg. The people behind me start to tut so I tell them to get lost and the girl at the till laughs so I tell her I'll report her if she does that again.

I go back to the flat and switch the telly on loud so I can hear it while I make tea. As I make a cup of tea I see my pills, so I take one. I can't remember if I took one yesterday or not.

I remember Ian's mother had a posh voice too. He took me to Durham once to meet her. They thought I had gone upstairs, but I listened at the door.

'Oh, Ian,' she said. 'I can see she's pretty, but, my dear, you can do better than that.'

The buzzing starts in my head as I remember the way her voice sounded. I can hear her voice clearly and the way it made me feel.

I heard Ian laugh his cross laugh. 'Mothers never think anyone is ever good enough for their sons! Give her a chance, Mother.'

And his mother said, in that snooty voice, 'Background matters, Ian. You may think it doesn't, but I assure you, it does.'

'It doesn't matter a jot, Mother, not a bloody jot,' I could hear Ian hiss at her in case I was coming back. I pushed the door open and went into the room and Ian put his arm around me, kissed the top of my head. 'Hello, darling,' he said. 'All unpacked?'

I looked at his mother and I smiled at her, Ian was mine now. She did not smile back, she just left the room.

Ian loved me. He used to hug and hug me until I thought I'd break.

Now, I'm going to close the cupboard in my head to stop the thoughts falling out any more. I don't want them all over the kitchen. I don't want to think any more, it makes my head ache.

The mince looks a bit grey but it tastes all right. I might buy a cook book. I eat in front of the telly. Before the pubs shut I draw the curtains so no one can see in, so I am safe.

Chapter 12
Anna

Thunbergia alata. Black-eyed Susan. A
plant for southern or western climates.
Needs sun and shelter. The flowers are
creamy yellow with a very dark brown
or black centre or 'eye'.

Alice is a lovely, feckless, free-spirited girl with an infectious
smile. She is totally unpredictable but when she does turn
up she works swiftly and delicately, her hands moving
competently to New Age music. She has a long dark plait
snaking down her back and exquisite olive skin owing
something to Spanish forebears.

She turned up one afternoon two years ago, with two small
children called Oak and Elm, to buy herbs and we talked about
plants for two hours. She was with a group of travellers who
were moving on and she needed to stay in Cornwall because
her parents were ill and she wanted to stay near them.

I took an immediate liking to her and offered her a
job with me as a joke because, as we talked, she would
automatically pull weeds from the pots in the tunnels. She
jumped at my offer but warned me she would be unreliable
as she was with a group of tree people campaigning against
an extension somewhere near St Austell.

Ian thought I was mad, but I could see he was charmed by
her. She is a bit like an Indian princess with her nose-ring,

hippie cheesecloth clothes and fey, faraway manner. Due to pot, I've no doubt. The plants love her around and so do I.

Sometimes a fair dreadlocked boy called Jake comes and picks her up in a pink camper van in the evening. He has Oak and Elm in tow and they take off, head for some surfing beach. On the days she comes I feel younger and more carefree. I think I envy her a little. Part of her is how I would like to be.

Today, at our coffee break, she says she will read the cards if I like. So far I've resisted. She takes them seriously and I can't really believe in them although I know she earns money from doing readings. I laugh. 'Oh, go on then.'

We are sitting cross-legged on the grass and Alice spends a long time shuffling the cards and asking me to cut. Eventually she starts to turn them over, absorbed, tongue on top lip and I smile at her concentration. I have told her very little about my past life.

'A man in uniform keeps coming up,' she says. 'Someone important?'

'Yes,' I say quietly.

'Two more uniforms. Two young men. Soldiers. Younger than the first man.'

Alice is rocking and humming as she turns the cards. 'This card signifies travel, journeys. They are far away. Your sons?'

Of course Alice knows I have identical twins who are away backpacking, the whole village knows, but they certainly are not in uniform.

Alice turns another card, then another. 'Two women here who love you. Both passed on. This card here is wealth. You will never be rich but you will never starve. This card represents something that is going to happen soon. A judgement or a small windfall. This one, discord, or anger, which is unresolved.'

Alice, still humming softly, turns the cards. The sun goes in and I shiver, reaching for my sweater. 'This card here . . .'

The humming stops abruptly and she covers the card quickly with her hand and, under her dark skin, I see her face has gone pale.

'Oh,' she says breathlessly, gathering the cards deftly up so I cannot see the one in her hand. 'It's a . . . a . . . warning,' she trails off.

I am suddenly cold and pull my sweater over my head and begin to get up off the grass. 'Don't look so worried, Alice, it's probably a warning to get on with some work!'

Alice reaches out and, surprisingly firmly, pulls me back down on to the grass. She is not smiling. 'Please sit still, Anna, this is important.'

From the middle of a nest of velvet she uncovers a crystal ball. 'Look, love,' I say gently, 'I'm not into this and I must get some work done.'

She is very still, gazing into the glass ball. When she looks up I see she is upset.

'Anna, I have to finish this reading. I don't want to, so there must be something you need to know. Please just sit still.'

I sit back on my heels reluctantly and wait. 'There is a picture of two young men with long hair near a temple or palace. It is hot . . . shimmering. They are happy. The older man in uniform has passed over. He is smiling, there is peace surrounding him . . . Now the young men are both short haired and in uniform again. Different uniforms. They are marching about on a cold, windy square in blue and gold and there is a big white horse going up some steps.'

Alice closes her eyes, is silent. Then she says, 'They are now in a strange and violent place with mountains. There are tanks and large snow-covered fields full of danger. The boy is crying because of something I cannot see. The other boy is in a helicopter and they are attacking something on the ground.'

Alice looks up at me. I am afraid now and hypnotized by her voice. 'The place is very evil. The boys are in danger, but the older man wants you to know that no harm comes to them. Your sons will be all right. They will come home safely. They will marry, have children, grow old. Life will not repeat itself. It will not.'

As I sit here in the still garden, the pictures Alice is giving me are as clear to me as if I am watching television. And I have no doubts at all about the truth of the visual images I have of my sons. For I feel Ben's presence everywhere in a thrill of excitement.

Alice is silent again, gazing into the glass ball. When she speaks again her voice is husky and tired. 'There are three people who represent a danger to you, Anna. The man loves you but is careless. The girl is troubled and unthinking. The older woman . . . The older woman . . .' Alice looks straight at me. 'The older woman wants everything you have, Anna. There are violent colours all around her representing imbalance and if she can she will take your husband and child. She will, Anna, and you must fight and watch your back for a very long time. Promise me you will be careful.'

Alice reaches out and urgently takes my hands in hers. There are two red spots high on her cheeks and she looks exhausted and afraid. Our eyes meet and hold.

Something has happened here this morning and I know suddenly that my long-buried fear has a name. 'I promise I will be careful.' We smile at each other and Alice topples over on the grass fast asleep and stays that way for half an hour.

I cannot doubt now that Alice has powers, for the images of my sons are so vibrant and strong. Disturbed, I walk up towards the house. Strangely, I do not feel fear. Alice is a gentle soul. The vibrations Hester gives out would upset anyone. If she glimpsed tragedy in her crystal ball, it was Ben dying at forty.

I look up towards the house from the trees. It stands in a glade with a slant of midday sun shining on the front.

From a distance I can see the pink haze of geraniums on the sitting-room window-sill framing the small tabby face of one of my cats.

White paint frames the original windows and flushes of red-leafed Virginia creeper softens the dark grey granite. My house. The place I live. It looks like a house in a fairy tale, surrounded by roses in bud and late camellias. Hansel and Gretel's gingerbread house in a wooded clearing, hidden from the world.

I stand and look up at it from underneath the monkey puzzle tree brought from the gardens at Tresco fifty years ago. I feel I am stepping into an illustrated children's story book to a perfection I have made that is not real. As if I have made up a story that cannot have a happy ending and I am now inside it, trapped, in an elusive completeness I cannot hold on to.

Am I about to lose all this? Is this what Alice saw? Some cruel throw of the dice that will make me lose all that I have for the upkeep of a madwoman?

Yet it is not the images of Ian, Jessie or Hester that fill my mind and heart. It is the images of my sons that makes my heart soar with a strange incandescent joy. They are as clear to me now as when Alice was talking.

It is as if I have received a long letter from them telling me of their plans. The feeling is just like the happiness a letter brings when you know your children are safe and well.

The boys and I sat and talked of their lives before they left for India. They knew, even with good degrees their career options are limited. Perhaps they have both decided to go into the forces already. Or perhaps I have had a glimpse into something they do not yet know. Liam will fly, like Ben. Dan, colour-blind, will stay earthbound.

I know that that terrible and violent place is Bosnia. But they won't be hurt. They will not die. How can I be so reassured of that? Because of Ben. Because he is here in the garden with me, in this surge of happiness, in this strange glimpse into something I don't understand.

Our sons will go on to lead happy useful lives. Standing here I feel as if I am floating just above the ground in an unreal state having had a privileged and wonderful rare glimpse into the future. As if I have had a private message from the people I love most, telling me something I could not otherwise know.

It makes anything else that happens in my life secondary and unimportant.

When Alice wakes she is her old self and we happily weed the tunnels to her pinkle-ponkle music. In the evening she goes contentedly off in her blancmange camper, hitching her flowing cheesecloth skirt above her grimy bare feet and waving to me cheerfully as she lights up.

As evening comes I begin to wonder whether Alice put anything in my coffee. The phone is ringing as I reach the house. I run to pick it up but again there is only silence. But this time I hear Hester breathing.

I go out to greet Ian as I hear the car turning into the drive. His face lights up as he sees me. I won't tell him about Hester yet, he has enough to cope with with this move of his.

'Wot! Not down in the garden?' He grins at me.

I bat my eyelids and flap my arms about like a hen. 'I am being the little woman and meeting you at the front door.'

Ian laughs and kisses me. 'How very unnerving!'

Chapter 13
Ian

The move has gone unbelievably well. We are installed. Away from the cramped conditions of my last office I can work a thousand times more efficiently. Sainsbury's representatives have come back to us. We are trying not to get too excited or get our hopes up, but they certainly seem interested in our tender.

The local county council have also approached us, they want to build a new sixth-form college and Nick and I are both working together on this as he is more conversant with planning consent down here.

I have had to start coming in earlier and going home later. Driving into work early has made me realize why Anna loves the mornings so, and of course, with no one to disturb me, I can get so much done before nine when the rest come into the office.

I should feel guilty not helping Anna more. In this heat the watering takes hours and she is looking exhausted. As I drive past the creek I glance to my right as if I might see her down by the greenhouses, but all I catch is the glimpse of the windows of the house. The sun has not yet burnt the mist off the water and the effect is eerie, like being enclosed in a thick blanket.

The interesting thing is, Anna and Jess seem to be getting on better. I have noticed Jess spends much less time in her room at the moment. Perhaps it's better if I am out of the way.

The other reason for working until I drop is that I don't have to think about this ruddy court case which is looming up like a fucking bad dream. I've had to dig into the loft to find my divorce papers for my solicitor and I deeply resent the time it has taken going over old ground with him.

There are things I want to forget. There are so many things I never ever want to remember and it is taking a huge effort of will not to shut myself away until it is all over. I do so as much as I can and I deeply resent Anna and Jessie's closed wary faces every time I emerge from my study.

Can't they just get the fuck on with it and leave me alone? I don't want to talk. I don't want to be sociable at meals. I just want to be left to my own sodding devices.

Seeing Hester again will bring it all back. The waste, the terrible waste of my life. The failure. Not just Hester. Me. The guilt that follows me down the years and will never leave me, for I am culpable.

Those first months of marriage. The only happy time. She was like a delighted child with a little rented house in suburbia, away from her mother. She would cook me lovely little meals. Surprisingly, she loved to cook. Eventually of course, it got out of hand and she spent far more than we both earned. Later, lethargy and drugs took away all her interest in cooking.

She still worked part time for the local tourist board and all I can remember of those early weeks is eating and sex. It was like being on an island, that first house. Hester and I against a hostile world, for she had a facility for making enemies which I could not understand, it seemed to happen so fast.

All I remember is I could not get enough of her body. The more strange she got, the more exciting she seemed. After sex she glowed like a child, her thin body clung like a limpet, she aroused me in a shocking and unnatural way.

I did not know then, in those early days, that making love for Hester was like having a cup of coffee. No more important than that. She had utterly no awareness, as if she had been born on another planet, that there was anything wrong in promiscuity. Like an animal, if you had an itch, you scratched it and it really did not matter with whom.

I was working long and hard, the virtual coffee boy in my first job in an architectural firm and she would ring me up all the time to ask me when I was coming home. She was lonely, she was sick, she wanted me. At first I found it flattering and amusing, this pretty little wife who could not live without my constant attention. Very soon I realized the obsessive, manic quality of it, but by then she was pregnant with Jessie.

A brief respite. Peace. Hester left work and blossomed, seemed content and excited about the baby. I pretended, in those early days, that she had never been unfaithful. I do not think she was during her pregnancy, but of course I don't know. I was papering cracks, desperately papering cracks to make it all right in my head. Because the reality of what I had taken on scared the shit out of me.

I watched the child grow inside her. Imagined the tiny skull and bones forming into a human being. I thought, this strange woman I have married is going to be totally responsible for this tiny life growing inside her. My child.

The random irresponsibility of human beings hit me even then, struck me as being wrong. You make love. You fuck. The biological time is right and a child is made, formed in your own image. No thought is given to the next twenty formative years in which this child will form his impression of life and will go on to make the next generation. A child again conceived, in love, hate, drunken stupor, or indifference.

Bloody terrifying.

I have not seen Hester for four years. Not since she was sectioned and stopped looming up out of the dark, lurching around our rented houses, peering in windows at Jessie and me. I do not doubt Hester loved me in her own way. Obsessive love, of course. Perhaps, if I am honest, no one has ever needed me or loved me as exclusively as Hester did in those early months of marriage.

I park the car, press the alarm and walk across a deserted early morning town. As I near the cathedral I have a sudden impulse to go in. I walk slowly up the steps and go into the shadowy interior. It is the end of choral communion and I slip quietly into the back and close my eyes to the music.

I can't pray. How can I pray to Something or Someone I do not believe in? But, just in case, I ask for help to get me through the time when I will have to face Hester and the flotsam of my past.

Suddenly, the pale face of Anna floats in front of me. Quiet, gentle and intelligent. Getting on with her life. Putting up with my moods, putting up with surly Jess. Awake before me, down in her garden, forever down in those gardens of hers. Creating something. Asking nothing.

I am stricken. I suddenly realize how much I admire her. All that she is and does. I can be such a shit. The thought of losing her makes an unfamiliar feeling akin to panic rise up, making my skin prickle. It's got to work, this marriage of ours. It's got to.

Voices. If only I could stop listening to the bloody voices in my head.

Chapter 14

Hester

On the train to Cornwall Mr Casey sits opposite me. He is quite young and stares a lot. He has bulgy blue eyes and he asks lots of questions. I don't think I like him. When I get tired of his questions I look out of the window and pretend not to hear him. He said it was unfortunate that Miss Hardy-Brown was not able to accompany us. He is frightened of women.

I walk up and down the train fetching coffee and I try to talk to people but everyone wants to read their papers. Mr Casey asks me questions like, 'How long were you and Mr Roberts married?' and 'I understand you suffered from ill health on and off during much of the marriage? Was he a sympathetic, understanding husband?'

Of course I tell him how I suffered. How Ian neglected me, how I was left alone for days and weeks with my baby while my husband had an affair with that woman. It makes tears come to my eyes just remembering and Mr Casey leans forward and looks sad. He says, 'Don't upset yourself, Mrs Roberts. I am going to do the best I can for you tomorrow. We'll see if we can't make life more comfortable for you.'

I don't mind some questions, but it is stupid him asking me about dates and money. It is stupid when I have been so ill. I look out of the window and ignore him.

Suddenly, there is the sea. We come out of a tunnel and

the train runs along a sea wall. The sun is shining on little boats and people are walking in the wind, blowing along a small beach. I press my face against the window and my stomach aches.

I remember. I remember I am out there on that wall with my father. We ran across the beach when we heard the train coming. 'Wave,' he called out laughing. 'Wave at those poor people in the train, Hester, while we are having fun out here beside the sea.'

I waved and waved and I saw little faces of people in the train and I thought I will never know who they are. I could meet one of them in a street and they would never know it was me on this sea wall with my father, waving and waving at them. When the train had gone, my father lifted me off the wall and I felt such love for him that I wound my arms round and round his legs and pressed my face against his prickly trousers. He looked down at me. 'What's all this?' he asked, laughing.

'Don't die,' I whispered into his legs. 'Don't ever die and leave me alone. Promise you won't die and leave me.'

He bent and gently pulled my arms from around his legs. 'I can't do that, lovey, you know that. I'm your dad and I'll die before you. But by then you'll have your own life, you'll be grown up and you won't feel like you do now. Now come on, I'll race you to that red sailing boat.'

But I did. I did feel like I did on the beach when he died. I was sixteen. He left me. He left me on my own with her. He shouldn't have done that. If he had loved me more than her he wouldn't have done that to me. I really thought he loved me more than anything in the world.

We are in another tunnel and the hurt is back and I moan because the noises are coming, a little rush of voices mumbling in my head. Daylight again and the sea is behind me. Mr Casey leans towards me. 'Are you all right, Mrs Roberts?'

I stare at him. His face is growing and growing. I stare

66

and stare at it. He goes red. 'I will go and get you a coffee, Mrs Roberts,' he says.

He gets up and goes away. I close my eyes, I am tired.

Why am I on this train going to Cornwall? I try to remember.

Am I going to see Jessie?

No, I don't know where she is.

I laugh suddenly, remembering, and the woman next to me gets up, gathers her things and moves quickly away up the corridor. I call out to her to try to explain but she disappears through the sliding doors.

I was only going to tell her that I'm happy because I am travelling to Cornwall with my solicitor. That my husband took my daughter away and now he has to give her back to me and money to look after her.

It would have been nice to talk to another woman about my husband and child.

I always find Jessie. I always find where Ian has hidden her.

Chapter 15

Anna

Althaea rosea. Hollyhock.
Alyssum maritimum. Sweet Alyssum.
Impatiens balsamina. Balsam.
Brachycome iberidifolia.
Swan River Daisy.
Gerastium tomentosum.
Snow-in-Summer.

I am surrounded by the last of the bedding plants. The air is dry, catching the back of my throat. The sun unable to burst through the thick layers of cloud heats the day obscurely from everywhere. I keep the sprinklers on all morning as the moisture keeps draining from the soil and the garden is beginning to resemble a garden in Tuscany.

The court hearing for the increase of Hester's maintenance is set for today at Truro Crown Court. Ian's solicitor wanted the case to be on home ground where he believes the court will be more favourable to Ian. Hester is appearing in person and we would all rather she stayed firmly in London.

As I water the plants my thoughts are with Ian. I should have gone to court with him for moral support, but the plants are my reason for staying away and I don't have any wish to see Hester in the flesh.

'I won't have to see her, will I?' Jessie has asked over and over the last few weeks. 'She is bound to want to see me, isn't she?'

'You don't have to do anything you don't want to do,' Ian told her. 'But your mother is supposed to be rational at the moment. It might be good for you to see her, Jess.'

'No,' Jess replied firmly. 'I don't want to see her.'

Surprisingly she had turned to me. 'Don't you agree, Anna? If she sees me once she will just go on and on wanting to see more of me. She'll never give up. She'll find out where we are and she'll appear at a window, looming up out of the dark at us, that's what will happen.' Jessie's voice had risen to a crescendo and I had been taken aback by her fear. Jessie has such contradictory feelings about her mother.

I remembered the letter and the times I have picked up a suddenly silent phone, something I haven't mentioned to either of them. Neither of these things square with Hester's miracle cure. If the imminent arrival in Cornwall of Hester does this to Jess, much better she stay away from her mother and I said so.

Ian had looked wistful. 'It would be so good if Hester has changed and you could have some sort of relationship with her, Jess.'

'Dream on,' Jess said. 'Do you believe you can have a normal, divorced relationship with her, Dad?'

'No,' Ian said quietly. 'I don't believe that for a moment. I'm afraid I'm dreading seeing her again.'

'Me too.' And they had smiled at each other, both looking guilty. For the first time I felt protection well up in me for both of them. They have had to cling together amid the wreckage Hester made of their lives.

When the vans have collected most of the bedding plants I go to the summerhouse. Everywhere is quite still and I wonder if there will be a storm. I make out some bills, fill in a few invoices but my thoughts keep flying to how we will manage if Ian has to increase his payments to Hester. I look up at the walls and June's cards, fading with the sun, look back at me.

Cottages and gardens, windows into rooms. Flowers.

70

People. A couple. Two fat people in a meadow, turned towards each other on their sides, bluebells at their feet, a haze of blue sky. Her dress is a Forget-me-not blue of a thousand washes. His shirt is white and his trousers the same insubstantial blue as the woman's dress.

They reach out towards each other with their arms and their fingertips touch. Just touch without being able to curl around the other's hand. In the position of their heads, lying facing each other on their curved arms, is a sadness that rises from that small postcard like a threnody.

Something like pain and wonder will start in my throat every time I look at it. 'Silent Noon' it is called. Mixed media. Who are those people who only just touch? The stillness of those recumbent figures turned towards each other is so poignant that I imbue my own loneliness into the bluey-green colours.

I walk up to the house to make a coffee. Ian has been very distant these last few weeks, retreating firmly to a place where I am not welcome. Polite, remote, burying himself in work. Looking surprised if I make him aware of me. Coming back from somewhere a long way in the past. Coming back a stranger. Looking at me with those cold blue eyes for a second as if he does not remember who I am.

I put the kettle on the Rayburn and put a piece of toast into the toaster and turn and look out of the kitchen window. Old trellis, disintegrating with the weight of sweet-smelling roses, forms a square outside the back door. I will have to replace the trellis soon but the new one will not look the same and I have put the moment off.

When the sun is out it shines through the trees on to this small square of sheltered roses, and the petals fall on the faded paving slabs like confetti. Beyond the square are the woods behind the house which are deep and thick. I can just hear the distant sound of cars from the narrow lane leading up from the creek road.

The sun cannot reach into the rooms this side of the house

71

but shines on the granite where a climbing pear climbs up the walls of the house and practically into Jessie's bedroom. The pear tree looks incongruous there, wrong. And I often wonder who planted it.

Jessie loves it and picked the rather dark little room because of it. She said the other rooms were not cosy and she liked small rooms. I turn and make coffee and butter my toast and walk up the stairs to the large front room which we have made into an upstairs sitting room. We can see the creek and it is sunny and light. My mother's mahogany table sits in the corner and both Ian and I work here where we can turn and see the water.

Jessie and I seem to have been closer these last few weeks, probably because Ian has withdrawn from us. We have chatted and walked together with Hebe and she has come down to the greenhouses to help me. I know it might not last. I realize, when Hester is safely out of the way, Jessie will probably go back to her old monosyllabic self, but it feels good to be friends.

I finish my coffee and before going back downstairs I suddenly go into her room, something I never do. The window is shut and the air stale. I throw open the window and notice her bed is stripped. I go to the bathroom but there are no dirty sheets in the linen basket. Odd.

I go to the airing cupboard and see there are hardly any clean sheets left. Back in her room I open her cupboard and they fall out, six dirty sheets smelling of urine. I want to weep. Oh Jessie.

She has put a polythene bag under the underblanket so the mattress is not wet. I pull the underblanket off and throw it into a corner and turn the mattress. I hunt for an old rubber sheet I know is in the back of the airing cupboard, then I remake the bed with the prettiest sheets we have.

I fill the washing machine and go out and pick roses from the trellis. Fat red roses, deep and wondrous as black holes. When their petals begin to unfurl the colour lightens

72

and turns to a translucent scarlet as they offer themselves to the sun like blowsy good-time girls. I mix them with a virginal single white adolescent and a creamy country cousin climber, put them in a vase and take them upstairs.

I know that Jessie will only glance at the vase, but if I pick them with love, security might filter into the room and into her sleep. As I place them on her bedside table, I look up and see a movement in the woods, a quick suggestion of a blurred face and then it is gone. The hairs on the back of my neck rise sharply. I look out into the blackness of trees and tremble and do not know why I feel such sudden fear. The woods are private, part of the unsold Trevillian estate, but people do go in there surreptitiously to shoot rabbits.

I go downstairs and shut and lock the back door. I take the cordless phone with me. Normally I never do this. I have as much business as I can handle and friends ring in the evening. But I have a feeling Ian will ring me during the day. I walk down the garden to the tunnels and the sun suddenly comes out burning the thick heat haze off the sky and I am calm again, in sunlight, happy as I weed to some Gregorian chants.

After an hour or so the phone bleeps at me making me jump. 'Hello,' Ian says. 'Are you up in the house? I didn't really expect to get you.'

'No, I'm down here with the cordless in case you rang. Why aren't you in court?'

'Hester hasn't turned up and, as we can't proceed without her, we've been switched with a custody case. I don't know why I didn't expect this. Her solicitor is rushing around like a headless chicken trying to locate her by two.'

'How did he lose her? He must realize she is unpredictable.'

'Well, he can't very well sleep with her, can he? She had disappeared from her bed and breakfast when he went to pick her up this morning. He was staying with friends, apparently.'

'What's he like?'

Ian laughs dryly. 'Like a little ferret. About sixteen, with slicked-back hair and that closed terrier look of a man determined to change an unequal class system single handed. Especially a system where professional men can abandon vulnerable, disadvantaged wives.'

'Oh, dear,' I say. Then, 'But you didn't abandon Hester. She left you.'

Ian laughs again. 'Well, I don't think little details like that matter much to men like Mr Casey. He would probably cite mental cruelty or some such reason for her leaving. Anthony thinks he's a wanker for supporting such a spurious claim in the first place and for losing his client and wasting everyone's time.'

'Ian,' I ask. 'Hester couldn't know where we are, could she?'

'No, Anna. It was the first thing I asked. Casey told Anthony no one at social services would be so irresponsible as to give Hester our address with Jessie still living at home. Don't worry.'

As I kneel on the lawn surrounded by plants I am putting in my border I can smell honeysuckle strong and sweet. I still haven't told Ian that Hester has our telephone number, of that I am almost sure. Ian is saying, 'Hester will be scouting around the schools looking for Jessie.'

'We mustn't tell Jess, Ian,' I say quickly. 'She won't think of private schools, will she?'

'I don't think so. But I have rung Jessie's school, just to be safe.'

Poor Ian. How long has he been doing this down the years?

'Are you ringing from the office?' I ask.

'Yes. I'd better go now, Anna.'

'I hope this afternoon isn't too bad, Ian.'

'I do love you, you know,' he says suddenly.

74

I smile. 'And I you. It will be OK. I'm sure of it.' But I wish I was sure.

'Hope so. See you tonight, darling.'

Ian rarely uses an endearment. I feel better.

I hear the unmistakable sound of the pink VW camper as it deposits Alice outside the house. I am glad she has come. The phone rings again. 'Hello,' I say. 'Ian?'

The voice is quiet and friendly, conversational. 'Hello, Anna. How are you? This is Hester speaking. Could I have a word with Jessie?'

My mouth goes dry and the palms of my hands are suddenly sweaty. Startled, I say faintly, 'Jessie is at school. Where are you, Hester?'

'Wouldn't you like to know?' she answers in her friendly voice.

'Hester, you are supposed to be in court.'

'That can wait. I want to talk to my daughter.'

'She is at school at this time of day. You must know she wouldn't be home.'

There is silence and I wonder whether to put the phone down. Her voice somehow doesn't go with the person who wrote the letter. She sounds perfectly reasonable. Just as I am about to say something she says, 'I'll just have to talk to you then, Anna, won't I? Are you happy? Are you happy with my moody, silent husband?'

Her tone is soft, interested. 'It is quite hard isn't it when he shuts you out for days and then looks at you with those icy blue eyes as if you are invisible? Do you find that too, Anna?'

The goosebumps start up on my arms and I am cold in sunlight. I start to say goodbye and she raises her voice a fraction. 'Does my husband pull Jessie on his lap, or is she too big now? Does he laugh at you over her head, rock her to and fro on his lap and sing, "My little girl, aren't you, my darling? Not silly old Mummy's. Daddy's little love, aren't you, my pet?" Does he still do that, Anna?'

75

Alice calls out, 'I'm here.' And runs down the garden towards me. She is multicoloured today, like a dancing patchwork quilt. I must switch the phone off. I must switch off that insidious, damaging little voice with the horrible London twang. But I'm hypnotized and she goes on, softly covering me with her poison, coating me like sap from the trees.

'One day soon, Anna, you will not be able to keep the scream in. You will scream out at him. One very long scream. Then he will smile at you with his mouth but not his eyes and he will whisper, "Anna, you really are quite, quite, mad."'

I am shaking so much I have to hold the phone steady with both hands. 'I am going to switch the phone off, Hester. Please just go away. Go to the court where you are supposed to be. You are the one who wanted to go to court. Well, go there and stop bothering me.'

There is a sudden explosion of sound. 'Whore!' Her voice is hoarse and harsh. 'You are just a common whore! I know your game. Jessie hates you. She wants to be with me. You are cruel to her, I know she's kept short of food, I've got the social services on to you, they are watching you, madam. They know what you are. They know you walk up and down the streets showing off your fanny. That's how you got my husband. Wiggled your fanny at him didn't you? Well it's my fanny he really wants.'

I switch the button and throw the phone across the grass. I'll never ever bring the phone down here again. I will never ever answer the phone except via the machine. I feel sick and contaminated.

'Hey, hey, Anna, what's up? What is it?' Alice plonks herself beside me, touches my arm. 'You are as white as a sheet. You're shaking.'

'Obscene phone call.' I manage a wry smile but Alice is concerned.

'Have one of my herbal teas.'

'I'm not that bad! I'd love a coffee, though. Stick some brandy in it, Ali, please.' I hand her the house keys.

She stares at me worriedly. 'I've got something better,' she offers.

I shake my head, try to smile. 'I'm tempted though.'

She goes on looking at me. 'You know who it was, don't you?'

'Yes.'

Still she doesn't move. 'Anna, you won't forget what I told you, will you? You had a warning.'

'I won't forget, Ali.'

'Lie in the sun. I'll be back in a moment.' She whirls away up the garden, all psychedelic colours against the green trees.

I don't want to be still. I want to be doing something and I go back to work. I feel literally stunned. I have never heard Hester's voice before. I quail at the accuracy of Hester's veiled half-truths, her dark echoes of my own misgivings, delivered with an uncanny surety of reaching their target.

Could Ian have ever been cruel to a vulnerable Hester? Could that coldness have fuelled Hester's vulnerability and inherent insanity?

Tiny pots full of sweet peas. Air Warden. Jet Set. Cupid. Comforting old lady, lace curtain, pelargoniums. Summer Shower. Alpine Glow.

I find under my fingertips, 'Pelargonium Hotorium'. 'Happy Thoughts.'

I smile and thoroughly water small shoots that must grow strong.

Chapter 16

Ian

The day is quite as bad as I thought it would be. The morning of the court case is heavy and airless. I drive straight to the courts to meet my solicitor who is looking cross. Apparently, Hester has gone missing. I spot her solicitor straight away. He looks very young and earnest. He is wearing small wire-framed glasses and shiny shoes and he is agitated. 'For Heaven's sake,' Anthony, my solicitor, says. 'Bloody man has lost his client.'

'So what happens now?' I ask.

'There will have to be an adjournment, until she is found. This case won't be until after lunch, I expect. Total waste of time and money.'

He is hopping mad, and I don't blame him. He will have cancelled all appointments to come to court.

The case is adjourned until two o'clock and I drive back to the office. It is a good thing I did not make any appointments today.

Nick's mouth drops as I walk up the stairs and through his office. I collapse into his visitor's chair. 'Hester has gone missing. The case had to be adjourned until this afternoon.'

'I don't bloody believe it! That woman causes mayhem wherever she goes.'

'True.'

'Coffee?'

'Please.'

He hands me a coffee from his machine and perches on his desk.

'Well, will they find her? Will she turn up this afternoon?'

'I've absolutely no idea, Nick.'

'What will she be doing? Will she remember where she is supposed to be?'

'She will be looking for me and Jess. And I really don't know what state her mental health is in.'

'She can't find you, can she? I mean she won't turn up and frighten the living daylights out of poor Anna?'

'No, she can't possibly find us out there. No one, not even her mother, knows our address.'

'Go and ring Anna, all the same.' Nick is a worrier.

I finish the coffee. 'I'll do that.'

Anna sounds content, she is in the garden. How she does love her garden. A surge of love for her surfaces suddenly, surprising me. Why am I such a sod, sometimes?

Talking to her reassures me and I get on with some telephoning and then return to the court at one thirty. Hester is there, standing with her solicitor, and it is a shock after all these years. She is faded, she is shabby, she is . . . old.

A lump rises in my throat. Pain and pity overwhelm me, so sudden, so strong, so unexpected I am alarmed. She rocks faintly on her feet, the pills I suppose. Shit, shit, shit. I don't think I can cope with this.

She turns and sees me, stares. Her expression does not change, but her eyes never leave my face. She looks triumphant, secretive, a look I know so well. A look that is so familiar it should chill. But it does not chill me, it excites me. She is very still. She reminds me of a cobra, swaying this way and that before it strikes.

I turn away abruptly, turn my back. Anthony gives me a quick, old-fashioned look. 'OK, Ian?'

'Fine. Let's get on with this bloody charade.' Thank God, anger is surfacing like a huge familiar and welcoming black wave. A terrible anger that comes from hopelessness and guilt and something I will never ever understand.

Something dark in me.

80

Chapter 17

Hester

Mrs Beale, the bed and breakfast lady, gives me a good breakfast. Last night after Mr Casey left me here I went down the town for fish and chips. I ate them in my room watching the telly. I felt cosy and warm. I could hear Mrs Beale talking below me and I could hear the people in the other rooms all around me, coughing and washing. It was nice as if I was in a family again.

After breakfast I fetch my things and give my key back. 'I understood Mr Casey was picking you up here,' Mrs Beale says.

'Oh, no,' I tell her, 'I'm meeting him at the court.'

I go out and up the main road, past the station, towards the big school I saw last night. I sit on the wall and watch the buses bring the schoolchildren in but I can't see Jessie. I begin to get angry because Mrs Beale told me this is the only school. Every time a bus comes in I watch but she doesn't come.

When the bell rings and the buses stop coming I walk back up to the station and suddenly a bus passes that has a name I remember. I run to the stop to catch it. I look in my bag for my piece of paper and show it to the woman next to me.

'The bus stops at the edge of the village. They don't go out to the Trevillian estate. It's right out in the sticks.'

I ask her to tell me when to get off. She tells me she is visiting her daughter and her new granddaughter. We talk about babies and things, it is nice to have a friend.

When it's time to get out she tells me to go and ask directions from the people in the Post Office. 'Ask in there, dear, they will have a phone book.'

The Post Office is just a front room of someone's house. It makes me laugh. I go in and buy chocolate, I am very hungry.

'I am picking up my daughter and taking her home,' I tell the lady behind the counter.

'She is staying with friends but I'm not sure of the address.'

'What is their name, dear?'

I feel hot trying to remember. Name? What is that woman's name? 'Anna!' That's it.

She clicks her tongue. 'Surname, I need, dear.'

I stare at her, then laugh. 'Roberts. Roberts, of course.'

'Incomers are they?'

'I think so.'

She goes down a list. 'Would it be a Miss Harriet Roberts of Willow Farm?'

'No.'

'What about Ian and Anna Roberts out at Trevillian Lodge?'

There is a great roaring in my head. I can't speak. Everyone will think they are married. Everyone will think Jessie belongs to them.

'Are you ill, my handsome?' She is peering at me.

'No, no. I'm all right. Yes, that's the one.'

'Sorry, my duck, I can't give you the telephone number, it's ex-directory.'

I smile at her. 'It's all right, I have it. Thank you. Thank you very much.'

She gives me directions. ''Tis a good, long hike,' she says.

I walk and I walk. The mist hangs over the fields so I cannot see much except the road. I don't meet anyone. After a long time I come to a sign post that says Trevillian but when I follow the road it comes to an end in a sort of track. All around me are woods and still I don't see a single person. She must be a witch, that woman. Jessie will be so pleased to see me. I'll take her to the shops.

I go down a footpath and when it ends I climb over a gate into some woods because I can see some smoke rising over the trees. How can there be smoke in summer? The trees bend to reach me. I don't know if I like it here.

Suddenly I come to a break in the woods and below me there is a stone house with smoke rising from the chimney. I don't know yet if it is my house. The house where my little Jessie lives.

I stand under the trees very still and watch the house. There is someone in an upstairs window but I cannot see their face. Just a movement, a white blur. I peer to see better and it seems as if the face looks back for a minute. It's not Jessie.

I feel strange. Something catches in my throat. I turn away. I feel frightened of something, but I don't know what. I'm very tired.

I walk to my left where I can just see a lane and hear a tractor. The sun suddenly comes out and I find a ditch full of dry leaves. I lay out my mac to have a sleep. I'm so tired and the sun is warming me, shining out of the sky in a great slant and catching specks of things which whirl down to my feet.

I like it here now, it's private and secret.

When I wake I walk down the lane towards the road. I must find a bus. I'm supposed to be somewhere. I'll remember soon. Suddenly I see a phone box and I burst out laughing and go inside and dial that woman again. I put a whole pound in. I'll speak to her this time. We'll have a nice chat.

Chapter 18
Anna

Mentha Suaveolens. Apple mint. *Mentha piperita*. Peppermint. *Citrata* (Eau-de-Cologne) mint. Keep it contained or it will become pervasive.

Ian rings me from the courts to tell me that Hester's claim for more maintenance has been refused but so has his bid for no liability at all. I suppose Ian will have to contribute towards Hester's upkeep until she dies.

Funny. If Ian dies first, will I end up keeping Hester?

He arrives home looking exhausted, his eyes are bloodshot and his tie pulled loose and I notice the fraying collar of his shirt, and affection and pity well up inside me. I turn quickly away and pour him a stiff drink.

Jessie is staying the night with Lily and I had thought we might go out and celebrate the end of Ian's ordeal, but I see Ian is clearly past it so I go and raid the freezer.

After Ian has showered we open a bottle of wine and sit together upstairs where we can watch the sun set. Two swans are sailing delicately on a high tide below my greenhouses. I rarely get to watch the sunset from here as I am usually watering and it never ceases to astound me with its power.

Ian cannot relax, he paces the room as if exorcising something and his anger permeates the mellow room as the blood-red sun disappears into the slate-grey waters.

'Tell me what happened. Then let's try and forget Hester, at least for tonight, Ian.'

I hate the effect Hester has on him, although after today I am beginning to understand it.

He looks at me, then past me at the sky. 'Hester is always here between us, isn't she?'

I had wanted this to be a happy evening after the pressure of the last few weeks, but I am tired and shaken by the events of today and I begin to distance myself, become detached as I do when I am unable to cope.

I long suddenly to be peacefully watering.

Ian sits down. 'Oh, it's just her solicitor tried to discredit me to obscure the glaring fact that Hester already had a substantial settlement from me when we divorced. She also had all the proceeds from the house.'

'Why did she?'

'Because I wanted out, Anna, and it was easier to let her have everything. I just wanted to walk away from it all, sever all contact with a good conscience.'

'How could you sever all contact? When you have children, that's impossible.'

Ian glares at me. 'Are you going to let me finish what I am trying to tell you?'

'I'm sorry.'

His suppressed fury is making me miserable. I am in the middle of someone else's story and I don't want to be there. I have had enough for one day.

'Casey, her solicitor, insinuated that I had given Hester a good settlement because of a guilty conscience. He suggested it was her marriage to me that triggered her breakdown. My fault she is in the situation she is in. My overbearing attitude and lack of affection caused her to leave because she had no alternative.'

I am appalled and Ian grins at me grimly. 'He had to get a sympathy vote for Hester.'

'I don't understand why all this came up at all? I thought

it was purely a case for increase in maintenance, not another chance to dig over the bones of your marriage.'

'Come on, Anna! The two are inextricably linked in all divorce settlements.'

I get up. I need to be doing something. 'Come and talk to me downstairs while I do some pasta,' I say and Ian follows me down with the wine.

I put some prawns and melon on the table and some pasta on the Rayburn and we sit at the table. Ian pushes the pink prawn and yellow melon into his mouth in sharp little movements. From across the table his anger reaches me like a hot draught and I am silent, waiting for him to continue.

'The judge then asked Hester a question and it became obvious to everyone in the room that she was two shillings short of a pound when she started to ramble on about me reducing her to the streets, to beg in order to feed herself!'

I burst out laughing.

'It's true, honestly. The judge asked her what she did with her benefit and Casey jumped up and said his client was apt to get confused.'

'The judge said it was indeed confusing, especially as he had Hester's medical notes in front of him, to understand why the DSS had backed Hester's claim for more maintenance which had been extremely ill advised, and he was dismissing it forthwith. He reduced my payments but said it was beyond his remit to nullify it altogether. And that was that, Anna.'

I let out my breath in relief. 'Well, it's not so bad is it. It's over, done with, forget it. It's not worth getting angry over what was said in court, Ian, you know the truth of things.'

'You're right,' he says and gets up and goes to the fridge for more wine. 'Sorry, darling.' He hugs me quickly.

I drain the pasta and search my mind for what it is that disturbs me. Is it the relentless, excited, obsessive quality of his anger? The sort of anger people have when they cannot let go of the cause of it?

It is on the tip of my tongue to tell him about Hester's phone call.

Ian is saying, 'I'm sorry, Anna, I should have taken you out, given you a break from cooking. Still, shall we get quietly drunk instead?'

I smile and we sit down again. I want to ask him what it is he still feels about Hester. I want to understand why, after all this time, he is still so angry and bitter. But I know it is not the right time. It never seems to be the right time. Or am I afraid to ask the question? Ian is silent. He forks pasta into his mouth as if it is a punishment, or an excuse not to talk. The silence lengthens and I realize suddenly I am clutching my wine glass with anxiety. We have got to that time of night when we are tired and have had too many drinks and the evening could dissolve suddenly, fragment into frightening and unmanageable pieces. Ian comes back from wherever he was and puts his fork down and reaches across to touch me. 'Anna, this is delicious. Is there a film on later we can watch?'

'Yes . . . Yes, I think there is.'

We both make a tremendous effort and I tell him about Alice and Jake and Ian tells me about Nick and work.

We are rather like two people standing on the edge of a precipice. If we step forward we will plummet, so we gingerly edge backwards to safety and ground we can manage.

We watch a film and then, determined to rescue a precious evening on our own, we sit in the bath together getting steadily drunk. The bath is a huge enamel Victorian one with taps in the middle. We tipsily soap each other and water goes everywhere. We are like silly children let out of school.

I watch Ian from the other end of the bath as if I am seeing him for the first time. Fair, going very grey. A big heavy man, but somehow vulnerable, the shoulders slightly stooped, as in men who do not take much exercise. He is not conventionally good looking, he is too brooding, does not smile quite enough, but when he does it is like the sun coming out.

His life shows in the lines of his face and the droop of his mouth when he is tired. Stress is etched in the fine lines around very pale blue eyes. It is this which attracted me. This mixture of vulnerability and aggression. An unknown quantity.

What attracted Ian to me, I wonder?

Ian throws a sponge at me. 'Don't look at me like that, you little blonde hussy.'

Because I am small, I have never been as thin as I would like. Now, I am very thin and brown from being outside so much.

When Ben died I let myself go. I didn't care. I threw on the first things that were handy, hardly cleaned the garden out of my nails. Now I am trying hard to bother again, find time to care how I look. I buy potions for my face and Indian scarves for my untameable hair.

'What is this stuff in the bath?' Ian asks now, sniffing suspiciously.

'Aromatherapy. It is supposed to help you relax.'

Ian's eyebrows shoot up. 'If we relax any more we will drown.'

I laugh and drink some more wine. 'This is wonderful, lying here on our own, getting amazingly drunk.'

Ian bends to my breasts and takes a nipple carefully into his mouth. As he does so his penis rises out of the water between my thighs like a monster of the deep and we both shake with laughter. We get out of the bath and throw towels round ourselves and make a dash for the bedroom.

Ian is as abandoned and sexy in bed as he is buttoned up and silent out of it. It has made me look at buttoned-up men in quite a different light. With Jessie out of the house there is such freedom in making as much noise as we like, being silly lovers for once, with no responsibilities.

I fall asleep almost immediately like a replete cat. I feel such relief that we rescued the evening. I have always been a contented person, it does not take much to make me happy.

The last thing I hear is the barn owl hooting outside on the granite gatepost.

I wake again and find the bed empty, the room in complete darkness. I lie for a moment trying to get my bearings, wondering why the room is so dark, then I see it is Ian's body that is blocking the light from the window. He is standing quite still, looking out, his body tense.

'Ian, what is it?' I whisper.

After a moment he backs carefully away from the window and comes back to the bed. 'I heard something. Someone on the gravel, but I can't see anything. Perhaps it was just an animal.'

But I can tell he doesn't think so. After a moment he says, 'I think I'll just go outside and check around the house and go down to the greenhouses.' He is pulling on old cords and a sweater.

'I'm coming with you,' I say and pull on my jeans quickly before he can stop me.

Hebe is waiting by the back door, tail wagging eagerly. I wonder if she too has heard something, but being a rescued dog she rarely barks.

Ian collects a strong torch and we walk around the house shining it. If there had been anyone here they would have been long gone by now. We make our way from the locked house down to the greenhouses, Hebe snuffling cheerfully ahead of us. Ian shines the torch on the lock of the summerhouse and we check every greenhouse and tunnel.

There is a strong breeze and the trees, huge in the dark, wave and bend like wild arms. There is a wonderful smell of herbs and honeysuckle and something else I can't quite place, but seems familiar. There is a heavy dew but only our footsteps leave a crushed imprint on the lawn.

'Nothing here,' Ian says and we make our way silently back to the house. As we reach the front door I smell that scent again. It reminds me of something, of someone, but I cannot catch the memory.

Inside, we put the kettle on the Rayburn, leaning against it for warmth. I say, looking out at darkness which is just lifting over the trees, 'Ian, Hester did go back to London, didn't she?'

Ian pulls me to him. 'I made sure. I watched her get on the train. Darling, it was just a fox or badger.' He smiles at me. 'Remember when we woke up and found those two lads camping down in the garden, thinking it was a public park?'

'Ian, I haven't told you before, but Hester has our telephone number, she has rung here.'

Ian's arms grow stiff under my fingers, a fleeting look of defeat passes swiftly over his face. 'Oh, God!' he says. 'Why on earth didn't you tell me before?'

'I wasn't absolutely sure until today. She rang this morning wanting to speak to Jess. She was very abusive.'

'I'm sorry, Anna. What time did she ring?'

'This morning, just after you. I presumed she must be ringing from the courts or a box near by so I didn't ring you.' The truth is I didn't think of ringing Ian I was so shaken. 'Ian, how has she got our number?'

'I just don't know. The only place I can think of is her mother's, but Mai is unlikely to have been careless.'

Hester's mother, Mai, has our number supposedly hidden, for emergencies. Hester is as big a burden to her as she is to everyone else.

The kettle boils and I make tea. 'I'll ring her in the morning,' Ian says. 'How many phone calls have you had, Anna?'

'About four. Until today she never spoke. I could hear her breathing but she would just replace the receiver. Today she rang and spoke for the first time, asking for Jessie. It was a hell of a shock. She was quite calm at first. Then hurling abuse.'

'I'm so sorry,' Ian says again. 'I suppose I will have to change the number yet again.'

'Ian, if you change the number, the boys can't reach me.' I look at him anxiously.

'Of course, I was forgetting . . . We will have to make sure they know before we change it.'

We drink our tea looking out of the kitchen window on to darkness. For the first time I wish it had curtains. 'I thought I saw someone staring in at the house from the woods earlier,' I say. 'For some reason I felt really frightened.'

'Anna, listen to me. I know what you are thinking, but there is no way it could have been Hester, believe me. Please don't let Hester unnerve you like she does Jessie. She may have our telephone number, but she doesn't know where we are. She would have turned up, not rung, I assure you, I know her.'

'But Ian, telephone numbers and addresses go together.'

'Hester's mother has never had our address. She did not want it for this very reason. She promised she would not put our name by our telephone number either.'

Ian takes our mugs and puts them in the sink. 'Come on, let's go back to bed. I'll phone her in the morning.'

Back in bed I lie on my back, stiff with tension, unable to sleep. Ian, beside me, is wide awake too.

I hear myself say suddenly, 'Were you ever cruel to Hester, Ian? Did you ever taunt her for not coping with Jessie?'

Ian is very still beside me, then he says quietly, 'Of course! How could I forget how very plausible Hester is?'

I can feel his hurt. Wrong time, wrong day. Stupid.

'She told you I taunted her?'

'Yes.'

'You feel you need to ask me that, Anna?'

'I just want to hear you say you were not unkind to her, Ian.'

'Unkind?' He sits up so violently I jump. 'Now then, let's see, was I unkind when I came home from work to find her in bed with the plumber and Jessie alone downstairs? Is it possible that I was a little less than civil when she came into the office and accused me in front of my staff of having affairs with my secretary, next-door neighbour, anyone I even spoke to? Was I unkind to defend myself when she

92

came at me with a garden rake for picking up Jessie for a hug? Perhaps, you would prefer that I had been kind on all those occasions, Anna?'

He is shaking and turns violently over on his side away from me, his voice becoming as icy and distant as a stranger's. His back emanates a stiff fury and bitterness I shrink away from.

'I'm sorry.'

I should not have spoken. But it is this, this constant layer of terrible anger that lies just below the surface of his character that unnerves me most. Alarms and alerts me to the possibility of great coldness and cruelty to those he no longer loves.

I do not want the dry seed Hester has planted in my mind to take root. But threads of Jessie's stories filter like cobwebs through my mind. When Ian distances himself, withdraws, instead of helping me understand, making me understand, I quail, I feel totally confused by the conflicting messages I am getting of the man I married. I am not equipped to deal with all this suppressed anger.

Was it so wrong and disloyal to ask such a question?

My heart hammers away with misery at how the evening has ended. I will never know what Ian was like before the years with Hester covered him like a dark cloak. It is a pity. I lie on, sleepless in the dark, very still, beside a stranger. As dawn comes, as the birds start slowly to sing, I tell myself Ian's anger need not be guilt. It could be a defence against being hurt again, against hopelessness. And I acknowledge that my fear and misgivings of this second marriage are my own baggage that I carry with me.

Hester only pressed clever fingers on a bruise of doubt I already have. On the wisdom of taking on two damaged people and my ability to cope with things I have no understanding of. I have led a sheltered life in comparison to Ian and Jess. I just want to be happy. I just want to garden.

I smother a silent scream of loneliness.

I want Ben. I want Ben alive. I want Liam and Daniel. I want

June. I want my mother. I want my old, my own life back. I want to be safe.

In the half-light I move my hand slowly to Ian's back and place my fingers tentatively there like a whisper, to feel the warmth of another human being. He turns immediately and scoops me gently to him as if I am a child.

The stranger, the man I do not know, disappears.

Thankfully I relax, close my eyes. Before I fall asleep I suddenly remember that evocative smell in the garden tonight. My mother used to spray it on the sheets. I am sure it is 4711 cologne.

Chapter 19
Hester

Melanie sits at her desk, looking at me without saying anything. I must be careful.

'Well, Hester,' she says after a while, 'I am very disappointed.'

I don't answer. I watch a wasp on the window pane trying to get out. Its buzzing is very loud. 'Let it out,' I shout.

She gets up, opens the window and flicks it out with an envelope. When she sits down she says, 'Hester, why are you not taking your pills? Do you just forget or do you think you can do without them?'

'They make me tired, they make me muddled.'

'They are exactly the same pills you had when you were here, Hester.'

'They are not! You've made them stronger so I can't think straight.'

'Why would we want to do that?'

'To stop me finding my own child, that's why,' I shout.

I get up, I don't want to talk to her any more. Melanie gets up too.

'Hester, there is no reason why you can't see your daughter, but not when you are like this. Not while you are abusive and aggressive. It lies in your hands. The medication we give you is to make you better, not to confine you . . .'

'Who told you I was abusive? It's not true. It's that woman making trouble, so I can't see Jess, isn't it?

'No, Hester, it is not. You disappeared from the accommodation we found you in Cornwall and held the court case up. You apparently made an abusive phone call to your ex-husband's wife. You disappeared again before the train left Truro station, causing a lot of worry and trouble for the local social services agency. And you had to be bailed out of the local police station for refusing to pay a taxi fare. You have repeatedly frightened your mother by phoning her in the middle of the night from various phone boxes all over London.'

'Piss off.'

'Hester, I'll talk to you on Sunday. Hopefully you will be feeling better by then.'

She presses a buzzer and two nurses appear. A sudden dread fills me. My head is suddenly quiet. What have I done?

Melanie comes towards me. 'It's all right, Hester,' she says gently and touches my arm. 'We are going to give you an injection which will work much faster than the pills. Then you can go into the day centre for the weekend. You'll be surprised to see one of your old friends there. I'll see you tomorrow.'

In the Day Centre is my friend Wendy. I feel so happy. She is the best friend I have ever had. There are a few mental cases in but we sit together and have our lunch. She is having trouble with her parents. At first she said she felt very glad to be home, although she missed me. Then she said one morning she caught her mother putting something in her food. She began to watch her and realized after a while her mother was poisoning her. It's dreadful, and of course no one believes her.

I tell her about Cornwall, about seeing Ian again, knowing he still loves me and is trapped with that woman. I tell her I think I have found my Jess, but I am not quite sure. I tell her how clever I was about getting off the train again just as it started and they thought I was in the toilet. When it was dark I got a taxi near to that house. I walked in the dark and found the house again. I waited until all the lights went out and then I tried to get in to see Jess, but I was not sure it was the right house and the door was locked and it was very dark and an owl frightened me and I ran and my feet made a noise on the gravel and my heart thumped and I felt sick.

I found the call box on the main road again and I rang for a taxi and the bastard taxi driver drove me to the police station because I couldn't pay the fare.

Wendy says I am very brave.

In the afternoon we both have to go back to the ward to have a sleep. In the evening we watch a lovely film on the telly together. I suddenly have a very good idea. Now, Wendy could come and live in my flat with me. She says it would be lovely.

I go to bed early because I have a headache. The nurse says it is the injection. She says the pills take about seven days for the body to absorb, but an injection works in twenty-four hours and I will feel fine in the morning.

After lunch next day Melanie comes to see me. I ask her about Wendy and she says it sounds as if it might be a good idea in a few months but she wants me to get back on my feet first and Wendy has to stay on here for a little while longer.

'How do you feel?' she asks.

'I'm fine. I've had a lovely weekend.'

'Do you feel heady or muddled?'

'I did yesterday, but not today.'

She looks at me. 'Hester, I would really like to increase your home visits for a while. I am going to see if it is possible. Ideally we would have liked you back longer, but we just don't have the room. Do you think it might be a good idea to come in for monthly injections as you have trouble remembering to take your pills?'

'No,' I tell her. 'They give me a bad headache. I'll take the pills. Why can't I stay if Wendy is going to stay?'

'She needs to be here for a little longer. You don't, Hester.

Tell me, would you really want to live back here? Isn't it nice to have your own little place?'

I think of the flat. I think of the empty feel when I wake. I think about the silence. I think about remembering to get milk and bread. I think about when it gets dark and lights come on when I am outside and I feel everyone is in the light together shutting their curtains against me.

'Hester, don't cry. Please don't cry.'

I didn't know I was. 'I don't know what I want,' I say. 'I don't want to be alone. I don't want the noises in my head.'

'I know,' she says. 'I'm trying to help you all I can, Hester. If you will only help yourself by taking your pills. Everything is all right then, isn't it?'

I don't know. The voices in my head are not so loud. But the Hester I know goes too. I am frightened that the real Hester will disappear and I won't be able to get her back, ever, and they will have won, then, they will have won.

I must be careful.

'There are lots of things I want to do,' I tell Melanie. 'I think I'll get a picture for the lounge. I'll take the pills every day. I might travel. I might go for a holiday.'

I watch her carefully.

She lets out her breath with relief. She smiles. 'That's it, Hester. That's the spirit!'

Chapter 20
Ian

I often look at Anna and wonder what Ben was like. If his name is ever mentioned her face lights up, becomes soft. I hardly know the twins, but when they were at home I used to hear them in the kitchen round the Rayburn. 'Hey, Mum, do you remember that time Dad came home on leave with all that Irish whiskey and he and June got totally plastered and went swimming with nothing on and the old lady in the beach house got up and yelled into the darkness, "What on earth is going on down there, you are disturbing my pugs!" We all fell about. Oh God, that was funny.'

Ben and Anna could not have had time, I suppose, to get tired and jaded with each other. A husband forever young and loving. A perfect marriage? Well, that is certainly what Anna would like me to believe.

He died six years ago and she still can't talk about him, not to me anyway.

Nick and Pud have invited us to supper. Anna is too busy and I am relieved in a way. I enjoy going to them on my own. I can relax and not worry that Anna is feeling excluded. It also saves the trouble of finding a babysitter for Jess who believes she is too old to have one but would, in reality, hate to be left on her own.

Pud welcomes me as effusively as ever. She is a large, warm, comforting woman, the old-fashioned sort, who live their lives through their husband and children despite having a good degree.

She and Nick are sitting out in their large rambling garden with three Labradors, two black and a fat yellow one. The lawn is littered with grim-looking bones. 'Bliss, isn't it, this heatwave? Forgive the graveyard.'

Nick comes out of the house with a cold beer for me. 'How's that delightful girl of yours?'

'She's fine. She sends apologies, she is just so busy at this time of year.'

'Oh, Ian, we quite understand. Expect the drought is affecting her?'

'She is inevitably losing things and the water restrictions are a nightmare, we are having to use washing-up and bath water. It's a lot of work.'

'Poor thing! Watering must be hell. We must all get together later in the summer, have a barbecue or something, she must come to that and relax.'

Pud goes off into the house to see to the food and Nick and I talk about work. Through his apple trees I can glimpse the new marina glinting with expensive yachts. I feel myself relaxing for the first time since Hester's visit. Here I can be myself, I do not have to worry that I should be doing something to help, I can just sit.

Pud comes out with an enormous salad and puts it on the table, then goes back and brings out steaks on large oval dishes while Nick wanders into the house for the wine.

'What a wonder you are, Pud!' I say.

'Isn't she?' Nick says fondly, coming back.

We eat, talk about mutual friends, and get through copious amounts of wine. 'Everything quiet after the court case, Ian?' Pud asks suddenly.

'Is it, hell! Hester rings all the time, usually during the day when Anna is alone. Anna won't answer the phone any more in case it is Hester, who then becomes abusive. We don't want to change the telephone number because of Anna's boys. They are away backpacking.'

'I thought you looked strained when you arrived, Ian.'

100

'Oh, I'm all right, Pud. Nick and I have a lot of work on at the moment.'

'I know. But Nick hasn't got a batty ex-wife lurking about. Well, not that I know of.' Pud laughs shortly. 'What did it feel like seeing her again?'

'Dreadful. She looked so shabby and old and . . . odd. I don't know what I expected, but it was a shock.'

'How did you remember her?'

'Well, odd, always odd, of course, but youngish and still attractive.'

'Was she still like that when the marriage ended, then? Or have you just remembered her as you married her, before Jess?'

'I suppose I must. Stupid, isn't it?'

'Darling,' Nick says gently, 'Ian is here to relax, not to be gently quizzed about Hester, even by you.'

I smile. 'It's OK, really.'

'It's just,' Pud says in a rush, 'I know you, you will bottle everything up, close up, not let anyone near you, and we are your oldest friends and I thought it might do you good to talk, that's all. But only if you want to, of course.'

I get up and kiss her. Nick said to me once, 'Pud brings out the best in you, somehow.' And it is true, she does.

There is silence for a moment and a blackbird sings, loud suddenly in the garden which is becoming full of shadows as the sun goes. I say quickly, before I lose the will to say it, for I prefer not to talk about things, 'I felt guilt when I saw Hester again too. As if I had turned my back on something wounded, that I should have made better by taking more trouble, trying harder.'

'Christ,' Nick says, 'you tried longer than most of us fucking could.'

'Your language doesn't get any better,' his wife says dryly. She leans forward and touches my hand. 'You feel guilt because you are a nice man and you so desperately wanted things to be right.'

'No, Pud,' I say carefully, finishing up Nick's bottle of wine. 'I feel guilt because I knew almost at once I wasn't going to be able to give Hester what she wanted emotionally and I withdrew. Later in the marriage I was cruel. I enjoyed being cruel. I taunted Hester with her madness. I put my finger to my head and rolled my eyes. I used Jess to make her jealous. I listed gleefully her inadequacies. I despised her lack of intellect.'

There is a long silence. Only the blackbird.

'Ian,' Nick says firmly, 'you lived for sixteen years with a schizophrenic, for heaven's sake. You managed to keep down some bloody good jobs, look after a small child and an increasingly neurotic, damaged wife long beyond what was sensible. Don't interrupt. If during that time you said or did things you deeply regret, ask any long-term carer about guilt and the limited ability to endure mental illness without damage to oneself.'

'Nick is right, Ian. We can all be cruel. People drive us to cruelty by demanding more than we can give them.' This from Pud who I cannot imagine ever being cruel. 'You are not,' she says quietly, 'a cruel person, Ian. You need to believe that.'

I have drunk too much. 'Am I damaged, then?' I ask.

Nick walks away, embarrassed, across the lawn towards the water to see what one of the dogs is barking at.

'Perhaps. Aren't we all in some way?' Pud's voice is careful in the coming darkness, as if I am ill or a hurt child. I can sense her feeling for the right words. 'We both like Anna so much, feel she is good for you. Anna isn't Hester, Ian, you can talk to her as you are talking to me. It is so important that you do, that she knows how you are feeling, why you can be moody and difficult.' She laughs to take the sting out of her words.

'If I am damaged, is this why,' I ask before Nick comes back, 'is this why I want sometimes to be cruel to Anna then?'

There is another embarrassed silence in the dark garden. It is getting cold and Pud shivers and gets up.

'You have drunk too much. You can't drive home, Ian. You can have Hal's bed. Nick will ring Anna.' She turns to me and says sharply, 'Perhaps you'd better make sure your cruelty isn't becoming a habit if you want to sustain a second marriage. Perhaps you should look at whether it is a clever man's foil against boredom or misogyny, Ian.'

How very perceptive she is.

I lie in the bed. I think about what I so nearly told her. That Hester still excites me in a terrible nightmarish way. As if, somewhere inside me, I recognise her madness and it ignites some force in me.

Anna, beautiful and stable, faintly bores me in that stability and sense of purpose. I know what is going to happen, each day.

I watched to make sure Hester caught that London train after the court case. She was with her solicitor and a local social worker. She looked back over her shoulder as if she knew I was there. I saw that familiar strangeness in her face and I was shocked to feel that excitement.

Like my cruelty, it appals me.

Chapter 21

Anna

Camellia. Cornish Snow. Evergreen and
frost hardy. Grows to approx. H. 3m.
(10 ft.) Hundreds of small, single white
flowers in early spring.

Alice is talking to the camellia tree. She is reassuring it that
its move is really necessary. Ian, up on the hired digger, leans
down and asks if I think the hole is big enough. I measure the
roots, nod and carefully start to fill the hole with water. The
hole awaits, as big and deep as a grave. The camellia stands in
an old bath full of tepid water and I am praying I don't lose it.

Alice and I guide it in the home-made hoist we have made
and lower it down into the hole. We hold it steady and
straight, no mean feat as it is a big tree, and Ian scoops
and pushes the mound of earth back around its roots with
the mechanical shovel.

Meanwhile Alice goes on softly talking up into the shiny
green leaves.

'You will be much better off here, tree, there is plenty of
shade and you are not crowded. If we don't move you, you
will die. If we had a choice we would have left you where
you were. We've picked the place carefully, this is the right
place for you. OK, tree?'

Ian still up on the digger, sweat running down his face,
raises his eyes to the sky and touches his forefinger to

his head and asks dryly, 'What sort of reply are you getting, Alice?'

Alice treads earth around the trunk and says placidly, 'Wouldn't you like a few encouraging words if you were being uplifted to a strange place? This camellia has grown in the same position for maybe ten or fifteen years. It will go into shock and without love it will die.'

I stroke the dark, waxy leaves. By this evening they will be slightly curling in protest and the colour infinitesimally faded. It will require all its strength and all the care we can give it to survive. 'Beautiful tree,' I mutter anxiously.

It is unfortunate it has to be moved. The old man who lived here before us misjudged the size and width of trees and shrubs when he planned the arboretum which lies between the house and the garden I now have my greenhouses and tunnels on.

Alice crouches down in front of the camellia and starts to chant, her nose-ring flashes in the sun and I am reminded suddenly of India. Of holding two little blond boys by the hand as I watch Indian women in saris of bright, fading colours, working on a building site, crouched by the monsoon drains at noon cooking on a Primus, plaits of dark hair snaking across brown shoulders as they sing to the babies folded on to their backs.

Ian moves the digger away then jumps down wiping his face on his T-shirt. 'I'll get you two women a cold drink, shall I?' he asks and disappears up into the trees. I turn back to the camellia. I am very afraid it will die.

As if reading my thoughts, Alice stops singing and says, 'Only think positive thoughts around it, Anna, nothing negative.'

'I am trying,' I tell her. 'But we are in the middle of a heatwave and the ground is parched.' I turn off the water and we bank a little more of the soaked earth up around it.

Ian comes back with three cold lagers and we sit on the grass drinking them in exhausted silence. After a while Ian looks at

106

his watch. 'I'd better have a shower and go and fetch Jessie,' he says, but doesn't move. Alice, lying on her back, seems to have fallen asleep.

'I can't get hold of Hester's mother, there never seems to be anyone there. For some reason she's got herself an answer phone, so I've left a message. Odd though, she's always hated machines.'

He gets up slowly and pats the top of my head. 'See you later. Thanks for coming and lending a hand,' he says to Alice who props herself up on one arm.

'It's OK. I wasn't doing anything,' she smiles, then calls after him. 'You should do yoga, Ian. It would relax you, you're never still for two minutes.'

Ian gives a honk of laughter. 'Candidate for a heart attack, am I? You concentrate on your tree. Much more rewarding, Alice.'

For a while Alice and I lie in companionable silence, then she suddenly rolls over towards me and says slowly, 'Anna? You never mention him, but they told me in the village that your first husband was shot down in the Gulf War.'

'Yes, he was,' I say. 'His flying days should have been over, but they needed his experience. It was a training reconnaissance flight to take aerial photos.'

'I'm really sorry, Anna. How old were the boys?'

'Fifteen.'

'It must have been terrible.'

'It was.' I wonder why Alice is suddenly curious about my past. She tugs daisies out of the grass nervously, in case I take offence.

'I . . . I was just wondering if . . .' she peters out, and I look at her and laugh.

'Alice, dear Alice, what is it you are trying to ask me?'

'I've no right. I'm invading your space, I know I am. It's just . . . I needed . . . wondered . . . if your first husband and Ian were alike?'

The wind gets up and moves the branches of the trees

above us creating a wonderful breeze. Clouds have suddenly collected while we talk. There is going to be a storm.

'Not alike at all. Ben was mad. A mad Irishman.'

Alice sits up. 'What did he look like?'

I pull my raffia bag towards me and take out my wallet and the fading photo of Ben and the boys and hand it to her. She stares at it for a long time. 'He was exceptionally beautiful,' she says quietly. 'What was it like being married to someone who looks like that?'

'Hell,' I answer.

She waits for more but I don't give it to her. Instead I go up to the house and get us both another cold lager which we sip in silence.

But the photo of Ben, which I can still hardly bear to look at, has triggered memories and suddenly I find myself talking in the way I have only ever done with June. June who picked me up off the floor many times in my marriage and finally got me to see there was another way of coping with infidelity.

'Women loved Ben and Ben loved women. Most women. All women.' The first time I have ever said that.

I press my face against the cold glass and it burns my cheek. 'I loved him so much it hurt, Alice. When he smiled at me, threw back his head and laughed with the pleasure of being home; when he caught me and the boys to him as if we were the most precious things in the world I could have forgiven him anything. He adored us, his family, he was truly Irish in that way. But he was constantly unfaithful and once or twice he nearly broke my heart.'

Alice stares at me. 'But you never stopped loving him.' It is a statement, not a question.

'No, I never stopped loving him.'

'So did you sleep around, too?'

'No,' I say slowly.

'Because he would have minded?'

'Because he would have minded. And because I wasn't interested in anyone else. You see,' I try to explain, 'I sort of understood, Alice. Ben liked to live dangerously. He'd flown in Northern Ireland, he'd been through the Falklands and as a pilot he was well aware of the dangers, so he embraced life absolutely and that included beautiful women. It didn't mean he didn't love me. And he was right to live life to the full, wasn't he? He died at forty.'

Alice stares at me. 'But he made you sad.'

'Yes, he made me sad and jealous and angry. But he also made me amazingly happy. When he was home, huge, mad and Irish, filling the small cottage and my life, boundless with energy, my throat would constrict with love. All pain was worth this. This moment of his return. Alice, he was part of me, part of the air I breathed. I could forgive him anything. But he died, he left me and the sun will never shine so bright, life will never be so intense, vivid and searing again.'

I close my eyes against the cloudless sky, the rising wind, and Alice. I do not say, it is as if I am living in twilight.

Alice is silent. When I look up she is running her fingers along the rim of her glass, and I see a tear slide from under her dark glasses. Dear Alice. I say brightly, 'I am sure part of Ben's unfaithfulness was because we got married so young. He never got pretty women out of his system.'

'Ian? Are you happy with Ian, Anna? He doesn't look the unfaithful type,' Alice asks suddenly.

I smile. 'No, I don't think he is. Yes, I'm . . . happy. Trying to be happy.'

Alice looks at me shrewdly. 'It's not the same thing.' She pauses. 'I think he's a nice man, Anna, who's been in the dark too long.'

I am surprised, it is a mature comment for a twenty-one year old.

'His life shows in his face,' she says. 'Sometimes his face seems full of shadows. Sometimes when I look at him I feel as if there is another man, very different, just inside him, longing to get out.'

I am silent, suddenly infused with sadness at her insight.

Filled with angst at the knowledge that men who deserved to be loved often aren't. Men who take your love for granted, like a wonderfully safe cloak, nearly always are.

I lie back on the grass beginning to wish we hadn't started this conversation. 'Alice, you are much too young to understand, but the trouble is second marriages are entered into with such a lot of emotional baggage. No landmarks . . .' I trail off.

Alice's voice reaches me softly beneath the waving branches of the trees. 'I do understand, Anna. I see and sense things about people I often don't want to.' Her voice is wistful. 'I'm only twenty-one and I've already had two failed relationships. I know about baggage.'

I hear the unmistakable sound of the VW. Alice begins to gather her things together and I open my eyes and smile at her. 'What a dear and lovely little witch you are, Alice.'

We walk back up to the house together and the waiting pink camper. Suddenly she turns, drops her bags on the ground and hugs me fiercely.

Startled, I hug her back, then look into her face. I see tears in her eyes and something she desperately wants to say and cannot.

She blinks and tries to smile. 'You are the nearest to a mother I've ever had, Anna. My mother didn't have me until she was forty-five. She's always seemed old and now she has Alzheimer's. You are special to me, I want you to be happy. If you hadn't given me a chance I wouldn't have survived.'

'Oh, Alice.' I hold her away gently. 'Why didn't you tell me before? I'm so sorry.'

She shrugs and lets me go. 'Nothing you can do, Anna.' She grins and flies towards the van calling, 'I'll be in to see the camellia tomorrow.'

I wander back down the garden and crouch before the camellia as Alice has done earlier. I send good thoughts its way but do not speak. As I crouch there I feel strange. I feel as if I am turning into Alice. As if for a moment I am Alice. I feel the weight of the nose-ring and her heavy black hair hanging down my back. I feel her long flowing Indian skirt around my brown ankle which has a thin gold chain on the right foot.

I am shimmering above the tree, looking down on myself. Or Alice. I am no longer sure. The moment evaporates as if it has never happened, but I am filled with a strong feeling of being linked with Alice in a way I cannot understand.

I remember how she read the cards for me. How she gave me a warning and the goosebumps rise on the back of my neck and down my arms as if I should pick up, deep inside the primitive, intuitive, part of me, something Alice has not said today, but I can only sense something I am unable to comprehend.

I walk briskly up to the house. I can hear the phone ringing on and on. I won't answer it. I will not answer it. I must shower and get supper for Jessie and Ian. Clouds are massing and the wind is beginning to fling itself through the trees. There is going to be one hell of a storm.

Chapter 22
Ian

Jessie comes home from a weekend with Lily in a foul mood, not because she hasn't enjoyed herself, but because she has and she does not want to be back here, miles away from civilization, when she could be with Lily and her two brothers on a farm within spitting distance of the beach and a short bus ride from Truro and the shops.

She sulks and sniffs her way through supper, pushing the food around on her plate and whinging her way through the meal Anna has cooked until I itch to slap her. Eventually I can bear it no longer and snap, 'For heaven's sake stop behaving like a spoilt brat, Jess. Anna and I have had a lovely weekend too, and you are spoiling the end of it.'

Jessie immediately gets up, leaving her food and flounces out of the room looking martyred. She and Anna have been getting on so much better, why on earth does she have to spoil it? I thought she was growing up, but the pleasant girl of the last few weeks has suddenly disappeared again.

A minute later the phone rings and I move quickly to pick it up before Jess, but she reaches it first and it obviously isn't Hester because Jess talks animatedly in stage whispers for a while. Anna is looking as if she longs to be away from us, back down to the peace of her garden and I really cannot blame her. I try to lighten the atmosphere. 'Lily is presumably hearing what rotten parents we are,' I say as we clear the table.

Jessie shouts, 'It's Gran, Dad.'

Surprised I go out into the hall to speak to Mai. I have not spoken to her for ages and it seems funny to hear her familiar London accent. She apologizes for the answer machine. It is an anti-Hester device, she says. Hester has begun to ring her night and day and she just could not take it any more. 'Are you afraid Hester will come round?' I ask.

She tells me that she has a strange feeling that Hester has been in the house, but nothing seems to be missing and Hester has never been round when Mai has been there. She says that she rang the social services because she felt nervous and Hester's social worker rang her back to say that they were about to re-admit Hester for a long weekend to monitor her drugs. She reassures me that there is no way Hester could have found our telephone number from her.

When I have said goodbye I relay all this to Anna, who says crossly, 'Well, she's got it from somewhere, Ian, hasn't she?'

'I realize that, Anna,' I say equally irritably.

I pour the rest of the wine left from the meal and take it over to her. She is flicking through the Sunday papers and I sit beside her. It has been such a good weekend I don't want it to end on a bad note. 'It isn't just us she has been making a nuisance of herself with, she's been ringing her mother constantly too. They will check whether she is taking her drugs properly, we may never get another irrational call again, darling.'

I am trying hard to be cheerful and upbeat but Anna's face remains unusually closed. She looks up at me and is about to say something when there is a vast clap of thunder which sends Jessie flying into the kitchen and Hebe under the table.

I get up and say to Jess, 'I'm afraid your mother is being a bloody nuisance once again. Not only is she constantly ringing here, she is upsetting your gran too. We don't know how she got our number, Jess, so just be careful what you say when you have to speak to her.'

Jessie glares at me. 'I don't need this! I've got exams you know. She'll turn up on the doorstep. She'll bloody well embarrass me with my friends.' She strides to the door and throws it open.

I get the feeling Jess is thoroughly enjoying being dramatic, she is in that sort of mood tonight. 'Jess, just try to be pleasant and let's hope she will get bored and go on to something else.'

'Bloody, bloody hell!' Jess shouts. I am saved from more histrionics by another clap of thunder and I take the chance of exiting stage right and go to get on with some work.

Chapter 23
Hester

When I wake I can't remember where I am. Then I see the bare yellow walls of the flat. I used to have pictures. I used to buy them in Boots, they were really nice.

I get up and make some tea. It is pouring with rain. Miss what's-it-Hardy-Brown has stuck up a great big notice on one of the cupboard doors. PILLS 9 A.M. AND 5 P.M. I take one out of the packet and swallow it with my tea. I don't want monthly injections and I hate needles.

I go back to bed, there is nothing to get up for.

Wendy is still at the hospital. She is still my friend. If it stops raining I might go and see her. I lie with my eyes closed and make up stories. When I was a child I had a best friend called Alison Goodwin. She used to make up stories in bed too. We called them our Secret Lives . . . doing our Secret Lives. At school we would tell each other our stories of the night before, but no one else.

My dad kept pigeons in the garden. I loved the sound they made when I was in bed in the early morning. I would lie there warm and listen to them cooing and then a train would rattle past shaking the house and I would feel safe and happy.

I wasn't any good at school, I hated it, I hated the teachers. I couldn't wait to leave. My mother would get mad at me, but Dad would smile and say, 'Never mind, lovey, just do your best. You'll be all right, you're a pretty girl.'

A pretty girl. He always made me feel pretty. I was small and dark like my father. My mother was bigger than my father. Big and round like a hen. Too big for the house. The house would have been just right for him and me.

Sometimes when I couldn't sleep I heard sounds in the night I didn't understand. I could hear my father's quiet voice pleading with my mother and her voice would hiss, 'No!'

Sometimes she would cry very quietly, but I heard her through the wall.

Some nights I would hear my father get up and go downstairs. After a while I would get out of bed and tiptoe down the stairs and I would smell his pipe. He would be sitting in the dark smoking his pipe.

'Hello, lovey,' he would say. 'What are you doing up and awake?'

'I can't sleep,' I would say and climb on his knee and cuddle in. His dressing gown was prickly against my face and I would put my thumb in my mouth and bury myself against him and fall instantly asleep. I felt so safe. My dad would never let anything happen to me.

In my Secret Life my dad and I lived on an island in the sun with just natives. He didn't need a wife because he had me and if he died I would marry one of the huge black natives and I would get excited thinking of that.

My dad always had one afternoon a week off, a Wednesday. I can't remember why. He and my mother would go somewhere, down town shopping or to the cinema. I always went to Alison Goodwin's after school and they picked me up on their way home.

One Wednesday Alison was ill and didn't come to school so I caught the bus home. I always carried a key and I thought it would be exciting to have the house to myself for the first time ever. I let myself in through the back door and was making myself a sandwich when I heard something from upstairs.

I froze, thinking it was burglars and then I heard my father laugh softly and my mother made a strange noise deep in her throat. I crept up the stairs so they wouldn't hear to see what they were doing and their bedroom door was open and they were both in bed in the middle of the day with no clothes on.

My father's hand was round my mother's breast and he was kissing her neck. Her chin was up in the air and she was uttering strange little moans. I could feel the blood rushing in my head and a pulse beating there.

Then my father pushed the bed covers back and my mother spread her legs out and looked up at him laughing and he knelt up and I saw his thingy and he put it inside her and they thrashed around making horrible noises. It was revolting. I felt sick.

I wanted to run but I couldn't move, my legs wouldn't work, they sort of crumpled under me at the top of the stairs.

When they had stopped thrashing around he rolled off her and with his hand he gently pushed her fair hair away from her face. 'I love you, Mai,' he said.

I could feel a rush of voices in my head.

She half sat up. 'I know, John,' she said. 'I know you do, and I am trying. I know you are a good man. I've told you it's finished for good this time, and it is.'

My father didn't say anything, he just bent and kissed her on the mouth and her hands came up around his neck and pulled him down on her as if she was a cushion and the kiss went on for ages and the noises in my head got louder and louder and I turned and ran down the stairs and into the front room where all my mother's china was kept on shelves, not to be used, because it was valuable and I climbed up on a chair and threw it all on to the floor, I smashed it all to smithereens.

Serve her right. My father loved me, not her. She never loved him, she loved that other man in uniform. She should have gone away with him and left my dad and me together.

I didn't want him near her. I didn't want him to put his thingy in her. All the time I smashed I screamed and they came rushing down the stairs with hardly any clothes on.

I don't want to think about it any more because the whispering is coming back in little rushes and whispers. I get up quickly. I find my purse and go out into the rain to a call box. I push the money in and he answers.

'Hello,' I say. 'I expect you are surprised to hear me. How are you? How is Jess? I thought I would just ring and see how things are going for you.'

There is a long silence, then he says, 'I'll get Jess, Hester, but these phone calls will have to stop, otherwise I will have to change the number.'

'She's my daughter, why shouldn't I talk to her?'

'No reason, Hester, if you ring occasionally, but you are ringing all the time.'

'No, I'm not.'

I hear him sigh. 'I'll call Jessie.'

'Just a minute, we need to talk.'

'We have absolutely nothing to say to each other.'

'You are my husband!' I say angrily.

'We are divorced, Hester. I am married to someone else.'

'To a whore!' I shout. 'You are married to a fucking whore . . .'

He puts the phone down on me. He puts the phone down on me.

I put more money in and dial again but he has taken it off the hook.

I run out into the rain shouting because I can't keep the anger in and some children on bicycles shout something back at me and laugh. They are laughing at me and pointing. I run at them and they look frightened and ride quickly away yelling, 'The witch is in her nightdress . . . the witch is in her nightdress.'

I look down. I forgot to get dressed.

It's all her fault. It's all her fault. That whore he lives with.

Chapter 24
Anna

Salix Chrysocoma. Golden Weeping
Willow. Beautiful deciduous tree with
graceful golden hanging foliage which
brushes the ground.

I can feel the day shimmering outside, the heat gathering as
it used to in the tropics. I get out of bed carefully so I don't
wake Ian and take my clothes to the bathroom. I love this time
of day before anyone is up when I have the world to myself
and it is burnished with possibilities.

I make coffee and take it out into the garden with
a cheerful Hebe trotting after me. Delicate cobwebs are
slung between honeysuckle and rose, on the surface of
large nasturtium leaves and threaded between the slats of
an old green lichen wooden bench. They shimmer like
delicate sculptures across the garden.

I check the greenhouses and open the flaps and go to see
how the camellia is doing. Alice is practising Reiki healing
on it. It is her latest thing and it appears to be working because
its condition is remarkably stable.

It is Saturday and I collect the two boxes of plants I am
delivering to a friend who is starting a garden from scratch
and walk up the garden to the van. I cannot afford to take
the day off to help her but I want to offer moral support. I
should be back before Jessie or Ian are up.

121

The roads are empty and the sun is emerging in an orange glow ahead of me. I cut across country, down the narrow lanes towards the yacht harbour, past the daffodil fields. I take the steep hill down towards the water. It is like driving into the sea and I hold my breath with excitement as I roll down towards it glittering ahead of me.

For some reason I suddenly remember a day years and years ago. Perhaps it is the sense of freedom of being on an empty road going some place when you should really be working.

Ben had been flying in from Singapore and I decided to surprise him, drive up to Brize Norton and meet him. June had lent me her four-wheel drive as my car was past making the trip. I bowled along, sitting high up above the hedgerows full of red hips and trees clutching the last burnished leaves, feeling as if I'd just been let out of school. I can still remember that happiness clearly.

I had broken the journey at my sister Jane's in Gloucester and she had laughed at me. 'Honestly, Anna, how can you still be so potty about Ben after all these years?'

'Easily,' I said, watching her feeding an array of noisy, pushing dogs collecting round her Aga.

She is six years older than me and married to Tom. They live in a lovely, imposing Georgian manor covered with Virginia creeper. The Malvern hills roll in the background and, beyond the old walled kitchen garden, orchards of small fruit trees rise up in hilly fields, startlingly beautiful, especially in spring.

Their relationship is loud and affectionate and goes with their lifestyle which seems to consist of hunting and arranging huge shoots or organizing business conventions. Jane was the clever one, the child my mother loved most because she had the capability of fulfilling all my mother's own thwarted ambitions.

In childhood I was a disappointment, the dreamer, the late achiever, partly because Jane's cleverness was rammed down my throat all my childhood. She did a law degree and had only just began to practise when she met Tom at a ball. She fell hook, line and sinker for him, surprising even herself, I think.

He came from a wealthy Gloucestershire landowning family and, to my mother's horror, they married almost immediately and Jane gave up a promising career to become the Hon. Mrs Brinkley.

They had four sons in quick succession, all brought up randomly, like the Labradors and Jack Russells called Jasper and Harvey, Conrad and Trollope. Their sons have all been absorbed into running the estate and farms.

Tom is large and attractive in an outdoor sort of way and obviously adores Jane, though I doubt whether an endearment would ever pass his lips. Jane has helped him build up the estate, crippled by death duties and a series of lords hopeless at business, and it is now a thriving concern.

My mother never could see that this was much more satisfying to Jane than becoming a barrister.

The whole family shout at each other as if suffering from terminal deafness.

I love Jane dearly but one night there is always enough.

I had smiled at her. 'At least you didn't say, "The trouble with *you*, Anna, is you still love your husband."'

Jane had looked up from the dogs. 'What *do* you mean, Anna?'

'All my childhood you and Mum said, "The trouble with you, Anna is, you don't think, are too sensitive, have no ambition, are so scatty . . ."' I smiled at Jane, the memory had no sting any longer but I could hear my mother's voice as clear as day, 'Darling little Annie, you really are so wet.'

'Did we?' Jane had looked startled. 'How rotten for you, I am sorry.'

I laughed. 'Don't be daft. I disappointed her by getting married so young.'

Jane peered at me. 'Didn't realize you had a bit of an inferiority complex.'

123

'I don't think I have, well, not any more.'

'I should bloody well think not, Anna, with that man of yours, adoring you from afar, making every day Christmas!'

I joke, embarrassed, 'Only because he often isn't there for Christmas!'

She had laughed and shooed the dogs out of the kitchen. 'Bugger off, you lot, and take your muddy paws elsewhere. Gin time, I think.' She had grinned at me, ruefully. 'Well, I may have been a bit of a favourite as a child, old thing, being organized and . . .'

'Winning scholarships all over the place.'

'Much bloody good it's done me, all I do is push food into people and animals.'

'You love it!'

'Yes, I do. What I was going to say before you interrupted? Oh, yes, maybe I was Mum's favourite as a child, but it is your lifestyle she relates to now. She cannot abide coming here, we are all too noisy and bohemian for her. Well, I can't help it, that's how we are.'

I could hear the hurt in her voice. I thought how frightening being a parent is: whatever you do you will hurt one of your children it seems.

'Jane,' I said, 'I do love you, and I adore coming here.'

She handed me an enormous gin. 'Bloody liar. Make yourself useful, take this to Tom in the office and tell him we'll eat at eight and I'll expect him in to carve.'

As I walked across the cobbled yard towards the stables which house Tom's office, I thought, how strange, the sister I remember from childhood is so different from the one before me.

Of course she was bossy, I was the annoying little sister, but she was so conventional then, so boringly, narrowly academic. She minded what people thought, she dressed carefully, with no imagination, even at university. When she came back for the holidays, I would be tie-dying and

124

jangling with cheap jewellery. I would embarrass her. She thought I was vulgar and had no taste whatsoever.

I thought she was a prude and knew I amused her university friends, and she hated it. It had not occurred to me before, through marriage we had both changed. As a naval wife I had been forced to tone down my excesses. Jane, secure in a conventional marriage, away from pleasing our mother, had become more unconventional, and totally uncaring about what people thought.

The next day I drove down the straight and beautiful Oxfordshire road to Brize Norton where light shone on white Cotswold stone and glinted on a vast array of autumn colours that I miss in Cornwall. I ached with excitement. In two hours I would see Ben. I had a weekend booked in a plush hotel and I wanted to shout and sing because life, as Jane said, was bloody good.

At Brize Norton it seemed both strange and familiar to be mingling with uniforms again. I checked the flight was on time then sat with a coffee, watching people. I immediately noticed one girl in particular. She was very attractive with long blonde hair. She had a little boy of about a year tucked under her arm and she walked up and down nervously. Both were very brown as if they had recently been abroad.

Eventually she came and sat near me and we struck up a conversation. I asked her if she was meeting her husband and she went pink and shook her head. After a minute she told me that she and her husband had just split up and she was meeting a friend. She suddenly looked very young and miserable and I felt sorry for her.

She told me her story in a little relieved rush, as people do to strangers who they will never meet again. She was married to a REME captain and they had been living in Singapore for the last fifteen months. Her husband sounded a dreadful bore and she said she suddenly couldn't bear him any more and decided to fly home.

It must have taken courage. The forces did not like

125

errant wives. 'What decided you, finally?' I asked, curiously.

She went pink again and said that she had met someone who had helped her have the courage to do it. Another man. I said, suddenly surprising myself, 'Be careful. You are very vulnerable at the moment.'

Tears welled up in her eyes, grateful for any concern and I sensed the misery of months about to erupt. Knew suddenly she was hanging in there for whoever she was meeting.

At that moment the flight was called and we both walked over to the huge glass window where we could watch the plane land.

As people streamed off the plane my excitement returned. I strained to see Ben and moved over to the gate where he would come in. The girl beside me moved too. Suddenly I caught sight of him, brown and beautiful, turning and laughing happily to someone next to him. My heart soared and shivered with longing. He would be so surprised to see me. I turned to the girl beside me and her face too was alight, sparkling with life, transformed by love. I followed her gaze.

It was on Ben.

Ben turned and peered as if looking for someone. I jumped and waved and so did the girl and her baby. He raised his arm and beamed as he saw her. She was taller and more beautiful, more noticeable than I was. A second later he saw me and his smile disappeared. He literally stopped dead in his tracks. He didn't know what to do.

It was like being hit by a truck. The girl turned and stared at me, horror on her face. I turned and stumbled blindly away. Ran across the airport and out to June's Land Rover where I heaved myself up into it and sat there quivering, rocking sickly with my arms round myself, waiting for the terrible pain to ease enough to drive away.

My mother always said you should never ever try and surprise anyone. Well, she was right. I had had the surprise.

126

How can happiness be so complete one moment and gone the next, never to be replaced in the same way? Never to be so joyous, innocent or encompassing again?

I managed to start the car, but could not see to back it out of its slot. I sat there snuffling and wiping my nose across my sleeve because I didn't have a tissue, and suddenly Ben appeared at the window. His face was white. I couldn't bear to look at him.

'Go away, you bastard!' I yelled.

'Annie. Let me in, I must talk to you. It's not quite how it looks.'

I laughed then and put the Land Rover into reverse.

'You can't drive like this, Anna. For God's sake, get out and come and calm down, let me talk to you,' he shouted.

I wound down the window. I wasn't crying any more. I was beside myself with fury. I dug the hotel reservations out of my bag and threw them at him 'Go and talk to that girl, Ben. Here you are, do it in comfort. You're an absolute bastard and if you don't get out of my way I'll run you over.'

I revved up and reversed, very nearly catching him. He looked ashen and in shock as he very well might. The burst of fury got me to the first motorway service station where I stopped and went for coffee. I had twins of eight and I wasn't going to kill myself for that adulterous bastard.

I drove all the way back to Cornwall without stopping once, a nightmare journey. June was sleeping in my house with the boys and when she heard me she came rushing down the stairs. Ben had rung her. She had been worried sick. She hugged and hugged me and bundled me into a hot bath and then into bed with toast and Marmite and a vast brandy. I lay motionless all night, catatonic with exhaustion and shock.

The next day we talked. She made me let Ben come home to explain. She helped me face the pain head on, not avoid it. She helped me make it a part of my everyday life until it shrunk to a size I could just manage if I was busy and

127

careful. And when Ben had gone back to his ship after his leave ended, we reviewed my life. She helped me start a new life that was mine and not dependent on Ben.

It was a horrible leave. But I couldn't keep up the anger. I loved him. There were the boys thrilled to have their father home. There was my heart turning at the sight of him coming out of the shower, running across the beach, hugging June. There were the endless conversations. 'I wanted to help her . . . It just sort of happened.'

I asked him what she thought, the girl. 'She thinks I'm a bastard for hurting you. She thinks I'm a bastard because she believes I misled her. She asked me what it felt like crucifying two women.'
Good for her.

I asked him if he loved her and he hesitated a moment too long. He said she was special in a way he didn't understand but that he loved me. Cut to the quick, I told him he could have a divorce. 'Oh, for God's sake, Annie,' he said, 'I don't want one. My life is here with you and the boys.'

But he had to take responsibility for the predicament the girl and her child were in. She might never have left her husband if Ben hadn't encouraged her to leave. Eventually she did go back to her husband and I made myself stop asking if he still saw her.

The following summer Ben flew the boys and me out to the naval base in Singapore. His ship was having a refit. It was a wonderful and happy summer, but I often wonder if our marriage would have recovered if June had not poured her life into loving us better.

I believe when I started to have a life of my own and a successful business, Ben started to see me differently. I was no longer the child he had married and moulded, biddable and loving, but a woman called Anna, earning her own money.

Now, so many years later as I drive towards the sea, I wonder why memories dance about like motes in beams of sunlight, apparently randomly. Is it because Ben and I came down this road to the pub at the bottom that awful leave. Here, where no one knew us? Or is it some familiar smell? Huge blue cedars line the road like the ones at the bottom of June's garden.

Or is it my joy in this day which reminds me of another long ago when it was whipped away?

I decide it is probably all these things. I do not often leave the house and garden and driving is a freedom that takes me to neutral territory where the voices of my past are clearer and bound to colour my morning.

When I have delivered the plants and arrive home, Jessie is on the cordless phone, sitting on the steps outside the front door in the sun. 'Mum, look, I can't meet you, it's too far. I'll get Dad, then. I'm all right . . . Yes . . . Yes . . . Please . . . Look, I'll write, OK?'

She sees me and grins. Gets up and does a little jig, holding the phone away from her ear and making faces, rolling her eyes to the sky. She is wearing the most ridiculous outfit which seems to be made up of frail pieces of material she has tie-dyed finished off with her enormous black lace-up DMs or some such boot.

I grin back at her. It is going to be about a hundred degrees, she will expire.

She puts the phone down. 'Hi. Dad is going to give me a lift into Truro, to the swimming pool.'

I laugh. 'Oh, I see, silly me, I should have guessed. You have got all dressed up to get undressed again.'

Jessie giggles and tosses her mass of dark hair about. She is in a good mood. 'No need to be sarcastic. Alice is here, she has just gone down the garden. Dad is carrying some water down for her.'

I leave the front door open and walk down into the garden. The voices of the past fade gently away and I am firmly back in the present planning my day.

Chapter 25
Ian

Anna is up and gone before I wake properly. I lie for a while enjoying the prospect of Saturday. Then I get up and put my head round Jessie's door to see if she wants tea, but she is dead to the world.

No one is about so while the kettle boils I walk down the garden in my dressing gown. It is a still and marvellous morning. Down here hidden almost from the house it is like a little kingdom. There is colour everywhere, bedding plants have wilted but vast pots of geraniums remind me of a house I once rented in Tuscany.

Anna has made a little arbour with a seat and divided the gardens like small rooms which lead into each other, shielding this part of the garden from the tunnels and greenhouses. I am again filled with admiration and something else. Envy? Perhaps. Envy for something so imaginative and complete and creative. Anna's ability to move outside herself and make an external statement which is linked to what she is. A fecundity in nature. This garden, I suddenly see, is how Anna exists and thrives, endures and flourishes.

I get up and walk about noticing more and more what she has done since we came here and it is incredible. I *am* jealous. Jealous that she has not needed me for any of it. I do not exist in this, her kingdom. I smell the roses and see cloudy clumps of colour, flowers I do not even know the names of, falling over small dry stone walls. The wind rattles palms and the early morning sun, arriving up through a creek mist, shines on the glossy leaves of huge camellia trees, showing up cobwebs glistening with dew, linking flowers and branches.

I am intrigued by her facility to be inside something I can only view from the outside. Walking on a beach at sunset with Anna once I was amused and struck by her total immersion in the pink sky turning pale purple like a bruise and reflected like a mirage in the sea below. I could see the colours, I could admire them, I could describe them. I could see they were spectacular. But I wasn't *in* them. I was on the outside looking in. Anna was completely submerged, unaware of me, part of the sea and sky.

For the first time in my life I wondered if I had been born without a second eye. I felt I was missing something. This feeling sets me apart from Anna.

I feel as if I am trespassing. I am adrift in someone else's life. Does she dream of Ben here? Is all this a shrine and homage to a life that is gone for ever for her? A life when she was happy and young. Do I think she is unhappy with me then? I suddenly realize that I do and the thought is as sad and confusing as my feelings about Hester.

I should come down here more. Here is the spirit of Anna. Here is the heart of all that she is and does. I do not know her. I really do not know or understand this woman I have married. I like her very much. I admire her. I fancy her. I love her as much as I am able to love anyone.

But is it enough? I really do not know whether I have the energy to expend on intimacy any more.

Pud wrote to me urging me to talk to Anna, to try to explain my guilt and confused feelings about Hester. But how can I explain something I do not understand myself? Here, in Anna's garden, Hester seems as far away as if she never happened and there is such a peace in the feeling, yet I know it will not last. That bloody phone will ring, linking inextricably that life with this.

132

I can hear Jessie calling me. 'Dad, Dad.' In an irritated voice. Then she comes running down the garden. 'The kettle is boiling its head off, Dad. What are you doing?'

'I was enjoying the peace.'

'Oh.' She sits beside me. 'Where's Anna?'

'She's gone to deliver some plants. Jess, would you say you are happy?'

Jessie stares at me. 'Why? Now, this minute do you mean?'

'I mean, in general.'

'I'd rather live in a town.'

'Apart from that?'

She bites a nail and sniffs. 'You mean is it OK living with Anna, don't you?'

'I suppose I do.'

'Yeah, it's all right. Dad, can I have a lift into Truro? I want to meet Lily, a whole lot of us are meeting at the swimming pool.'

I look at her. I suppose she is very much my daughter. She likes to keep her thoughts to herself, that way they can be controlled.

'I suppose so. Though I imagine there is a perfectly good bus. I'll trade you for coffee and toast.'

'Done! Dad, you'll have to get on though, I've only got an hour.'

She disappears through the trees humming and I smile. I've got my answer. Jess is fine.

I start to walk back up the garden when I hear the pink camper van. I see Alice leap out and the camper turns and she calls out to two small boys as it disappears in the dust from the drive. I am irritated. I didn't know she was coming today and I am embarrassed to be caught in my dressing gown.

Alice throws back her head and laughs as I try and slink past her and round into the kitchen door.

'Well, well,' she calls, 'a bit of decadence, a bit of slumming from the executive class this morning is there?'

I grin at her. Alice amuses me. Few people have the courage to tease me. I have the sort of face which discourages it. Alice is afraid of no one.

Jess hears her and shoots round the corner, her face lighting up at the sight of the way-out Alice. 'Come on, Alice, come and have coffee and toast with us.'

I leave them and go upstairs to shower. I feel suddenly cheerful. I will try to talk to Anna. I have too much to lose not to.

Chapter 26
Hester

Janice what's-her-name bangs on my door before I am up. She wakes me up. The bloody woman wakes me up. Gives me a fright too. I can't think where I am for a minute.

'What sort of time do you think this is?' I ask her crossly. 'I was fast asleep.'

'It's ten thirty, Hester, and you were expected at the clinic to pick up your prescription at nine o'clock. Remember?'

'No.'

She sighs and comes past me into the house without being asked in. She draws back the curtains in the lounge and looks around. I can see she is in a mood. My head aches, it thumps like someone is inside it.

She lifts up my supper plate from the floor and some cups and things I left there which are nothing to do with her and takes them into the kitchen and bangs them down. I can hear her fiddling with my packet of pills, the silver foil goes plop as she presses the holes to count my pills.

She sighs again. I am getting sick of her sighing. I go into the kitchen. 'Hester,' she says, 'you only have two pills left. You should have one week left. Is there another packet somewhere?'

'I don't know, do I?'

'Did you take one, last night?' She peers at me. 'Or more than one?'

'I can't remember.'

Her voice rises. 'But you have been told, Hester, over and over. You must only take one at a time. Taking two, if you forget, doesn't work.'

'It's not my fault. Sometimes I forget the morning one, so I take two in the evening. It says on the packet, two a day, doesn't it?'

'TWO A DAY, MORNING AND EVENING.' She is almost shouting. 'We have been through this time and again, Hester. The pills now come in foil containers, much easier for you to remember. I know you understand perfectly well the importance of the dosage, so why are you being perverse?'

She clutches her long hair back with her hand and closes her eyes for a minute. There are big dark circles under her eyes. I have never seen her like this before, almost as if she might burst into tears.

She turns and plugs my kettle in and says quietly, 'Go and get dressed please, Hester. I'll make you tea and then give you a lift to get your prescription.'

That's quite kind of her. I feel sorry for her. I don't know why.

'Make one yourself. You look tired,' I tell her.

She smiles at me. 'Thank you, Hester. Can you hurry? I am supposed to be at an important meeting.'

I go and put on my clothes and while I am drinking my tea she watches me. After a bit she says, 'Hester, it is important, don't you think, to try and keep your flat clean and tidy. It is such a nice, bright flat, something to take pride in?'

'It's all right.'

'The other thing is, you must put your rubbish in the green bins provided, Hester, not just outside your front door, where it will smell and animals can get to it.'

I look at her. 'Who's been saying I do that?'

'I can see that you have. And I think some of your neighbours have asked you to use the bins, haven't they?'

'Them! None of them like me.'

'I'm quite sure that is not true. I'm sure they want to be

136

friendly and helpful, but you are rude to them sometimes, aren't you, Hester?'

'They whisper and their children call me names. They shout things at me.'

I can feel the anger starting. I hate them all, they think they are so posh and la-de-da and they aren't.

Janice whatnot leans forward. I would like to cut all that awful frizzy hair right off.

'Please try to get on with people, Hester. Life will be so much easier for you then.' She gets up and says, 'The thing is, I am not going to be able to visit you as often as I have been doing. I have an enormous caseload and I just cannot get round everybody. This is why it is so important for you to start taking responsibility for your own medication.'

I look at her, my heart starts to thump. 'You mean you are not coming again, don't you?'

'No, I don't mean that at all. I am still your social worker and you are still in my care. But will you please come to the centre regularly, for your follow-up care, Hester? It is there purely for the benefit of people who have been in hospital and you can air any problems, get help with anything worrying you.'

'It's too far.'

'It is not too far. Are you ready? It is less than fifteen minutes on the bus from here.'

I get my bag and we lock the flat and get into her car which needs a clean and she says, as we drive off, 'I had hoped I might get you some ancillary help, someone to help you with the housework and things, but I'm afraid with the cutbacks . . .'

'Do you like your job?' I ask.

'I used to, Hester, when I started.'

'You are only young now.'

She smiles. Her face is much better when she smiles. 'I'm not, you know. I am nearly thirty-six.'

'You don't look it, but you have got black rings round your eyes.'

'I have had to work a lot of extra hours this month. One of my staff is on sick leave and one on maternity leave and they haven't been replaced.'

'You need a holiday.'

She laughs and sniffs. 'Indeed I do! I am going off camping in France with my boyfriend in two weeks.'

'That's nice. Have a good time.'

'Thank you, Hester, I will.'

'I used to work for the tourist board in Oxford. It was a very good job.'

She seems surprised. She parks outside the clinic and turns and looks at me. 'Did you? That must have been very interesting indeed.'

'It was. But my husband made me leave. I met so many people, you see, he was jealous.'

She makes a funny little smile with her mouth that isn't a smile because it makes her look sad. She says, 'Have a good day, Hester. They are expecting you inside. I'll see you again soon.'

I get out and she shoots off. She's not bad really. I don't want to go inside, they go on and on about the bloody pills as if I am a child. I am not and I can do as I like, it's up to me. They like to control people, the social services, everyone knows that. I am just going to creep away when I see someone I know from the hospital so I go inside. I suddenly think of something nice. Janice Hardything is going on holiday. Why shouldn't I?

I haven't had a holiday for ages either. I'll go camping too. It is a very good idea. I will have to buy things I need. Then I'll catch a train to Cornwall.

I won't tell them I'm coming, I'll ring when I get there. I'll tell my husband to have Jess all ready. She loves camping, does Jess.

Chapter 27
Anna

Chrysanthemum parthenium. Feverfew.
White petals round a yellow centre. The
foliage has a pungent smell so this is not
a flower for cutting.

The phone is ringing and ringing. I hear it as I start my watering and it is still ringing as I go up to the house to turn some chicken in the Rayburn. I hear Ian say tightly, 'I'll get Jessie, but these phone calls will have to stop, otherwise I will have to change the number. If you ring occasionally, fine, but you are ringing all the time, Hester.'

Jessie and Lily come bursting in the front door giggling, and rush upstairs. Jessie has been on holiday for weeks and I dread her getting bored or falling out with Lily, then I really will have problems.

There is a hosepipe ban and although I am exempt because I have a business I still have to be careful. Water is a problem and I have had to use bath- and washing-up water which has to be lugged all the way down to the greenhouses.

Alice has been wonderful, coming in for extra hours, but we are both exhausted, working in this heat. Ian has helped me every evening carrying the buckets and filling the water butts outside the summerhouse. But he is under pressure as he has a big tender coming up with the council which he is desperate to get to build up the reputation of the firm and to ease some of our financial problems.

We see each other briefly during the week. I am in the garden until it is too dark to see and Ian is working late, long after I have collapsed into bed. I am up and out before him in the morning, so we meet briefly at supper which I have begun to dread.

Hester seems to dominate supper. Her timing is unerring. No matter what time we sit down she manages to interrupt the meal. The answer phone infuriates her and Ian has to switch it off or she uses all the tape up which in turn infuriates him.

We sit steeled for Hester's call, trying to be normal and pretend it might not ring. If we take it off the hook, which we often do while we eat, the abuse when she does get through is much worse. I have got to the stage where I refuse to answer any calls in case it is her. Every evening I go straight back down to the greenhouses, away from those endless calls which puncture our lives. Disrupt, unnerve, mar the atmosphere of wonderful long summer evenings.

If Jessie has Lily staying the call has drama value and can be discussed endlessly in the safety of bedrooms. But the Hester Jessie talks about to Lily is not the one she talks to me about, or the one she dreads arriving on our doorstep. It is a sanitized version for schoolgirl consumption.

Tonight, when I go up to the house for a break I pour a glass of wine, get Ian a beer from the fridge and go upstairs where he is working. He sits tight-lipped at his desk. I see he has had enough of Hester.

He takes the beer and downs it almost in one go. 'Have you got time to sit for a minute?' he asks.

'Of course I have.' I collapse in a chair opposite him. 'Getting up again will be the problem!'

He smiles at me tiredly. 'How are you doing?'

'I'm losing far too many plants. I'm going to lose money this year, Ian, without a doubt.'

'Well, there's absolutely nothing you can do about a heatwave, unfortunately.' He fiddles about with a pencil distractedly.

'What's the matter?' I ask. 'Apart from the obvious.'

'It is the obvious,' he says. 'We can't go on like this, Anna. I was wrong. Hester's calls haven't stopped, they just go on and on.'

'If only the boys would ring, I could tell them we have to change the number.'

'It isn't just the boys. I'm bloody fed up. We are both running businesses. We shouldn't have to be ex-directory. If people can't get hold of you they go elsewhere. Fat lot of good it did us being out of the phone book anyway. She got the number somehow.'

'But there isn't anything we can do, is there, apart from changing the number?'

'I could go to the police. We are being harassed, Anna, and there is a law to protect us against this sort of thing.'

'But doesn't that mean an injunction or something? Going to court, with logs of calls to prove she is being a nuisance?'

'Yes. I thought if I rang the police they might use some influence on social services to take some responsibility.'

'But is she their responsibility?'

'Presumably. I don't know. They are responsible for her medication. They were responsible for letting her out of hospital. They judged she was fit to be out.'

'I'm not sure it's quite as simple as that, Ian. I suppose we are all expected to absorb and care for people like Hester. That's what Care in the Community is supposed to mean, isn't it?'

Ian looks at me. 'Even if people like Hester ruin lives, go on ruining them?'

I get up and go over to him and he winds his arms round me and leans his head against me. He is heavy and I feel his exhaustion in his bent head.

'I should never have married you, Anna. It was very wrong of me.'

I pull away. 'Come on, you're getting maudlin. Let's go for a walk before it gets too dark. You're exhausted, Ian.

141

Come and relax for half and hour and then we'll go to bed, together for once.'

He laughs and gets up. 'Unfortunately, I think I am only capable of sleeping.'

'Don't worry about it, so am I.'

We call out to Jessie, collect Hebe and walk down the lane towards the burnt-out manor. The night is so still you can hear a leaf fall. The track is hard and cracked and the verges bursting with cow parsley. We walk up to the manor without talking. Eventually, as we reach the gates leading to the burnt-out house I say, 'Would you like Hester to be readmitted?'

Ian leans on the gate and looks up towards the sad house with its gaping windows.

'I don't know. I suppose I would be sorry if she had to be.'

'I don't understand, Ian. What do you want for her? What do you think should happen to her?'

Ian does not answer and the silence between us grows.

I remember the other night, the night of the storm when he told Jessie that Hester had our number. There was something in his face I did not understand.

Then I glanced at Jessie and saw fleetingly a strange, sly, kind of excitement flicker across her face. It was quickly replaced by conventional horror, but it was there.

A look of fervent suspense passed between them as they faced each other against the background of the storm. I wondered suddenly if they needed the constant challenge of Hester in their lives, like battered wives returning for more.

Is it like me, dreaming of Ben and my old life? Is it what they perceive as their real life, now gone?

Do they yell too loud, protest too much? I feel the same agitation as that evening, with the lightning zigzagging over the trees and as disturbed as the claps of thunder which followed it.

Is this what Hester knows, deep, deep inside her?

142

I say quietly, 'What is it that you feel for Hester, Ian?'

He turns his back on the house and faces me. 'She is the mother of my child, Anna. I just feel profound and utter sadness. She's stuck in the past. Jessie is five and I am still her husband. She can't move on. She's stuck in the past.'

I feel emptiness in the pit of my stomach. And I am startled. I hadn't expected this. I feel suddenly isolated and yet it is perfectly natural for him to have these feelings, Hester was his wife. It's just I believed he didn't have any feelings except anger for her any more and I feel shock that he does.

I feel bewildered.

We walk on, turn and cut back through the woods, the woods I am afraid of. The light is going and I am walking at dusk with someone I don't know at all. I share a life and a bed with a man whose feelings are skilfully hidden. Pain rises, pressing against my chest.

Suddenly we come upon badgers, little, big-bottomed babies and we freeze excitedly as we watch them chase about and play like puppies. They quickly see us and disappear but Ian keeps hold of my hand. 'Anna, I feel sometimes, maybe I should have remained responsible for her. You know? For better, for worse.'

I take my hand from him. 'Perhaps it was something to be considered before you married me. A bit late in the day to feel all this, isn't it?'

'Oh, Anna, I didn't mean it like that! You know I don't mean I wish I hadn't married you. I mean I sometimes wonder if I had any right to.'

'Any right to divorce Hester? Or any right to marry me!'

I am very angry.

He makes me turn to look at him. 'Anna, I'm tired. Any right to marry you and put you through this. But, yes, I do feel guilt. Perhaps Hester should still be my problem.'

I am cold and it is dark and I do not like these woods at

dusk. I do not like them even in sunlight. Now I can feel them closing in on me, trapping me into darkness.

'You think you should have had a life sentence, do you, Ian? Perhaps you should sort out what you really do feel about Hester. Where is the guilt coming from?' I ask angrily. 'Are you just being overwrought and sorry for yourself? Do you feel you are in some way to blame? Do you feel loss, despite everything, because Hester is the mother of your child? Perhaps you still love her? Is there some tie there I don't understand?'

Ian stops me. 'Anna, why are you so angry? Of course I don't feel love. I feel anger and frustration. I feel pity and I feel . . . useless. I can't prevent her intrusion. I can't prevent her presence in our lives. I want her to leave us in peace. Then, sometimes when I hear her voice, I remember how she was when I first saw her, when I married her, slim and dark and pretty. That's when I feel guilt, Anna.' He turns me to face him. 'Anna, I feel horrified sometimes of my feelings about Hester. I loathe how she makes me feel. I have got to such a pitch that I wish someone who was once my wife dead.'

'Ian.' I shiver. 'I'm sorry, I can't go on with this conversation now. I'm cold and Jessie is alone in the house.'

We stumble on in silence and come out of the wood on to the narrow overgrown path which follows the fence that separates this part of the woods from the private woods behind the house.

As we start to descend I feel the hairs rise suddenly on the back of my neck. Hebe starts to grumble softly under her breath. I stare into the darkness but can see nothing. I turn and hurry down towards the lights of the house. They look welcoming. Jessie has her curtains closed, she always does, but light is streaming out from the kitchen and spills out on to the flagstones. Below me I can see, shining in the dark, the white of nicotiana and roses, standing out clear against the shadows.

144

Round at the front door Jessie is shining a torch down the lane looking for us. All the lights in the house are on. 'Where on earth have you been?' she yells. 'I've been worried sick!'

Both Ian and I burst out laughing. She has a pinny on and huge great dog slippers on her feet. She stands in the doorway, hands on her hip as light spills out on to the porch. 'It's not funny!' she says. 'I've been really spooked on my own. You shouldn't leave me for so long.' But she grins at us, glad we are back.

'Sorry,' Ian says.

'I hate all that blackness. I wish there were houses out there with twinkling lights.'

'I'll just check the greenhouses. Can I have the torch, Jess?'

Ian says to Jess, 'I'm just going down the garden with Anna.'

I look at him. 'There is no need, I do it every night. I am often still down there at this time.'

'I don't care,' he says, following me down. 'Tonight, I am coming with you.'

I wake to horrible screaming. Ian is out of bed before I can even gather my wits. When I get to Jessie's room he is hugging a sobbing Jessie curled into him as if to bury herself.

'She was in the room.' She is sobbing. 'She was here in my room, Dad. She was . . . she was . . . I saw her.'

'No. You were dreaming, Jess. You were having a nightmare. There is no one here. No one can get in. It was just a horrible dream.'

'I'm sure she was standing by the bed. I'm sure she was in my room. I felt her.'

'Jess, stop this,' Ian says firmly. 'Your mother cannot get into the house. She does not even know where we live. She is in London. You should not eat cheese on toast last thing at night.' He tries to make her laugh.

145

Jessie turns and looks up at me. 'I'll go and make some tea and I'll check all the doors again, Jess.'

'And the windows,' she calls after me.

I check everywhere. Everywhere is locked. Jessie looks relieved.

As we huddle round the Rayburn I decide I will make curtains for the kitchen windows. Ian takes Jessie back to bed and tucks her up like a three year old. She is enjoying having his attention. I realize suddenly, we are both so busy, Jess is feeling neglected, despite her friends.

Ian is ages coming back to bed and I get up to see what he is doing. He is checking the front door and the little windows each side of it. I watch him check the door that leads out to the wooden garage, built when we did the extension. His face looks white in the dark. He does not see me standing on the stairs.

I remember suddenly what he once told me.

'The odd thing is, Anna, that before Hester appears, Jessie always has the most awful nightmares. As if she knows deep inside when her mother is near.'

For the second time tonight the hairs rise up on my neck. I turn and stumble back to the bedroom. I walk through it into the little dressing room and firmly shut the door. I switch the little lamp on and it shines on the photos of my smiling sons. On Ben.

I close my eyes. I will pretend. I will pretend he isn't dead. I will pretend I am back in the cottage by the sea and that I am safe. Lamps are on everywhere and Ben and I are laughing as we move about cooking a meal. Upstairs there is loud music from the boys' rooms and Ben turns and smiles that amazing lazy smile that turns my legs to water.

June is in her large house and if I open my eyes I will see that ancient cedar and hear the noise it makes in the wind, like the sea breaking on white sand. Like the soft whispering sound of familiar voices filtering down through sweet-smelling branches.

146

Chapter 28
Hester

It is dark and the night is very hot. I can't sleep. I get up and look at the picture I bought. It is of a little girl in an old-fashioned dress with a puppy and a kitten. It is like my Jessie. I put it on the chair because I haven't got a hook to hang it yet.

I think I will pack now. I will make some tea first. I do not know what time it is as my clock has stopped but it must be very late because it is quiet outside. No one is shouting or swearing out there.

I bought a track suit from that cheap factory shop. I will need one for the country. And I bought a sleeping bag and some polythene. I remembered that you have to have polythene from when we used to go camping. Jessie was only a baby then and we had to keep her very warm.

I bought a present for Jessie in case it is her birthday. It could be. It's a dress. It's very pretty with smocking. And I bought a skirt for me for her party and a T-shirt. I used up all my money.

The tea tastes horrible, I think it is old. I don't know what to put my things in. I will have to go to her house and find something. The sun is coming up so I can go now. I will have to walk because I have no money.

It is nice outside, there is no one about except the old tramp who is slumped in the newsagent's doorway. I feel sorry for him although he can get quite nasty and shout.

When I reach the house I ring the doorbell but no one answers. I know she is there because the bedroom curtains are drawn and she never gets up early, she is too fat and lazy.

I ring and ring and then I start to bang on the door and shout for her to open it. She really is a bugger. People in the next-door houses start to look out of their windows and shout at me to be quiet. A man opens his window and calls down to me. He is black with grey crinkly curly hair. 'Hester,' he shouts, 'do you know what time this is, woman? It is only five thirty in the morning and your mother is fast asleep. Now go home like a good girl until morning.'

'Bugger off and mind your own sodding business,' I shout back. I can't remember his sodding name.

The curtains are drawn back and she appears at the window. She has got very old. She looks down at me without a smile, as always. 'Hester, be quiet, you are disturbing the whole street. What on earth do you want at this time of the morning?'

'Let me in. I want a bag to put my things in. I want that soft bag thing of yours. I am going away.'

I hear someone shout, 'Alleluia.' And I bang on the door again. I am going to get angry.

'Let me in!' I shout at her. 'Let me in, you old cow.'

'Don't!' the black man shouts to her. 'Shall I call the police?'

'No!' she shouts back. 'All right, I'm coming down, Hester. Just be quiet, will you?'

The black man disappears from the window too and, as she opens the door, he comes out of his door and walks across to us.

'It's all right, Ronald,' she says. 'I'll be fine.'

He looks at her and says, 'That is what you said to me four years ago. Let me come in this time, Mai.'

'What is he talking about?' I ask her. 'Tell him to bugger off, will you?'

She stares at me and I notice her hands are shaking. She really is old.

148

'Well,' she says after a minute, 'he could make us tea, while we look for your bag, couldn't he? He could even make a bit of toast if you are hungry.'

I am hungry. 'OK,' I say and I go into the house and the black man follows me.

She starts to climb the stairs slowly, holding on to the rail with one hand and holding her dressing gown up with the other. She tells me to stay down and she will be back soon. I go into the kitchen and sit down and the black man looks at me.

'Hester,' he says, 'your old mother can do without these disturbances.'

I don't answer. I see her bag on the chair, half hidden by the tablecloth. There are two clumps from upstairs and the man gets up quickly and goes out, shouting that he will carry the bags down. I have to be quick. I open her bag and see her wallet. I open it and pull the notes out quickly and push them in my pocket and shut the bag.

The man comes back with two canvas bags but they are not what I want. One is too big and one is the wrong shape. She sits on the chair the other side of the table.

'They are the only soft bags I have, Hester. What sort of bag are you after?'

I can't remember the proper name for it but I tell her I want to be able to fold my sleeping bag in it and carry it on my back.

'Knapsack!' the black man says. 'Stay there! I might be able to help you.'

When he has gone my mother makes the tea and says, 'Where are you going, Hester?'

'I'm off on holiday, camping. Just like we used to.'

She stares at me. 'Who with?'

'Wendy, from the hospital. We are going together.'

'Does the social worker know, Hester?'

I look at her. She wants me back in there away from my family. She is part of it all. I have known all along really. Those pills are to keep me muddled so I can't go anywhere. She is worried that I won't take the pills too.

149

But I must be careful in case they stop me. Jessie needs me.

'Of course,' I tell her. 'And Melanie. I have injections now, to save taking the pills. One a month.'

She passes me a cup of tea. 'Oh good. So you are feeling much better?'

'I'm fine. Why shouldn't I be?'

She sits down at the table heavily, making it rock and my tea spills into my saucer. She was always fat and clumsy. She was never beautiful and smiley like my father thought she was. It was a mask. She pretended. Like she is pretending now to care how I am. I am getting a headache, my head is starting to buzz. I don't like her. I don't like being near her. She makes me sick.

She has both hands round her cup of tea and she is staring at me again with something in her face I do not like. 'Hester,' she says, 'I hope you can find peace and happiness. I hope you will take advantage of the help offered to you. I'm sorry if you feel I've failed you, somehow. You were always your father's child, I'm afraid. I've never understood you.'

The voices rise, rise, whispering to me.

I remember. I remember running down a garden path towards her. She had a long fair plait hanging down her chest. She was smiling. As I reached her I threw my arms around her legs and looked up into her face. The smile disappeared. She did not scoop me up. She bent and prised my arms away from round her legs. She walked away. She did not like the feel or touch of me.

I never ever went near her again.

'You never loved me,' I say.

Her eyes fill with tears. The black man comes back with a knapsack that has cobwebs on but it is exactly what I want.

I smile. 'Thanks. Thanks a lot. It's great.'

I'm happy. I walk down the passage to the front door. 'Bye,' I shout.

I hear her say, 'Oh, Hester, Hester,' very quietly before I slam the front door.

Chapter 29

Anna

Dianthus. 'Gran's Favourite' Old-
fashioned pinks. In summer masses of
sweet-smelling white flowers with a
deep-pink edging.

Every year Ben's mother, Naimah, flies in from Belfast to go
to the Chelsea Flower Show with me and catch up with her
friends in England. She books into her club near the West End
and I catch the train up to London. This year I had to miss the
flower show but we meet in August to go to the theatre and
have a meal. We plan to spend the following day together,
then I will catch the night train back to Cornwall.

Naimah meets me at Paddington. She is just the same. She
ages so gracefully and has such formidable energy. She used
to be a sculptor and is very Irish and eccentric. Ben's father
by contrast was a very conventional military man, but the
contrast must have worked for they had a wonderfully happy
marriage.

Ben was one of five children, the only boy, and when he
was killed, for a while, I thought Naimah was going to give
up and die too. But she didn't. Instead she started to paint,
wonderful pictures that sold.

She hugs me tightly then holds me away and stares at me
critically. 'My darling girl. Lovely as always you are, but so
thin and brown. Like a little Indian!'

151

I laugh and look at her still beautiful face with that unmistakable Irish colouring, pale, almost translucent, where the veins and shadows show underneath the fair skin.

'And you,' I say, 'are quite amazing, Naimah. The rest of us age but you remain the same!'

'Do you know, darling, I am eighty. Isn't it horrendous?' She links arms and we move slowly down the platform. She walks with a stick now and I feel her brittleness, her ageing in her arm in mine. I cannot bear the thought of Naimah dying.

'Everyone says *The Master Builder* is very good, so I've booked. Is that all right, darling? You do like Ibsen? Not too heavy?'

'I may live out in the sticks, Naimah, but my brain still functions, just.'

Naimah laughs. 'It's so good to see you, child.'

Sitting in the theatre is like old times. If Ben was home on leave when Naimah came to London, he would come too. But, mostly, the Chelsea Flower Show was Naimah's and my time together. The play is marvellous and I feel myself relaxing and enjoying the buzz of London. Naimah has booked a table at a Greek restaurant near the theatre afterwards and, as we sit facing each other, discussing the play, she suddenly says, 'Darling child, are you happy?'

I am taken by surprise. 'Naimah, why do you suddenly ask that?'

'Because when you got off that train you looked so tired and tense. So lost. I've felt you relaxing, becoming your old self as the evening has gone on. But the chatty, little bouncy Annie seems to have gone for good.'

I do not know what to say. As I look into her beloved face I wonder how changed I have become. My feelings, kept in careful check, rise suddenly to the surface and are in danger of swamping me. I do not know what I feel, I do not know what I want or who I am any more. I seem to live a life of trying to forget, trying to pretend. I seem to think people won't notice if I try hard enough.

She reaches for my hand. Hers is very pale with brown age spots on the back and I take those delicate, capable fingers and turn them in my palm. She doesn't speak, she is waiting for me to. So I try. I try to explain what it feels like to be out of my depth. What it feels like to live with two people I do not quite understand. To daily live with the voices in my ears of people I do understand and who are no longer with me.

Yet the essence of those people that made up my life, a life that is gone, are so much more real and more familiar than the ones I now live with. So that it is hard to know what to hang on to because the ground constantly shifts. It feels as if there is no safe ground. I have forgotten what it feels like to be safe. I am forgetting what it feels like not to feel anxious. It lives inside me this anxiousness, it has become a part of me.

Only to Naimah can I speak of such nebulous sensations. Of feelings which shimmer and dance just out of reach. Of a dread that lives within me that I cannot name, whose face I dimly recognize. Yet I do not want to cast a cloud on our time together. I see that she is troubled. Suddenly she looks the old lady she is. I smile quickly. 'Naimah, I'm just tired, take no notice, honestly, I'm just tired.'

It is important our time together is happy, for her and for me, so that I have it to hold on to later, when I am back in Cornwall.

Naimah says slowly, 'I can see that you're tired, darling. Gardening is tiring. Looking after a teenager is tiring. Adjusting to a second marriage is tiring.' She leans back, letting go my hand. 'I would expect you to be tired. That wouldn't worry me. It's something else. I sense you are speaking, child, of fundamentals, that you are making abstracts out of absolutes in order to cope. To feel safe we usually mix and mate with people we understand and are comfortable with. From the same background and culture. Or failing that they are familiar to us on an emotional or intellectual level. If we live with someone who meets none of these criteria, the alienation must be total and confusing.'

153

Naimah leans towards me. 'But, darling, why would you have done that? Married someone totally unfamiliar? Unless you misread the signs. Unless you made a mistake or married on the rebound, for all the wrong reasons.'

I tell her. I admit to the terror of the loss of Ben, my mother and June. Of the boys leaving for university. I tell her of the quiet sad architect who looked over June's house but couldn't afford it. Who took me to admire the new County Court at Truro, the Tate at St Ives, who could talk passionately about architecture, about space and light, about texture and dimensions. His voice would rise with excitement as he showed me books on buildings he had designed and helped to design.

A man who fixed things in the house for me. Who began to fill Sunday afternoons. Who eventually told me about his wife who was mentally ill and his daughter who was being looked after by his mother in Durham while he got his business off the ground in Cornwall.

A man who was kind to me and seemed honest, lonely and interesting.

And I tell Naimah about Hester, how suddenly, once he had introduced the subject of Hester, how rarely we spoke of anything else. The interesting man I had married seemed taciturn, shut in, obsessive much of the time, struggling with something and seeming to expect me to cope with his daughter on my own.

Naimah listens, then says slowly, 'Your husband . . . I feel very sorry for him, Anna darling. I cannot see how it could be possible to love, marry, have a child with a partner who is unbalanced without it affecting your own state of mind. Impossible to live with any member of a family who is mentally ill without viewing life a little askew yourself. Perhaps, darling, he married you too soon, before he is able to leave his wife behind him.'

We take a taxi back to the hotel and sit in her room drinking brandy and talking of the boys and happy things before we finally go to bed. As I kiss her goodnight she says, 'You remember? A Chinese kiss is pressing a nose to a cheek and smelling the scent of the skin?'

'Yes.'

'Have you forgotten, my darling, it is done because the person has to smell familiar. Smell and feel and touch. The chemical balance has to be correct. All has to feel right before the old Chinese contemplated a relationship.'

I smile. It is true. The twins' amah, Ah Heng, told me that. I had forgotten.

I know what Naimah is telling me.

The next day Naimah and I have the most wonderfully tiring day visiting Kew, the National Gallery, Waterstones and taking tea at the Ritz. There is so much to see we hardly have time to talk. She finds flying visits to London as thrilling as I do and there is never enough time to do all that we plan.

We have a late supper together, then Naimah insists on coming with me to Waterloo to catch the night train. I don't want to leave her. As we stand waiting she says, 'Darling, I just want to say this. If you have bitten off more than you can chew, don't be afraid to get out. Don't look back. Don't feel pity. Just go. Quietly and single-mindedly leave. Come to me.'

I feel like crying.

'But,' she says, 'be sure, Annie, that the echoes of Ben and of your life with him are not becoming louder than the voices of those you are now living with. Make sure the past does not cloud your future. So that you cannot hear or appreciate the rhythm and possibilities that lie ahead. Happiness lies within us all, my darling Annie.'

My train is called and she clutches my hands to her chest and closes her eyes for a minute. 'You are so precious to me. I love you and the boys so much. I know you adored my son to distraction, but he wasn't a saint, he didn't always make you happy. He was beautiful and selfish and fun and you had

155

a good life, full of love for the most part. But don't make him a faultless hero in your mind and memory, will you? A barrier to your future. Run, run, child, or you will miss your train.'

I start to run then something makes me turn back. I run back and hug her fiercely to me. We are both crying. It is as if we both suddenly feel we might not see each other again. Then I run – bolt – for my train. I look out of the window, strain to see her departing back in the dark, but she is gone and my sense of loss is overpowering.

It is early when I get back to the empty house. Alice has put the last of my sweet peas in the earthenware vase we dug up in the garden. They are faded purple like the pansies she has placed with them. It warms my heart, her thought and the beauty of those little turned-up faces.

In my bedroom she has placed deep blue cornflowers. She knew how I would be feeling when I returned. I walk round my room touching my things like a talisman. I walk past the breakfast things piled on the draining board and go down into the garden for the first of the day and breathe and breathe with relief to be back in the place I have created. A thing completed. Something I have taken sole responsibility for, and for which I have not asked for advice.

For once I have not been deflected or let this business of mine, or my garden project, take second place to what is happening in my life. It occurs to me suddenly as I garden all day, listening to the curlews on the water below me, that all my life has been lived through the lives of men. Ben, the boys. Now Ian and his life encroaching, as invasive as ivy, into my world.

How many wasted hours I spent crying over Ben when I was young when I should have been creating my own life. All that wasted energy in loving too much and weeping uselessly. June showed me the way out, the only way out. And what did I do as soon as she died? Jump into the first pair of arms that came along, grateful for succour.

Dusk comes. No one comes home. There must be a message

on my answering machine. I garden on and on with my thoughts.

As the days of summer start to peak and my garden becomes overblown and blowsy with the heat, I finally acknowledge what June so often tried to show me by example. Taking responsibility for my own life. Having the courage to admit I may have made a mistake. Having the courage to leave if necessary, despite any fear of financial hardship. What I have made here I can make again.

I could run away, find a little place for me and the boys. Home again, safe again. Just me and my sons, me and a garden. It is tempting.

Or I could stay and make this marriage work.

The moon sails out of a cloud, is reflected dramatically in the water below. Far, far away seabirds call out, making me shiver with a soft sadness. I hear the distant growl of Ian's Saab coming up the lane. I imagine his tired face in which hope is almost extinguished, but not quite. I imagine his face if I left, a face in which there would be no light left.

Of course I will stay.

As I walk up to the house to meet him I hear the sound of the phone. I hear it even over the slamming of the car doors.

Chapter 30
Ian

The YTS girl has done the most appalling typing I have ever had the misfortune to see. She has not managed to type one letter for me this week without a mistake and I am heartily sick of it. I just do not have the time for ineptitude. An eight year old could do better.

I go storming down the bloody staircase, nearly breaking my neck and tell her it just is not good enough. Badly typed, misspelt letters reflect on the firm and, if she isn't up to it, she should not have taken the job, anyone applying should be computer literate, which she obviously isn't if she cannot even find spell check. She tries to say something but I hold my hand up. I am not interested in excuses, I tell her, I would just like the few letters I do give her to be able to go straight out to the post.

Before I turn to go back upstairs I see tears well up in her eyes, but I can't help it. If Nick is too soft to do anything, then it has to be me.

I glance at Nick as I gallop through his office once more and he raises an eyebrow but says nothing. The phone is ringing as I reach my desk. The planning officer from Penwith in Penzance wants a meeting with Nick or me. Could one of us make it by midday? I know Nick has a meeting with the Sainsbury's group so I tell him I'll go.

My secretary, Miriam, comes up and we go through the week's appointments. She is cool and I know she is annoyed with me for shouting at the young YTS girl.

159

I should not have done that in front of the others. I am tired. The meeting went on and on last night.

I decide to leave for my appointment early, I need to get out of the office. 'I'll keep my fingers crossed for this afternoon, Nick,' I tell him as I go down.

'They can't stall much longer, they will have to give us an answer soon. It will be a relief to know either way. The waiting is getting me down.' He looks at me. 'I don't think it's what is getting you down though, is it?'

I laugh shortly. 'No. I am just honing my wonderful capacity for upsetting people this week. I am doing amazingly well at it.'

'Anna?'

'Yes. I took your wife's advice, tried to talk to her and completely ballsed it up.'

He looks at me unsympathetically. 'Well, you will just have to keep trying, won't you? Until you get better at it.'

'I usually get more sympathy from you, Nick.'

He swivels round on his chair and takes his glasses off, a sure sign he is annoyed.

'Ian, everyone in the office is very aware that Nancy's typing leaves a lot to be desired and there is every possibility that she will have to be replaced or her duties changed to filing until she improves. But she is seventeen years old and has lived all her life in care. She was so proud to be taken on. We were going to say something to her, gently, on Friday, so she could keep her dignity, not lose confidence.'

'Oh, God! I'm sorry.'

'Perhaps you could tell Nancy that at some point, Ian. The thing is, in a small office, it is important to check things out. If one person is upset then the whole team goes awry. There is enough stress at the moment just waiting to see if this job comes through.'

'I'm sorry,' I say again. And I am. For bringing my domestic problems to work with me, which is what I have done. 'I take your point, Nick. I'll talk to her later.'

*   *   *

160

Nancy is nowhere to be seen, but Miriam and Lucy glance balefully at me as I go out. I get in the car and, as I have plenty of time, I decide to take a detour home.

Anna is down at the bottom of the garden with Alice. There is strange music, some sort of Gregorian chant with cymbals, coming from the summerhouse. I stand watching them, before they see me. One dark head, bent repotting and one fair one, tied with an Indian scarf. They are absorbed in what they are doing, they look so peaceful and fey, almost of another world, bent with this music against the colours and textures of the plants and flowers around them.

I feel as if I am intruding.

Then Anna looks up, startled to see me. 'Is something wrong?' she asks, getting up.

'No, nothing.' I smile. 'I had to go to Penzance and I thought I would drop off for a cup of coffee. I don't want to disturb you.'

'Don't be so silly. I'll come up to the house with you. Would you like one, Alice?'

Alice grins at me. 'Hi, why don't you both sit in the garden and let me make the coffee? I expect it's good to get outside your office, isn't it?'

'It's very good. Especially as I have been upsetting everyone with my bad temper.'

'Oh, dear,' Alice smiles, as she disappears up the garden. 'Perhaps you need a whiff of happy baccy!'

'I certainly do not, Alice!'

Anna is laughing. 'Come and sit down and tell me why you have come home at lunchtime, when Penzance is in quite the opposite direction and could not in all imagination be called a detour!'

'I wanted, needed, to see you.' I have to say it quickly, in a rush, or I won't say it at all.

She looks at me. 'Oh Ian.'

'Anna, the other night . . . We haven't talked since . . . I

161

was overtired, not thinking straight. Please . . . Can you forget it? All I know is I love you. I missed you when you were in London last week. I want things to be all right between us. I want us to be happy. I want us to be united over Hester, over all the difficulties. I don't want to lose you.'

For the second time today I see tears in someone's eyes. She does not say anything, simply holds out her arms and I hear her say, 'You won't lose me. Just keep talking to me. Make me understand.'

'I'll try.' I hold her away. 'What on earth is this music? It is like being in the middle of a Tibetan monastery!'

Alice swirls down through the trees with a tray. 'Don't be rude! I bet you have never been in a Tibetan monastery!'

I laugh. 'I haven't actually. What's all this?'

Alice glances at Anna. 'I hope it's all right. I microwaved that bit of risotto for Ian. I hope you weren't saving it for anything. I thought you might miss lunch.'

Anna smiles. 'Sweet Alice, thank you.'

I am struck suddenly about how close these two women are.

'Sweet Alice, thank you indeed,' I echo. 'Now, you can both help me to make amends in the office.' And I tell them about my popularity state, my lack of sensitivity and team spirit.

'Flowers! Plant or chocolates, or both,' Anna says.

'Not a plant,' Alice says. 'She is seventeen, she is unlikely to be into plants. But flowers are romantic and grown up.'

'And you will probably need two boxes of chocolates. One for Nancy and one for the others,' Anna adds. 'And possibly a bottle of whisky for Nick.'

'Hang on! Don't let's go mad. I don't want to take out a mortgage for all this. We will have Nick over sometime. He is quite used to me.'

I finish the risotto and my coffee. 'I must go. I'm going to be late now. Thank you both for my lunch. Delicious.'

As I drive away I hear the music begin again. What a funny

162

little pair they are, totally content in their own little world. I wonder if Anna ever smokes pot when I am not around?

Back at the office I slope in with flowers and chocolates and apologies. I take Nancy aside and tell her I am not giving her flowers for typing badly, but for being rude to her in front of other people, which was unforgivable. She is deeply embarrassed and pleased at the same time. And I see in her eyes how right Nick was. She is astonished that anyone should bother about her feelings.

For this public and humble apology, I am awash with cups of tea all afternoon and there is a suspicious amount of crackling paper down below as the chocolates are opened. I am always amused at how easily these small acts of contrition please women.

At five thirty Nick puts his head round the door. 'Come on, you can buy me an early drink before we go home and I'll tell you about my afternoon.'

As I tidy my desk I am reminded suddenly of a shoot I was taken on long ago. At the end, as we all sat drinking round a log fire and the keepers brought in steaming pies, a little boy had a book in which he wrote at the end of each shoot. He had written quaintly, in beautiful handwriting, 'And a good day was had by all.'

That is exactly how I feel. I am looking forward to my drink and I am looking forward to going home.

Chapter 31

Hester

Hundreds of people get on the train at Reading. The train fills up with them. It is a good thing I got on at Paddington. Some wear coloured shoes on their feet, some have half their heads shaved and earrings everywhere. Some have long hair to their waist, men as well as women.

I sit and watch them. Their children run up and down the corridor and some people look annoyed but I think they are lovely, like bright, chirpy parrots. After a while a young woman gets some fat crayons out. She calls them face paints, and begins to make the children's faces into animals with whiskers and eyebrows. Changes them into little furry animals.

She is very clever, but I look at the children, at their large eyes peering out of the paint and I feel strange, afraid. They remind me of dreams I used to have long ago. I get up and go to the buffet car for a coffee.

It takes ages to work my way up the corridor, queue for a coffee and walk back and when I get back to my seat one of the children with a ginger cat face is sitting in my seat. She stares up at me cheekily and does not move. I must not get angry.

Suddenly her mother notices and laughs. 'Get up, Poppy, and let the lady have her seat back, you cheeky baggage.' The little girl gets up cheerfully and smiles at me. I smile back.

'They get bored, don't they?' her mother says to me.

'How far are you going?' I ask.

'Totnes,' she says. 'There is a Festival of Light there, it goes on all week. It should be great. Where are you going?'

The plastic cup is hot and the lid seems stuck and the train is going so fast I am frightened of spilling it. My hands begin to shake. I can't remember where I am going. The woman is staring at me. I say, 'Oh, I'm going there too. Just for a day or two.'

'Oh, great,' the woman says. 'Hope this weather holds, we can all sleep out then under a ceiling of stars.' She bursts out laughing and turns to the woman beside her and gives her her scruffy-looking cigarette.

'One last puff,' the other woman says and starts to laugh too. I can't see the joke.

I turn to the window and look out at the fields flashing by. The sun catches the window and glints in at me blindingly. I close my eyes feeling a bit sick and I must have fallen asleep.

I wake and everybody is gathering their things together and shouting and complaining. The children are making so much noise I can't think. I sit there and try to remember if this is really where I'm meant to get off. I can't see the station sign. I can't see where I am. Is it Totnes?

The little girl with the ginger whiskers leans towards me over the table, peers into my face. 'You've got to get off here. You've got to get off. You better hurry up or you'll be left behind. You will.'

Her painted face looks like a little devil, a little ginger cat devil, I don't like it. Her mother leans towards me too. 'Are you OK?'

'I've got a headache. Why is everybody shouting? What's happening?' I ask.

'This train has developed a fault. It is terminating at Exeter. Everybody has to get out.'

I remember my things. Where are they, what have I done with them? 'What have I done with my camping things?' I start to get up but I can't get out into the corridor. I'm trapped and the buzzing starts up in my head.

The woman reaches out and touches my arm. 'Hey, don't panic,' she says. 'There is plenty of time. All these people have got to get off, it'll take ages. We'll help you find your things. I expect you left them in the baggage compartment by the door, yes?'

I have. I remember now. I smile at her. She is very nice. I look at her hand on my arm. I can't remember when anyone last touched me who wasn't at the hospital.

The train stops and people pour out like a huge wave. 'Bloody Nora!' someone says. I reach the door and grab my knapsack and sleeping bag and the woman helps me climb out. 'You are well prepared,' she says as we are pushed along the platform by a crush of people towards the exit.

Outside she helps me put on my knapsack. I look around and feel sick. There are so many people milling around. No one knows what to do. I don't know what to do now. How will I ever find Jessie to pick her up? The loudspeaker keeps blaring and I can't hear what it says. What shall I do?

The woman is watching me again. 'Would you like to hang around with us for a while, till you get your bearings?'

I feel a rush of love for her, I want to hug her. 'Yes, I would. Thanks.'

She grins. 'Right. This is Ed and that is Bill. Next to him is Fee and that's Andrea and Paul. I'm Zoe and this, as you know, is Poppy.'

'I'm Hester.'

'Hi there, Hester,' they say and we all walk in a clump along the platform until we find a wall in the sun quite near the station buffet and everyone puts their things down and sits on them and someone starts to sing and the sun is on my back and I feel happy again.

I sing too.

It is very dark and music is playing somewhere a long way away in the darkness. We are back on the train; we had to wait ages and ages at that station for the train to be mended.

A lot of people went off in buses, but my friends didn't. I don't know how long I have been asleep. All round me people sleep, the children lie very still. It is very quiet. I stare up, up at the stars. I have never slept in a train before.

There is a strong sweet smell a bit like a herb and the smell of curry powder and joss sticks. Somewhere in the train I hear low chanting.

When my head got bad at the station, Zoe gave me a head massage. It was wonderful. I fell fast asleep and when I woke I felt light as a feather. I brought my pills but I can't find them. When I was searching Zoe asked me what I had lost and I told her I had been in hospital and was supposed to take these pills.

'Antibiotics?'

'No, just pills to make me feel better.'

'Hey, I bet they were tranks. You don't need them, Hester. You don't want to push chemicals into your body. Now, I'll give you a massage, better than any pills, you see.'

These are my friends, my real friends. I want to stay with them for ever. It isn't lonely here, everybody is together all the time. I feel safe. I feel happy. Everyone laughs and sings a lot.

I sleep and I dream about my dad. I dream he is alive and here with me, but when I open my eyes I am alone. I sit up and there are clumps of sleeping people all around me, but not my dad. It is cold. No music plays. Even the children still sleep.

I shake the person next to me, but they groan and won't wake up. I get out of my seat but I can't wake anyone up. I get my sleeping bag and put it over me and I lie shivering as the sun comes up. It's like everyone has died. Then I remember my pills. If I could find them they would make me sleep again too. I get up again and walk to the luggage place and pull my knapsack towards me and search in the pockets. I find them right at the bottom and I take two with a swig of lemonade I bought at the station.

After a while I feel strange and dizzy but it is better than being alone. After a while my head fizzes and I can feel my heart hammering loudly in my chest. After a while I feel the darkness coming towards me, rushing like a tunnel and I fall towards it.

My head aches when I wake. I feel muzzy and don't feel like moving. The train seems to have stopped again. The sun is on me and I am hot under my sleeping bag. A lot of people seem to have got off. But Zoe is still here. She is painting the faces of the children again, trying to keep them quiet. I watch carefully as she covers their cheeks with thick paint. She makes them all look like little animals.

They sit over the arms of the train and on the floor and giggle and push each other. They stare at me and some of them rock backwards and forwards in front of me laughing. I don't like them. I should explain to Zoe not to do it but she wouldn't listen. I don't think she would understand.

'Hello there.' Zoe smiles at me. 'You slept for a long time, and so did I. We've both missed Totnes, I'm afraid. We are coming into Plymouth.' She laughs, she throws back her head and laughs. 'This must be the longest train journey in the history of the world. This train has changed engines or drivers, or both, three times since London. Hester, we've got to get out in a minute. We have to change at Plymouth.'

The people left in the train get out. No one hurries because the train isn't going any further. I think about Jessie. I have to get to Jessie. I don't want to miss her. I don't want her worrying.

'I have to find a phone. I must find a phone,' I tell Zoe.

She points. 'Over there,' she says. 'I'll look after your things, Hester, go and make your call.'

I trust her so I leave my things. When I put money in the phone box the number won't ring so I ring the operator. 'It is not a local call,' she says. 'You will have to put more money in. It is a Truro number.'

169

Truro, that is where I am supposed to be, not Totnes. I should be at Truro.

'Do a reverse call to this number,' I tell the operator.

It rings for a long time then I hear my husband's voice. The operator asks if he will accept a transfer call from a call box in Plymouth. She should not ask, she should just tell him.

'No,' he says. 'No, I will not accept a transfer call from Plymouth. I'm sorry.' And I hear him put the phone down.

The stupid, bloody operator starts to say, 'I'm sorry . . .'

The buzzing in my head drowns everything. 'You fucking stupid idiot. I'll report you. You don't know your job. He's got my little girl.' But the phone goes dead. I come out of the phone box. People are looking at me and I shout at them too. I have to get to Jess.

Zoe is suddenly beside me and takes my arm. 'Hey, hey, Hester, what is it? Come on, stay cool. Come and tell me all about it. Come on, let's sit over there.'

So I tell her. I show her the scar on my face where Ian hit me. I tell her about his affair with that woman. How they planned for years and years to go off together and take Jessie with them. How they have hidden her somewhere again. But I always find them. I tell her that. I always find them.

Zoe listens. She sent Poppy off with someone. I am glad. I don't like her staring. I will have to wash the paint off her face soon to show Zoe what I mean about devils hiding. You have to be very careful.

When I have finished telling her she stares at me for a long time, then she says, 'Hester, you have only got one life. Look after yourself now. Men are mainly bastards, let him go.'

'I've got a daughter. It's stupid to say that when I have a little child.'

'How little?'

I feel hot. I can't remember how old Jessie is. I can't remember.

I stare at her. She has gone black and white like when the

colour goes on a television. I feel the tears coming. I need to get to Truro. I have to get to Truro.

She touches my arm. 'Don't cry, Hester. Come on, let's find out which platform the Truro train goes from. Poppy and I may as well go there too. Plenty goes on. I know people there. I'll come with you.'

'Why?' I ask. I have to be careful. After all she paints all those faces. She could be in on it.

'Because,' she says so quietly I can hardly hear her, 'I've been where you are.'

I don't know what she means.

We are on the train again, but I cannot keep awake. Zoe says she will make sure we do not miss Truro, and even if we do there is not much farther we can go unless it is into the sea.

When I wake, Zoe is going through my knapsack. The cow, the fucking cow.

I keep very quiet and watch to see what she steals. She is riffling though the pockets as if she is looking for something and suddenly she pulls out my pills and looks at them. She opens the packet. Is she going to take one? But she replaces the pills in the carton and reads the label on the outside. Then she goes to her own bag and pulls out a little book and looks down it, her finger trailing the pages. Then her finger stops and she sighs and nods, closes the book and turns and puts my pills back in the rucksack.

She sees I am awake. 'Hi, Hester, how are you feeling?'

I sit up. 'Much better. My head has stopped whizzing and banging. I feel great.'

'Good,' she says and pushes her coffee over to me with two small white pills. 'Take them, Hester. I am not trying to poison you. In a different, almost forgotten life, I was a doctor. Then I got into homeopathy, natural medicine. It does work, Hester, if applied responsibly and in conjunction with other things.'

I look at her bare feet and nose-rings and I don't believe her. 'You a doctor? You're too young, anyway.'

'I'm afraid I am not. Hester, when you were asleep I had

a look at the pills you are taking, meant to be taking. I was worried about you. How many did you take last night?'

'I can't remember. Two, maybe three.'

'You must not do that, it is extremely dangerous. They have side-effects and they simply don't work when you take more than prescribed.'

'I thought you didn't believe in pills.'

She is silent and she sighs again. 'It is the pills that make you rock, Hester.'

'Rock?'

'Look, I was wrong last night to tell you not to take your medication. You should take them, but exactly as prescribed on the packet. Then they work, Hester. Aren't you feeling better than you have all day?'

'Yes,' I say. And I am. I feel good.

'Well, that is probably because you have the right amount of medication in your body.'

I am bored. She sounds like Melanie and what's her name who comes to the flat. I swallow the pills and look at her. 'Very odd for a doctor to paint faces,' I say, so she knows I know her game.

She laughs. 'I dropped out,' she says, 'before the system destroyed me and I stopped caring for people altogether.'

Poppy comes running up the train to her and she scoops her up and hugs and hugs her as if she will never ever let her go.

I can't breathe for the pain. Jessie. So small and plump but she never stops crying.

Zoe looks over Poppy's head and stops laughing suddenly. She reaches towards me.

'Hester, hey. Everything's fine. In an hour we will be in Truro.'

I laugh. Suddenly I'm happy. If it wasn't for the faces I'd ask Zoe to come camping too.

Chapter 32
Anna

Soleirolia. Baby's Tears. Mind-your-
own-business. Invasive perennial.
Small green leaves form a dense carpet
which smothers all other plants unless
restrained.

I am working in the summerhouse when Ian brings me down
a gin and tonic.

'Am I allowed to disturb you?' He knocks on the open
door, peering round it, his usually serious face full of suppressed excitement.

I fold my colour chart, surprised, for he rarely ventures
down here in the evening. 'Of course you are! What's happened?' I take the glass he offers.

He grins and lifts his glass to me. 'I've just heard, we've
got that contract with the supermarket group, Anna.'

I give a yell and get up to hug him. 'Wonderful! Oh, Ian,
well done, well done, both you and Nick.'

'It's bloody marvellous. Nick's just rung me, he's only just
got out of the meeting. Of course we need it in writing, but,
well, Anna, it's going to make such a difference, I hardly
dare believe it!'

I look at him, he is suddenly a different person. He looks
years younger. 'We'll have to celebrate,' I say. 'We can't let
this news go by without a celebration.'

He perches on my desk. 'I was thinking.' He pauses. 'I know you're busy, but it would be good to have a party before the summer ends, don't you think? You have neglected your friends and I have been longing for Nick and Pud to see your garden. Also, there are a couple of prospective clients it might be sensible to invite . . .' He trails off, watching me.

'Why not? Alice and Jake will probably help. I know they could do with the money.'

'Good. Alice keeps telling me about Jake's cooking! We'll plan it carefully, make sure it is not too much of a chore for you. Jess thinks it's a brilliant idea. A party before she goes back to school next week. She is up there making plans.' He moves towards the door.

I want to hit him suddenly. 'Oh, I see. You've already discussed it all with Jess, have you?'

He turns in the doorway, his face suddenly guarded. 'Does it really matter, Anna? Of course, I said it had to be all right with you.'

He makes me feel petty and left-footed. Of course it doesn't really matter. I turn and open my chart up without replying. Ian walks back up the garden and I stare at his back, surprised at my anger and resentment.

It is no good. I can't work any more. I close up the summer-house and now that it is cool I finish the watering which calms me down. Hebe comes looking for me and I bend and cuddle her and find suddenly I am fighting tears. I must try to have an early night. I am tired, my tiredness is making me childish.

It's just . . . I've kept everything going all summer, this heat has exhausted me. I don't want to socialize with anyone, I have got out of the way of socializing, I just want my garden, I just want to sleep.

As I walk up to the house I notice a difference in the trees, the leaves are bent ever so slightly. They are going to fall early because of the drought.

Jessie is watching television and Ian is on the phone again talking business. I pour myself another gin and take it upstairs where I can be on my own. I go through to my little bedroom and sit on the iron bedstead and look out of the window at the huge fir. I can hear music from the television downstairs. I hear Ian put the phone down.

I close my eyes and try to relax. With Ben I loved having people. But it was different then, we were all young, our children were small, the men were often away, so women were closer to each other.

I know I must have been lonely when the boys were young. I know I must have been lonely in those naval quarters on my own. I was probably lonely in the cottage when we first moved to Cornwall because we didn't know anyone. But I have never felt so alone as I do now.

It's my own fault. I haven't made time for people. When June was alive I didn't need anyone else. Other friendships were important but not vital, because June was always there for me.

The phone starts to ring. Neither Jessie nor Ian answers it and it goes on and on and on.

I open my eyes and look at the old casement window and the delicate cobweb-frosted glass of the door. The old-fashioned airing cupboard where I found that old laundry book dated 1918. This house is so special and suddenly, against the background of that ringing phone, I feel nothing, as if the joy in it all is fading away and I can't keep a hold of it.

I can't bear it any longer, I shout, 'Please, please, someone, answer that bloody phone.'

Nothing must take the pleasure of this place away from me. Nothing. No one.

Ian must have been coming up the stairs to find me. I hear him shout, 'Bugger it,' as he gallops down again in a fury.

I pick up my drink, I will have to go down.

'Yes?' Ian snaps down the phone. 'No, I bloody well will not take a reverse call charge from a Mrs Roberts in Plymouth! No, sorry, I won't take the call.' He bangs the phone down.

I go slowly downstairs as Jessie hares out of the sitting room. Ian looks at me grimly. No one says anything for a moment. Then I say, needlessly, 'Hester's in Plymouth. Presumably making her way down here?'

'Presumably,' Ian says and turns to Jess. 'Look, Jess, she won't find us. We've always lived in towns or villages before. There is no way she can find us, we are like a needle in a haystack.'

Jess is white, her eyes enormous in her face as she looks at her father. I go down the stairs to her. 'Jess, come on now, don't overreact.'

She stares at me. 'You don't understand, Anna, It's all my fault. When we moved here I sent a letter to Gran. Dad told me never to put the address on my letters, but I did. I wanted Gran to see what a posh address it was and be proud.'

She is crying now like a small child and I wrap my arms around her. Ian glares at her and picks up the phone again.

'Come on,' I say. 'I'll make you a hot chocolate. Come on, Jess, it's not the end of the world.'

But it feels a bit like it is.

Ian comes back before the milk has boiled and sits at the table next to Jess and ruffles her hair. 'It's all right, Jess. Your gran says there is no way Hester could have got our address. She decided she must destroy the letter when Hester got out of hospital. So, no more panic, and no more nightmares?'

Jess sniffs, embarrassed, and shoots a look at him from under her hair. She doesn't want to forgive him yet and I know how she feels and grin to myself as I cut her a piece of Alice's carrot cake.

'Apparently,' Ian says, 'your mother turned up at your gran's a few days ago looking for a knapsack. She said she was going on holiday camping with a friend.' He smiles at Jess, trying to make it better. 'I bet your mother has met someone interesting at Plymouth. You know: the bright lights, the entire cast of provincial *Cats*.'

It works. Jessie laughs with her mouth full of crumbs at Ian's silly voice. 'Yeah, Dad, that is very possible.'

'So no more worrying.' Ian smiles at her. 'Come on, it's late. Bed.'

As Jessie disappears upstairs, Ian says, 'Can I have a hug, Mrs Roberts? I seem to be upsetting everyone tonight. The evening started so well, too!'

I open my arms and laugh. 'Poor Ian! Come here.'

In bed, after we have made love, Ian gets up and goes and gets two brandies. 'I didn't know we had any!' I say, surprised.

'Grateful client!' Ian says and lifts his glass. 'Thank you, Mr Trevesko.' He looks down at his glass in a way I am getting to know.

'Spit it out,' I say. 'More Hester?'

'Yes. Hester's mother was worried in case Hester is headed this way. She rang the psychiatric social worker assigned to Hester who said she appeared to have left her flat and taken off somewhere. She hasn't been seen by anyone for a while, but they thought she was probably alone as the only real friend she made was back in the hospital.'

'Hester lived with her mother, didn't she, when you first divorced?'

Ian swirls the brandy about in his glass. 'Yes, it didn't work. She was found a council flat eventually. They have never got on, Hester adored her father. She always maintained her mother didn't like her. Mai told me that the social worker told her it would have been better if Hester could have shared a flat with someone else from the hospital, but no one could get on with her for long.'

'Poor Hester,' I say and mean it. I finish my brandy and lie down. 'It is a pity that Jessie and Hester can't have some sort of relationship. Hester's mother wouldn't lie about destroying that letter with our address on it would she, Ian?' I ask.

'It would be a very stupid thing to do, if she did,' Ian replies. 'Especially after what happened.'

'What do you mean?' I ask, pulling away to peer at his face.

177

He turns away to turn the lamp off. 'I only mean that Hester became so verbally abusive towards her mother that the social services eventually sectioned her. Neither she nor the neighbours could take any more of her effing and blinding at them and her odd behaviour. Now go to sleep, darling, I've had enough of Hester for one night.'

I turn into the warmth of his body, wanting to feel safe and happy. But I think Ian is lying about Hester and her mother. It's more than probable that a specific incident caused Hester to be sectioned.

Chapter 33

Ian

I lied. I did not tell the truth. Why? I just don't know. I have always tried to answer Anna truthfully before.

I have made the excuse to myself that I did not want to make her nervous or afraid, but the truth is Hester's violence that day was random, an isolated incident. The final crack in her psyche before she disintegrated totally and was carted away.

I was not there. I did not see it happen. I only saw the aftermath. Hester, pale, drugged and very frightened.

I do not want to talk about it. I do not want to think about it. I have trouble accepting it happened. Mai was too traumatized and I had to sign Hester's life away. Ensure she was sectioned.

I am being dramatic. Of course her doctor and a psychiatrist signed as well, but they had not been married to her, they were just doing their job. I imagine it is the same feeling when someone has to put a dog down. The same expression in the eyes. Pleading. 'I promise. I'll bark to go out. I'll try to be good. One more chance.'

It is something to haunt.

It was a betrayal.

It was a giving up of responsibility.

She was my wife. She was the mother of my child. She was a woman I once loved and had sex with. And I signed a piece of paper to say she could be drugged, incarcerated, have electric treatment, anything they thought fit.

I let her down.

I cannot speak of this, even to Anna, and if I go on thinking about it the black clouds will descend once more and engulf me.

Anna and I are driving into Truro. Anna has business and I am at last showing her my new office.

She loves it. 'You are so clever. It's a brilliant use of space. So simple, linking offices. I love it, Ian.'

She peers at the plans on my drawing board and I explain how we have to incorporate the old building into the new design and marry old and new and still keep it attractive to the planners and the public. She is so interested. I smile at her enthusiasm, it reminds me of when I first took her out. She makes some good points too.

I take her out to lunch. 'No, you can't come too,' I say to Jess when we meet in the town. 'Go and find Lily or something.'

I don't often say no to Jess and she goes flouncing off, sulking. I see Anna smile softly to herself.

I suppose I should say no more often.

I suppose jealousy is not just confined to me. I suppose Anna rarely has me to herself.

Chapter 34
Hester

I never knew trees whispered. I never knew the night isn't really dark when you are in it. It is so quiet I can lie and listen to the leaves rustling and whispering and the voices have come out of my head so I have no trouble hearing them.

I have a private place and I do not get cold because at night when I am in my sleeping bag I pile all the dry crinkly leaves on top of me. Zoe gave me a bedroll to stop the damp coming up from the ground.

In the daytime I leave in case people come, and I go into the town and buy a cup of tea and some food. There is quite a big market and I take packets of biscuits and things without anyone seeing. I save these for my supper, sitting in my sleeping bag, and I have one of those cardboard drinks with a straw attached. They are very good.

When I am lying in the dark sometimes the moon is huge over the top of the trees and the voices talk to me and I listen very carefully. They whisper that Hester should be living in a house with her husband. They whisper that that woman should not be with Jessie, because it is not right. The voices say, 'Hester has to be firm.'

'Firm with that woman?'

'Yes, Hester must be very firm. Hester should be in that house with her own child. The woman knows that, that is why she never answers the phone.'

Firm. That's what my mother used to say to my dad, when

I was a child. 'You must be firm with her. She needs a firm hand.'

My dad. If only he could see me now, he'd be here with me. My dad grew up in the country. He used to tell me stories. He couldn't have brought his old chair here though, the one he always sat in when I used to climb on his knee.

I loved climbing on his knee. Suddenly one day he told me I was too big a girl to sit on his knee. I knew what had happened. She was jealous even though she had a lover again, the same one. I know because I read the letters, where she hid them when she thought they were safe. Cow. Slut.

The buzzing starts in my head, it blocks out the voices and they go back into my head. I am angry remembering.

My dad sat in the dark, smoking, and I thought he was crying. I watched from the doorway and he didn't hear me. I went and climbed on his knee. I made him jump but he wrapped his arms round me, laid the top of his head on mine. 'Oh, Hester, Hester, Hester,' he whispered into my hair and his voice was thick and gargly and sad, like it was in a tunnel.

Suddenly I remembered a way of making him laugh and smile and be happy again. I reached down with my hand as I cuddled up to him and I touched his thingamy like I had seen her do, sort of stroked it through his pyjamas.

It was all soft and squishy. I heard him gasp and I felt excited, then it moved under my hand, sort of came up a bit and went harder and I felt wet between my legs, then all of a sudden I was thrown across the room and my father was shouting at me. 'Go to your room, at once, do you hear? Get out of here. Go, go.'

He had never ever shouted at me in my whole life. He sort of picked me up off the floor and pushed me away out of the room and I ran to my bedroom and cried and cried until I fell asleep. I was only doing what she did. That's all I was doing.

He never ever let me on his knee again. In the morning he came with a very serious face and told me it was something you only ever did to your husband and did I understand that?

I said no and he said it again and that I was quite big enough to understand it was wrong. I said if she could, why couldn't I?

My dad looked at me strangely as if he was seeing me for the first time and said, 'Oh Hester,' very quietly and went away.

The buzzing of voices is like bees, loud and it deafens me. It was her of course, jealous. It was me he loved. Me.

He never ever cuddled or touched me again. Never.

One day he went away and he never came back. A leaf drops on my face and I take my hand out of the sleeping bag to brush it away. My face is wet.

Hester is crying. The trees whisper, Hester is crying.

Chapter 35
Anna

Yucca aloifolia. Spanish Bayonet.
Evergreen shrub or small tree with
spiky sword-like leaves and large
clusters of white flowers edged with
purple in summer or autumn.

'Would you like to come to Penzance with me?' I ask Alice. 'I have to deliver some palms.'

'Great,' Alice says. 'You don't usually supply down there, do you?'

'No, but Mrs Penhilly is an old friend and likes to buy in from me. It's an excuse for me to go over. We'll give Hebe a walk on the beach.'

'Are you going to show me where you used to live?' Alice smiles at me.

'If you like.'

The roads are packed with holidaymakers and caravans. Living off the beaten track now, I don't notice the summer visitors so much. As we drive over the causeway the tide is in and Alice is enchanted. 'Anna, it's magic. Point in the direction your house was.'

I point across the water towards the church. 'You can't see the house, it's behind that clump of trees.' I ignore the turning into the village and keep on the Penzance road and turn off down a lane to Mrs Penhilly's cottage. She is over

185

eighty now and reliant on a gardener, but I remember when she did all the gardening herself. She would invite June and me over for wonderful teas and we would sit and talk in her beautiful subtropical garden for hours.

She is at the gate to greet us. 'My dear!' She hugs me. 'It is so good to see you again.'

'This is Alice. She helps me in the garden and I would be bereft without her.'

Mrs Penhilly's little black eyes regard Alice's offbeat appearance with interest.

'Hello, Alice. Now come in, come in, I've got tea all ready.'

She has laid it all out on a table in the garden and Alice wanders off in delight to look at her hardy exotics.

Mrs Penhilly peers at me closely. 'You look a little thin, Anna. Are you working too hard?'

I laugh. 'I'm just getting older and we have been very busy this summer. I'm negotiating for the field next door to me, I hope to expand next year and open up to the public.'

'Just you and Alice at the moment?' Her eyes are following Alice's bright progress through her garden.

'Yes.'

'Beautiful-looking girl.'

'Isn't she!'

'Psychic, is she?'

I stare at her. 'What makes you say that?'

Mrs Penhilly laughs at my surprise. 'Don't you remember, dear? I always used to tell the fortunes at the village fete!'

'Well, yes, but in fun, I thought!'

She pours the tea and instead of replying she calls Alice. They appear to have an immediate rapport which amuses me as Mrs Penhilly is a very grand old lady and my Alice is a lovely, fey, pot-smoking would-be traveller.

June had told me Mrs Penhilly had been quite a lady in her time and had got through four husbands.

After tea we unload the plants into her conservatory and

she shows me round the garden. It is not quite as magnificent as it was, but still very beautiful. 'It is not quite the same, not being able to do the toil yourself.'

She suddenly touches my arm. 'You must still miss June, my dear. You were so very close. Didn't we have wonderful afternoons talking shop!'

I smile down at her. At eighty I suppose many of her friends must be dead. When you are young you take your friends for granted. When you are older you remember all the times you could have called them up and didn't.

We say goodbye and, as I go to close the van doors, she bends and says something to Alice, quickly and secretly. I grin to myself. A couple of Cornish witches.

On the way back I turn into the village and we drive down to the beach. Hebe is raring to go and Alice runs off with her across the golden sand. It is late afternoon and people are beginning to pack up and make their way home. The tide is out and I walk across the pools in the deep rutted sand towards where the sea breaks in the distance.

The air is warm and humid and the sea reflects the heat, breaking in small delicate waves which turn gracefully, curling towards my feet and foaming in a creamy swirl. So different from a winter sea where there is an icy edge to the powerful turn of a wave and the noise of the surf deafens and quells and a bitter wind bites and blows at your face.

I stand a long way out on the vast empty beach at the sea's edge, blissfully alone. Far away stretches the deep blue, on and on to the horizon where one long stretch of wave breaks in the distance. My bare feet sink into the edge of the sea and I think, this is where we start and end. Here, at the edge of a force so powerful it blows your mind.

It feels so natural and right. I feel as if I could walk out into that soft velvety blue. There is a thrill in the thought of sinking into that unknown depth, to be swallowed by the infinite water carries a profound excitement of discovery.

I have a fanciful vision of vast blue arms widening up out of the horizon, widening as vaporous space to enfold me and make me part of sea and sky. Moulding me into amazing blues and yellows, so that I am part of a huge John Miller painting. It is a wonderful, ethereal sensation as I feel the water swirling up round my calves as the tide turns and begins to come in.

I hear Alice call loudly, urgently, like a seagull, and I turn, feel as if I am coming out of a trance and watch as she and Hebe run towards me. Behind me the beach stretches in a great golden arc, full of shadows, of soft echoes of childish voices. Of Ben scooping me up and running with me into the sea. Sitting close in the sand dunes watching the sun set.

'Oh, Anna.' Alice is out of breath. 'I thought you were going to walk into the sea. I couldn't see you properly, you were blending into sea and sand. You faded into the landscape. For a moment you disappeared.'

She is troubled, I hear the fear in her voice and laugh at her gently. 'Darling Ali, I wouldn't disappear when I owe you a week's wages!'

But she doesn't laugh. She stares at me and shivers. 'Too many shadows, Anna, too many memories. You shouldn't come back. The life you had here is gone. You have another life now and other people who love you.' She comes close to me and her eyes are bright and I am disconcerted by her vehemence.

'Can't you see, Anna? You have to fight your way out of the past into Now. Don't you see? The present will never become important unless you make it so. Unless you care enough.'

She puts her hands on my arms and gives me a little shake. 'If you don't fight back you won't survive. Stop escaping into your garden, making it into your whole life, putting all your love into it, keeping people at a distance.

Anna, please. Here, now, there are people who love you as much as those who have gone.' Her voice catches. 'Can't you believe in that?'

I stare at her and she stares steadily back. Her eyes are extraordinary, hazel, with flecks of green. Beautiful and disturbing and as familiar as breathing. Part of myself. I step back and, as if she is waking up, she says abruptly, 'I'm sorry.'

We walk in silence back along the beach and I try to absorb what she has just said. Am I preoccupied with my garden? Do I keep people at a distance? I have let my friends slide away into the background of my life. I am like the core of a deep bruise. All that surrounds me now is too raw and tender to let anyone place even loving fingers on. In my life now is a demarcation line. The past was where I was happy and safe and at home, inside warm lighted rooms with people I loved.

The present is where a note of unease beats constantly though my days, like a faint threnody. My garden has become more real than anything else in my life. It is me. Planning and planting, designing complicated patterns on graph paper have become the main joy of my life. It is what keeps me alive.

My head is always full of colour. I constantly view in my mind's eye sweeps of sweet-smelling white shrubs against a background of waxy green. I delight in my small newly planted blue cedar which will mark the boundary of my land with the water behind it.

I visualize it in years to come. Gigantic, with vast waving arms in the wind, to bring a thrill to people who follow me in the garden.

While I am bent with my hands in the dry soil or repotting thousands of small plants I can try and close my ears to the sound of that endless ringing that casts darkness on our days.

I can pretend I am not cold on the outside of lighted

rooms, nose pressed against the glass, looking in on lives too complex for me to understand.

'It's Ian's ex-wife that's causing problems, isn't it?' Alice says as I open the van doors and put Hebe in.

'It is a problem we don't know what to do about. But she has only prised open a hole that was already a crack.'

We climb in the van and I start the engine. 'Do you want to see where I lived or is that too morbid for you?'

Alice makes a face. 'I do want to see where you lived. I'm sorry, Anna, I shouldn't have said what I did. Who am I to know what's right for you?'

We drive past the cottage slowly, then turn and I show her June's house and where the greenhouses stood in the field with the horse. Then I can't bear any more. I drive away back towards the life I have now.

After a while I say to Alice, 'How about stopping for a drink somewhere?'

'Or two drinks.'

'Or two drinks and supper.'

'Or two drinks, supper and a spliff.'

'Or two drinks, supper, a sniff and arrest for drunken driving.'

Alice falls about. 'A spliff not a sniff!' She gets hysterical. 'Oh God. I must tell Jake there is a nice little number called sniff. Not snuff, not spliff. Sniff!'

Her laughter is infectious and I have to pull off the road and we sit there clutching each other, howling with laughter, while curious faces flash by on the dual carriageway.

Chapter 36
Ian

I cannot remember when I last had a party. Jessie has never had one. It was fatal, a recipe for disaster with Hester.

She cooked well, she could be vivacious and welcoming and all the time she would be targeting someone, working out in that marred little mind of hers who I might possibly like, be attracted to, be having an affair with.

As I am shaving a sudden wind gets up and rain splatters against the bathroom window. My heart sinks. Anna has arranged everything outside. Of course we have contingency plans, but I want to show off Anna's garden to everyone.

I feel as if it's coming right at last, all coming right. We complement each other, Anna and I. I understand her garden more than she knows. I am impressed by her use of space and light and colour. It all looks random and natural and yet it has been created by damned hard work.

When I go downstairs, Anna is leaning against the Rayburn reading a letter from her sons. She is absorbed, a smile on her face. I watch her, she suddenly looks so happy and young and relaxed. For a moment I feel irritated. Neither Jessie nor I can make her look like that. Then I recognize jealousy and stamp on it. I do feel threatened by her boys and do not like myself for it.

Anna folds the letter carefully and smiles at me. 'Hi, there.' She pours me a coffee. 'Now are you going to help me decide the exact position for the table?'

We walk down the garden and I see I needn't have worried. The sky is clear and cloudless. Later, as we position the table and throw a white cloth over it I pull Anna to me. 'I love you,' I tell her. 'And I am sorry that I can't change or make some things go away, it makes me defensive . . .'

'I know, Ian.' She hugs me, the top of her head fits neatly under my chin. 'Do you realize,' she says, moving away and fiddling with the cloth, 'that Hester hasn't rung for days?'

'Yes, you're right, she hasn't. That is why we are so bloody relaxed.'

We hear the camper van coming up the drive and Alice calls out and Anna moves up the garden calling back.

I sit and drink my coffee contentedly, listening to the birds. Later I have to take Jessie into Truro for a new dress and pick Lily up. Extremely tedious, but Anna has not got the time or inclination so I'll have to do it. At least I can drop into the office as I know it will take Jess hours.

In Truro I go to the cashpoint to get Jess some money. I give her too much and she squeaks with surprise, hugs me excitedly and dashes off to meet Lily. It feels good to be able to do it. But I feel guilty. I should have bought or given Anna something.

As I cross the market square I get a shock. I thought it was Hester in front of me, disappearing into the covered market. I follow and my heart is hammering ridiculously. Of course it isn't Hester, and relief makes me laugh out loud. But it is a measure of my past that makes me afraid to be happy.

For it is then Hester always turns up.

Chapter 37

Anna

Dianthus. 'Alice'. Modern Pink. A
flower with a herb-like scent and pale
ivory flowers with a clear crimson eye.

On the day of the party there is a smattering of early rain, but
the ground is like blotting paper and it is absorbed in minutes
and it makes no difference to the garden at all. We desperately
need water, but preferably not today as we plan to barbecue.

By ten the sun is blazing down again so I needn't have
worried. Both Jake and Alice are busy in the kitchen. Ian is
filling both fridges with drink and Jess is skittering about getting
overexcited as she and Lily have invited two boys to the party.

I have never seen Ian so happy. I have never heard him
humming about the house before. It has been a happy week
planning the party together, ringing old friends, deciding
who to invite, what we will cook inside and what out on
the barbecue.

If the boys had been home it would have been perfect.

But the next best thing, a letter from them, arrives. My heart
lurches for joy as the blue airmail envelope plops through the
front door. They are on a tiny island off Thailand, Phuket,
living in a hut on the beach. They are with a large group of
Americans and Australians and are having the time of their
lives. I fold the letter with their faces and voices clear in my
mind, as if they have just left the room.

Jake is a surprise. I have passed the time of day with him but I have never had a conversation with him. I'm not sure what I expected, someone shallower perhaps. He has a degree in anthropology and is doing a PhD on aquatic mammals. He is articulate and charming and I can see Alice smiling at my delight. I should have known my Alice better.

Cooking is Jake's hobby. Not everyday food, but the exotic Middle Eastern sort of cooking. He apparently supplements their income when they are desperate by cooking for people. 'You should be doing a PhD in food,' I tell him. 'By the smells coming from this kitchen you are wasted on mammals only interested in fish!'

He grins at me. 'I have considered it. As a hobby it's fun, it might not be if I had to earn my living at it.'

He and Alice take the van and go off to get the meat for me at the local butcher. How wonderful it would be if I were wealthy and then they could take over all the cooking for me.

Ian and I put little tables and chairs down in the garden with paper cloths and little pots of flowers to anchor them. Despite the drought the garden still looks lovely. I stand and look at it with love, remembering how it had been when I arrived.

Huge geraniums in urns, loving the dry weather, hang like ivy down the sides of the pots and trail along the ground. Great mists of white nicotiana and lavender fill the air and bedding plants tumble over Cornish hedges.

Ian, coming down the garden with a trestle table, smiles at me. 'When I have time to stand and just gaze, I realize how hard you have worked, Anna, how beautifully you have transformed this garden.'

I turn and look at the palms and formiums, bamboo and echiums round the pool. I look at the delicate and varying ferns I am beginning to produce and beyond them the group of greenhouses and tunnels bursting with life and I feel a sudden rush of contentment with my life.

My future is here. Now I have time to stop and take stock for a moment, I see all that I have achieved in two years and it is considerable. I have been working so hard, I have become unaware of how much I've done.

I cannot imagine now how I did anything else. Plants and gardens are my life. I have become passionate and obsessive and I long to expand. To successfully transform other people's gardens as well as my own. All this is in my grasp. How have I forgotten this fact? Why have I let Hester affect and spoil a life that has so many possibilities for joy?

I move towards Ian and he places the table on the ground and we hug amidst the life we are struggling to create together. 'I love you, Anna,' he says quietly. 'And I am aware of how much you have taken on. My frustration is knowing there are some things I just cannot change or make go away, then I become guilty and defensive.'

'I know,' I say, as we rock slowly like a dance sequence in the sunlit garden. 'Do you realize something?'

'What?'

'Hester has not rung for days.'

Ian grins at me. 'You are right, you are damn right, darling. Oh, bliss, this is why we are feeling so carefree and relaxed. Please God she's gone off and joined a commune or something!'

'Amen to that!' I pick up a trestle and we put the table together.

Ian says, 'Anna, do you realize we have spent more time together planning this party than in our entire marriage? We are going to have to remedy that, you know.'

'Yes, we are.' I hear Alice and Jake arriving back and Alice calls out to me and for a second as I enter the shadow of the hall, I wonder, is this real or are we playing happy families?

I go into the kitchen. 'Do you want me to put on a little lace cap and low-cut white blouse and little black mini-skirt with my little gold chain around my ankle to serve your guests?' Alice asks me, batting her wonderful eyes provocatively at Jake who is making leery grunting noises back at her in

195

a French accent, a black beret pulled sideways over his dreadlocks.

'No, I certainly do not!' I say, trying not to laugh. 'I want the Alice I know and love, thank you. What are you both on?' I ask sniffing.

They both pretend to be affronted, take off their aprons and walk towards the back door.

'Come back here!' I growl. 'I need you.'

'Anna needs us,' Alice says to Jake.

'Anna needs us?' Jake says to Alice.

Then they stand in the doorway gazing at each other lovingly. I suddenly have visions of guests arriving and nothing to give them to eat. If they were drinking I could remove the bottles.

Alice knows what I am thinking and smiles at me. 'It's all right, we are only fooling around, Anna. It is just the first time in ages we've been together without the boys.' She looks at her watch. 'We have to pick them up at five thirty. We must be on time. We'll only be half an hour, I promise.'

Oak and Elm are going to a birthday party but are coming on here. Jess and Lily have promised, and been bribed, to look after them. Jake and Alice have a horror of fire and will not leave the children at their campsite.

Ian is in the bath, Jess and Lily are giggling loudly and getting ready in their room. Alice and Jake and the little boys are having a shower in the extension we built for Liam and Dan's bedrooms. I wander round finishing the watering. I had offers of help but I don't want the tablecloths drenched and I love this time towards the end of the day and I need to see everything is just right.

It is so long since we had people I feel quite strange about it. I imagine it is the same for lots of people when they remarry. The friends you once had together don't necessarily gel with a new partner. Or you think they might not, so you don't ask them.

I stand for a moment, listening to the sounds from the house coming down to me. There is a smell of paraffin from the barbecue Jake and Ian have lit and I have a sudden painful sense of *déjà vu*. Ben and I used to barbecue all the time when the boys were little. The cottage faced south-west and we got all the evening sun.

Ian has put the small lamps on and although it isn't dark there is a little glow of warmth and light coming from the sitting room.

Ian has some music on and I smile as I hear Neil Diamond coming through the open window. It is so evocative of time and place somehow. When our children were babies and we carted them around to parties to houses where this music would be playing loudly.

He does not see me. He is smoking a cigarette and jigging about to the music with his eyes closed. I stand for a second watching his moment of complete happiness with an emotion I can't describe. I just know these moments have been too rare in his life and I am glad. I smile and creep away and go in the back door to have a bath and change.

The garden is full of people. Oak and Elm carry round little plates of sausage rolls and crisps and nuts. So do Jess and Lily but more self-consciously. The two boys haven't arrived yet, and I can tell both girls are on tenterhooks in case they don't come.

I introduce Ian to my friends he does not know and he introduces me to his clients and would-be clients. It is nice to meet Nick and Pud again and to see how fond of Ian they are. It is also interesting to see the ambitious side of Ian in action with clients. All seems to be going well, despite an eclectic collection of people. There is a constant buzz of chatter and a lot of laughter. Being outside helps. Barbecues always help people relax.

Alice fills the table with salads and the wonderful curry Jake has cooked in the kitchen this morning. Jake and Ian are manning the barbecue with Jess and Lily helping.

It is good to see people I once knew well, though inevitably there is now a gap and a slight formality where once there was ease. I do not feel uncomfortable exactly, but I feel totally detached from their lives.

The friends June and I had together are easier, but now, as then, gardens dominate the conversation. I am on safe ground. I see I have moved on from the friends Ben and I made together. Or perhaps I just don't want to be reminded of those days. Yet we have children in common, we hung about at school gates and sports days together and I don't want to lose touch completely.

Mrs Penhilly turns up with a driver and I am touched. As I show her round the garden I find I have a little gaggle of people following me and I realize I am probably going to pick up some clients too.

A flushed Jess sits self-consciously on the grass with a lanky youth who looks far too young to be showing off smoking. 'This is Darren,' she says. I smile at him, thinking Ian and I will have to get used to youths littering the place soon. I notice Jess has put on make-up and, frighteningly, she could be a good four years older than she is.

Lily is dancing to something noisy in the sitting room with a very spotty young man with a lovely smile. Oak and Elm are dancing with each other.

Suddenly, out of the blue, the feeling that I have stepped into another life, the feeling of being someone else becomes overpowering. I escape, slip out of the kitchen into the cool dark of the back of the house. Sounds of music and laughter ebb and flow round the house and I stand for a moment in the dark with the heavy scent of roses, stilling other voices before I go back inside.

I suddenly long for the boys to be here, anchoring me safely to my past.

The moment passes and, as I turn for the door, I catch again that strange scent on the evening breeze. It is not the roses, yet I cannot identify the shrub at all.

In the kitchen, Pud is stacking plates. She hugs me suddenly as if something shows on my face and I am immediately

198

warmed and touched and made better by that small spontaneous gesture.

By the time the last person leaves we are all very tired. Lily and Jess have put Oak and Elm to bed in either Dan or Liam's room and gone gossiping up the stairs to their room.

'I think you could say that all went very well,' Ian says happily. 'Jake, the food was out of this world. And Alice, you were wonderful, as usual.'

Alice and Jake grin, raise their hands and disappear to bed.

'You too,' I tell Ian. 'You can hardly stand.'

'I'm not leaving you to go on clearing up on your own.'

'I'm not doing any more. Everything important is in from the garden. I'm just going to make a cup of tea and unwind for half an hour or I won't sleep.'

'OK.' He kisses my forehead. 'Thanks for everything.'

Hebe and I sit on the sofa together and I smoke one of Ian's cigarettes. There is just a small lamp on and the shadows stretch across the silent room and I shiver suddenly, tired and cold. I get up as the kettle boils and make tea and take it back to the sofa.

I listen to the house move and creak around me. Cracking as it cools down and floorboards shift under the weight of bare feet hopping into bed.

The silence lengthens and reaches into me from the edges of the room as if it is whispering, trying to tell me something. I think about all the people who have lived out the pattern of their lives here.

A door opens and closes quietly and Alice comes in in bare feet. She is wearing a long kimono and her hair is loose and for a frightening second in the half-light I think she is a Red Indian squaw.

'Am I disturbing you?' she whispers.

I shake my head. 'Can't you sleep?'

'I was asleep, I woke suddenly. Are you all right, Anna?'

'I'm fine. I was just sitting here unwinding. I was just sitting here thinking about the ghosts of the past. People who have lived here before me.' Alice is silent. 'What is it, Ali, are you all right? Would you like some tea?'

She shakes her head and I try to make her smile. 'As you came into the room I thought you were a Red Indian squaw!'

Alice neither laughs nor seems surprised, she just nods. 'Did you know that in the spirit world guardian angels often look like Red Indians?'

I did not know. 'Are you my guardian angel, darling?' I smile.

'Yes, I am.' She comes nearer and I see she is crying. Comes to me, kneels and throws her arms round me and begins to sob as if her heart will break.

'Alice, Alice.'

I stroke her hair, deeply upset. This is so unlike her. 'What is it?'

She lifts her head. 'I don't know . . . Don't know . . . Woke up suddenly in this house to this terrible, overpowering sadness.'

Pot has a lot to answer for. I get up and make her drink some tea. 'You are exhausted, Ali. Now go back to bed and get some sleep.'

'Are you going?'

'Yes, I'm going this minute.' Her strange eyes are looking into me, pupils dilated.

'This house is . . . waiting,' she says.

'For what?' I am getting irritated and a familiar fear reaches out with a cold finger and runs along my spine.

Alice does not answer. 'Alice, shadows become threatening when you have taken substances you shouldn't have. I so wish you wouldn't. Goodnight.'

I blow her a kiss and go heavily up the stairs. Tomorrow is Sunday. I can lie in.

I turn at the top of the stairs and look down. Alice looks up, dark skin tight over her beautiful facial bones as she stands very still in the shadows, watching me.

Chapter 38
Hester

Music and voices. Car lights shine in an arc through the trees. Cars turn from the lane to the house below. What is happening?

My head aches. I don't want to move. Too hot for walking in towns. The trees are cool. I like the trees now. I lie and look up at the leaves, the branches move this way and that, this way and that. They whisper to me. Whisper. But tonight I can't hear their voices because of my head.

Car doors banging. I sit up, get out of my sleeping bag and see the house is all lit up below me. Every window has a light. There, through the trees the house looks nice lit up. I can hear people laughing and talking loudly round at the front of the house where I cannot see.

I'd better brush my hair. And put on some perfume, the sort my dad liked.

I make my legs move. I am a bit stiff and dizzy today. I walk to the fence that surrounds the wood. I keep to the trees and move down towards the house. I peer round the huge roses on a trellis which is breaking and I can look into a window. It is a kitchen. I see bottles of wine on the table and plates with foil over them. They are having a party. I was right, they are having a fucking party without me.

I crouch listening. I am sure that is Jessie's laugh. Two girls laughing. I am lonely. I am lonely. More and more cars come and the voices and laughter are like waves that come to me in bursts. I want to see, I want to see what is going on.

I am angry. My house. My husband and child. I ache and the voices are loud from the trees. I rock to and fro until I feel better. I cannot get near enough. I cannot see what is going on. I can only see moving, coloured dresses through the trees.

I could go down there, I could say, 'Hello, I'm Hester Roberts, Ian's wife, thank you for coming.' I could have got a dress if I'd known.

The smell of food is making me hungry. I edge towards the kitchen window. I wonder if the back door is open. I might try it. I could get food. I have every right.

A voice suddenly close by makes me jump and I turn quickly back to the shadows and scratch my arm on one of the roses hanging to the ground. The scent of it is so strong it makes me feel sick.

I am getting cold. I go back up into the trees and climb into my sleeping bag. I get inside it and I eat a packet of digestives and drink a can of beer. Very nice.

I lie down again and my heart hammers with hate for the whore who stole the people who love me. I fall asleep again to music and the murmur of voices in the distance.

When I wake all is silent and dark, but there are still lights on in the house.

I am hungry again. I make my way carefully down into the gardens. The tables are empty of food, but on the barbecue I find a sausage and I eat it. I move back up the garden, past the house and in amongst the whispering trees where I am safe.

I laugh. They don't know I am here.

As I reach my sleeping bag all the lights in the house go out.

Chapter 39

Anna

Erigeron. 'Darkest of All'. A spreading
plant with purple flowers like daisies
with yellow centres.

Sunday lunchtime and we are all lounging, still slightly
hungover, on the grass in the shade finishing off all the left-
overs from last night. Alice and Jake are still here and Oak and
Elm are playing on old bikes we found in the garage and dusted
down. One was Jessie's and the other either Liam's or Dan's.

It feels good having children in the house and garden and I
feel happy that Alice and Jake didn't want to rush home. Lily
and Jess are mooching about between house and garden deciding whether they have the energy to make their way to the
beach for a swim. Ian is sitting in an old deck-chair that looks
as if it will collapse any moment, reading the Sunday papers.

Jake is asleep and Alice and I are surrounded by seed
catalogues, planning sleepily next summer and the possibility opening to the public.

'How did the garden survive all the people?' Alice asks.

'Pretty well,' I tell her. 'Someone has been fiddling about
in the small greenhouse, a few flowers have been picked off
the plants and laid in little rows.'

Alice makes a face. 'Hope it wasn't the boys. I did notice
the geranium pots have been moved by the pond. Or was
that you?'

'No.' I smile at her. 'What does it matter? Just so long as they don't fall in, darling.'

Jake suddenly sits up and says, 'Anna, would you mind if I used your phone?'

'No. Go ahead, Jake.'

Alice looks surprised. 'Who are you ringing, suddenly?'

'My mum. Time I did, Ali.'

Alice watches his departing back with interest. 'Wonder what brought that on? He hasn't been in touch with his mother for ages. She doesn't approve of his lifestyle . . . Or me.'

'That's a pity.'

'Yes. Especially as he is an only child. But his parents are, you know, narrow, middle class with high hopes for him. Then he hitches up with me, parents live in a council house, two children and not married to the father. A traveller. Can't blame them, can you?'

I smile at her. 'If only they knew you.'

She sits up suddenly. 'It's you. That's what it is! Being here has reminded him of home and lazy Sundays on the lawn, roast potatoes, gin and tonic. All the things he misses, but would never admit to.'

I laugh. 'Thanks, Alice. Narrow and middle class, are we?'

'No! No, Anna! You know what I mean.'

'Of course I do!' I get up and pile the plates on to the tray. 'I'm just going up to the house to make a cup of tea.'

'Oh, good,' Ian says from behind the paper.

'I'll come and help you,' Alice offers.

'No, stay here and keep an eye on the boys, I don't want them in the creek.'

Jake is off the phone and looks pleased with himself. 'OK?' I ask.

'Yeah. Thanks for letting me use the phone, Anna. My parents have a problem with my lifestyle, and Ali is a part of that. But my mother has asked me to go and see them, with Ali and the boys. She is trying . . . She was so pleased to hear from me.'

'It is hard for mothers to let go, suspend judgement, take a back seat, you know.' I grin at him. 'Why do you think my two took off to the other end of the world!'

Jake takes the kettle from me and puts it on the Rayburn. 'You're OK, Anna. I admire you a lot. If you were ever possessive with your sons you had good reason. Ali says you and the boys are very close.'

'I like to think so. But I did have trouble letting go, Jake. They were and are my whole reason for living. And that is a hell of a burden for anyone to carry. I'm glad they got away for a while. If anything happened to them I would not want to go on living. It's wrong, but that is how it is.'

I shiver suddenly, the kitchen is cool after the sun outside. Jake looks at me. He is about to say something when the phone rings.

I go to answer it. 'Hello,' says the voice, 'Hester, here. Can I speak to Jessie, please?'

'Yes, Hester, I'll just call her,' I say politely, my heart sinking, for she sounds abominably near.

I yell for Jessie who comes running, Lily in tow, obviously hoping it is one of the spotty youths of last night. 'Your mother,' I tell her.

Her face falls, poor Jess. 'Oh, bugger, oh hell and damnation. Shit!'

'Jess!' I say automatically and go back into the kitchen where Jake is filling the teapot. We are both silent as we listen to the conversation.

'Hello!' Jess says crossly, then after a long pause, 'Mum . . . What? Of course I can't come on holiday with you. School starts again tomorrow. No, I can't . . . I failed two of my GCSEs . . . I'm working every hour God made for my resit.'

Jake and I make faces at each other and hope she does not turn into a pillar of salt.

'Yeah . . . OK. I'll tell him. What message? I don't know . . . Maybe . . . Sometime. Mum. Dad's not here. What?

205

Waiting for what? I can't understand . . . Oh thank God for that, her money ran out.'

Jess comes into the kitchen and eyes the cake I am getting out of the cupboard for Oak and Elm. 'Batty as ever, but she sounded quite happy for once. Couldn't understand a word she was talking about. Is there enough cake for Lily and me?'

Alice and I walk along the lane up to the burnt-out manor house with Hebe. It is late afternoon and Ian and Jake have taken Lily home and Jess and Oak and Elm on for a swim. It is too early to begin watering yet.

Alice has never walked up this far and is enchanted with the vast overgrown garden. She is silent as she gazes up at the derelict house. Again I catch that whiff of herbs and the sense of time standing still.

A blackbird is singing on the lower branches of a huge fir as if his heart will break.

Otherwise it is very silent here and after a while the silence bears down suffocatingly.

The house seems to look back at us, frozen in time, empty mullion windows like sorrowful eyes. There is a palpable sense of it waiting to be rescued from fifty-odd years of neglect. Yet someone cares, for every now and then the undergrowth is severely cut back so that the house is not totally reclaimed by nature.

Alice says slowly, 'It is such a beautiful house. Standing as if in mourning for something. I've never seen such vast rhododendrons and camellia trees, I didn't realize they grew so huge. Someone should rebuild this house, make it come to life again.'

'Perhaps they can't afford to. No one seems sure if the Trevillians still own it.'

Alice cannot tear her eyes away. 'I know the rumours. The estate was supposed to have a curse on it because things kept going wrong for the Trevillians. A child drowned in the lake in mysterious circumstances and then there was the fire and no one could tell how it started. After that, so my father told me, the family just lost heart and moved to other properties they owned.'

'I didn't know that. I know it's supposed to be haunted. The boys used to frighten themselves up here. I don't find anything creepy about the house, it is just sad and neglected.'

Alice glances at me, but does not see me. 'Rejected, Anna. Ghosts can be laid to rest. Once, once, this was a happy family house, children ran across the lawns and down by the lake. Once it was a much loved place . . .'

I watch her, remembering her sudden distress last night. Sometimes she looks so weary, like a little old lady. 'Alice, what do you see or feel or hear?' I ask. 'That the rest of us can't?'

She turns to look at me, leaning against the granite pillar. She is wearing a wine-coloured cotton skirt to her ankles and a cropped black T-shirt showing a bare brown midriff. Her hair is plaited down one side and reaches her waist. She looks like a beautiful Arthur Rackham illustration out of an old fairy story.

'My grandmother had it. My mother didn't. I've had it since I was a child, Anna. Sometimes I can't shut the voices up, whisper, whisper, whisper. It is a bit like I am blotting paper and absorb things . . . It's worse in old places or where things have happened. I do the cards, but lots of people can. But this sense of knowing, sensing without really understanding . . . I wish I didn't have it . . . I get sick of it . . .'

She pushes herself away from the pillar, tries to smile. 'Come on, let's walk away from here, the sadness is catching. Normally it's OK, I can handle it. It's just when I get tired. Let's go to the lake with the herons you told me about.'

'We need to follow the path to your left and through the wood, then we end up round at the back of the house.'

We start to enter the wood, Hebe bobbing about in the

undergrowth ahead of us. But suddenly she gives a frightened yip and comes rushing back to us, hair on end and refuses to go in further. Alice touches my arm. 'Anna, I'm sorry, there is no way I am going in there. I'm amazed you can bear to.'

I laugh nervously at her pale face. 'I agree the woods are spooky, but the lake and the birds are wonderful. Hebe often does this, frightens herself in the undergrowth.'

As we make our way back home down the lane I wonder where my lovely placid Alice has gone. As if reading my thoughts she says slowly, 'Anna? Can I ask you something? I know it's asking a lot, but I am getting like, really heavy. I'm missing travelling. Jake is going to take off to Newbury to join the tree people for a few days. I'd really like to go. Could you manage without me if I do lots of extra hours before I go?'

I look at her beautiful face and I just cannot begrudge her time out. My heart sinks but I will manage. 'Go, darling. But just come back my cheerful Alice. Promise?'

She laughs. 'You see, I am heavy! Jake says I am.'

Hebe is still nervous and yappy as we reach the house. It is unlike her. As I unlock the front door she suddenly skids round the side of the house and up the bank towards the wood barking furiously. Goosebumps rise up on my arms. 'It could be someone trespassing up there on the judge's land.'

Alice goes and picks Hebe up, staring up into the dark trees and I see the hairs on the nape of her neck rise too. She turns and looks at me. 'I think Jake and Ian ought to take a look up there when they get in. Jake says the old gamekeeper is past it, all he is interested in is breeding pheasants in the pens the other side of the wood. The judge is always away so he doesn't care much.'

'Do we need a glass of wine?' I ask as we make our way indoors.

'Definitely,' Alice says.

I must make curtains for the kitchen windows. I've been meaning to all summer.

Chapter 40
Ian

Hester is back to ringing two or three times a night. The conversation hardly varies. She always says she wants to speak to Jess, but I have the feeling she rings repeatedly either in the hope Anna will answer and she can be abusive, or I will pick up the phone and she can hear the anger in my voice.

I have rung social services and spoken to her harassed psychiatric social worker and Hester's mother but no one has a clue where she is. We suspect she must be in Cornwall now, but we can't be sure. She is muddled and cagey about her whereabouts when Jess tries to find out where she could be.

The one good thing is that Hester obviously cannot find us, hence the frustrated phone calls. I'm proud of Jess, she is growing up and beginning to cope marvellously with the calls, almost to take them in her stride, like swatting an extremely irritating fly.

Every evening we turn on the answering machine, but it does not mitigate the nuisance of the phone ringing or hearing her voice, it only saves us having to speak to her. The answering machine infuriates her and she will let out a stream of invective and I will have to leap up and switch it off. Often we just give up and leave the phone off the hook.

Tonight at supper the phone goes as usual, but it is not Hester. It is my mother. I get up quickly to switch the machine off. Something must be wrong for her to ring me. She will write regularly but rarely phones.

It seems she has fallen and broken her hip and the fact of her phoning is a call for help. Bloody awful timing. I am up to my eyeballs, but of course I will have to go up to see her. I speak to the sister at the hospital for a few minutes. Apparently she refused to let anyone contact me until now because I am always so busy.

I am anxious suddenly, she is a very old lady to break her hip. I explain to Anna.

'I am going to have to go up there, Anna. Poor old thing.'

'Of course you are. You must go as soon as possible, Ian.'

'Dad, I want to come with you, I want to see Gran too. Please. Come on, Dad, it's only study week, I can take all my work. She might die and I'll never see her again.'

'We'll talk about it. Come on, Jess, are you ready? We are going to be late.'

We are going to a parents' evening which I could do without. I think about the best way of getting to Durham.

'When is Alice back, darling?'

'Wednesday, tomorrow.'

'Good. Look, ask her to stay here on Thursday night, will you? I have to go to work tomorrow, I have a big planning meeting. But I will drive up to Durham early on Thursday and come back late on Friday. I don't want you in the house alone. We are too isolated here.'

'Ian, I'll be fine,' she says. 'And you must stay longer than that, it's hardly worth going.'

'I can't, Anna, I have too much on. Of course, I'll have to go up again, for longer.'

Jessie rushes in again and grabs some books. 'Come on, Dad, we're going to be late.'

I grin at Anna and pick up the car keys. 'I bet you she fell over that bloody cat of hers, he will sit on the stairs.'

210

Anna smiles back. 'See you in about an hour or so. Hope the evening goes all right, Jess.'

She stands by the door. I have the feeling she might be anxious to have an evening to herself for a change and wish I had remembered to leave the phone off the hook.

Chapter 41

Anna

Digitalis purpurea f. alba. Foxglove. A graceful perennial with trumpet-shaped white flowers in summer. Prefers shade and needs supporting.

How suddenly summer is ending, the leaves turning early because of the drought. The heat wave is over, the temperature has dropped to that of a normal September and every night the wind gets up and blows small yellow leaves on to the grass.

I used to love autumn, but Ben, my mother and June all died as summer ended. I don't mind when winter really comes and I can draw the curtains at four and sit by the fire with seed catalogues and gardening books, but I hate this run up to winter when it gets cold down here in the summerhouse as soon as the sun goes, and the garden begins to look wayward and wilting.

I dread the thought of being cooped up indoors with the sound of that endless phone ringing, listening to the answering machine whirring and waiting with resignation to see if it is Hester's nasal twang after the bleeps.

We use the answering machine as a barrier. We still have to hear her voice but we do not have to pick up the phone or make any sort of response to her and it does feel as if we are at least one step removed from the nuisance of her.

Sometimes she doesn't bother to speak if the machine is switched on, at other times she lets out a stream of invective and Ian gets up wearily to switch it off. We do give up and leave the phone off the hook, but if we do this it feels as if she has won and that she is blocking us from the outside world.

I have been touched by the way Jessie has coped with her mother's constant phone calls and her little reassurances to me.

'Don't let her get to you, Anna. Dad's right, she will stop eventually, she will get bored now she can't find us. She'll do something totally bizarre and get carted back to London by the social services.'

Maybe. But Hester is not stupid. When she rang us from London call boxes she never bothered to block the calls. She does now. We have tried 1471 regularly but we have never found out where she calls from. We do not know how near she is.

Jess sounds flip and hard, but I notice she does not go to meet Lily in Truro any more and when we do have to go into the shops she peers over her shoulder constantly, is jittery, chews her bottom lip, her eyes darting here and there as if Hester might manifest herself suddenly. It is no way to live.

Yet as the evenings begin to close in, the three of us draw together. Nothing is said, nothing is outwardly changed, yet there is a peace and affection that is new and real between us all. For the first time we feel and act like a family.

Tonight, I have been let off going to a parents' evening at Jessie's school and it is wonderful to have an evening with the house to myself.

Jessie wants to go with Ian to visit her grandmother and I think it is a very good idea for her to see her grandmother again. Ian wants me to ask Alice to stay overnight while he is away. She is due back tomorrow and I will be very glad to see her.

I clear the supper things and pour myself another glass of wine and the phone goes again. Ian has not switched the answering machine back on and I am torn between leaving it ringing in case it is Hester and the terror of missing the boys. I pick it up gingerly and it is my sister, Jane.

'This is a surprise!'

'I know. I suddenly longed to hear your voice. Probably the menopause!'

I feel a rush of affection. Jane always hides her emotions behind this jolly hockey stick façade which started as a joke and seems to have stuck.

'Is everything all right?' I ask.

'Oh, Annie, I got such a fright. You remember Rob suddenly decided to go into the army? He had a friend he hunted with in the Royal Lancers . . . Well, he went straight out to Bosnia after Sandhurst . . .'

I feel a rush of guilt. I had quite forgotten Rob had even left the farm.

'Did you watch the early evening news on Sunday? A tank went over a mine and killed three young soldiers. I was convinced it was Rob. He's out there with tanks, and I knew he was in the same place because he had just written. I was like a headless chicken, until we could find out which regiment those boys came from. I really believed Rob was the young lieutenant in that tank and I thought my heart was going to break.'

'Oh, Jane, I'm so sorry, I just did not realize he was out there.'

'They are all living in the most atrocious conditions, he is seeing the most barbaric things, Anna, dead bodies rotting, mines everywhere, villages burnt and razed to the ground.'

Jane cannot stop, the words come pouring out in an unstoppable flow. I have never heard her like this before.

I say carefully, when I can, 'I guess nothing can prepare very young men, even highly trained ones, for what they will encounter on active service in places like Bosnia.'

This reminds me of stomach-churning conversations from another life. Other nasty little wars.

'I'm sorry, I know, I know, I'm banging on. It's just I knew

215

you would understand. I knew I could talk to you. Tom thinks I'm overreacting, being a bit of a drip . . .'

'Oh, for heaven's sake!' I explode.

'Tom's right. I've had it too easy, Annie. I've always had my sons and my husband safe, with me. Suddenly, for the first time, I know how you felt all those years with Ben in the Falklands, in Northern Ireland . . . in the Gulf. And I wanted to say I'm sorry. Sorry, old thing, for all those years of smug self-satisfaction, when I rarely rang or wrote and still don't . . .'

'Jane, don't be silly, you've got absolutely nothing to feel guilty about. I've always known you are there, that's enough.'

'No, it's not, and I wanted to say now I really do understand, now I have someone I love in a dangerous place. And I wanted to tell you I admire you for all those years. I do think about you, Annie, and worry about whether you are happy. You adored Ben so.'

'I'm fine, Jane, so stop worrying about me, and try not to worry about Rob too much. Come and stay soon?' I say, touched by her words, suddenly longing to see her.

There is silence as she considers the possibility of actually leaving her farm. 'Yes. Yes, Annie, I will. Heavens, if we don't make the effort to see each other now, we'll be little old ladies unable to travel!'

I laugh. 'OK, then, let's make a pact to see each other regularly.'

'Done,' Jane says. 'Anna, I feel much better now, thank you.'

We say goodbye and I replace the phone. Jane and I have never done things together, it will be fun to start. Odd that siblings get closer the older they get. No rivalry I suppose.

I have a bath, then go into the upstairs sitting room to do some paperwork. I put Radio Three on and relax, enjoying having the house to myself for once. It is very silent out there, only the huge fir moving in the wind. I haven't seen or heard the owl for a while.

Suddenly, I hear something like the sound of a footfall on the gravel. I put my pen down and strain to listen, hear the noise again. Hebe lifts her head, gives a woof, listens too, then hearing nothing drops her head again in the silence.

My flesh creeps. I am sure there is someone out there waiting, listening too. I move carefully out of the sitting room, across the landing and into our bedroom where the light is off and I edge towards the window and peer down. I can see nothing there, yet if they are standing in my porch I could not see them.

Irrational fear clutches at my throat as I imagine whoever it is standing, as I am, quietly waiting. I am immobile, frozen to the spot, my mind careering around the possibility of an unlocked front door.

In a moment I will hear the click as the heavy latch is lifted and the person creeps in. I should fly down the stairs now and throw myself at the door and lock it if it isn't already locked. But my body will not move. I am in the grip of a monstrous and overpowering fear.

Suddenly, there is a crash in the porch, I hear my plants being knocked over and the next minute a fox flies out, veers off right and disappears into the trees. I let out my breath in a wail of relief and embarrassment at my absurd imagination getting the better of me.

I think I have been expecting Hester to find us for so long now, I can't really believe she hasn't. Ian and Jess used to say so many times, 'She always finds us.' Yet they seem to have forgotten and I cannot.

The phone rings again as I make my way shakily back to the sitting room. It will be Hester this time, for sure. But it is not, it is Alice.

'Anna? I'm really sorry, the van has broken down. We are totally stuck up here until we can get a part. I think it's going to be the end of the week. I feel really bad, Anna. Will you cope all right?'

My heart sinks. 'Yes, of course I will. Look, don't worry, there's nothing you can do about it.'

'Anna, you sound breathless. Are you sure you are all right?'

I hear Ian and Jessie turn into the drive and the comforting sound of car doors slamming.

'I'm fine, darling. Love to Jake and the boys and I'll see you at the end of the week.'

Alice pauses. She cannot seem to put the phone down. 'Anna, I'll be back as soon as I can,' she says quickly and hangs up.

I turn as Ian comes into the room and he sees me replacing the receiver. 'Not Hester?' he asks anxiously.

'No, Alice.'

'Oh, good,' he says. 'So you are all organized for Thursday night?'

'Everything's fine.' If I tell Ian Alice isn't going to be here, he won't go.

I go to him, needing the comfort of another body. 'I'm so glad you're back.'

He holds me away, smiling. 'I'll have to go away more often!' Then he looks at me closely. 'Are you all right, darling?'

'I'm just stupid. I got thoroughly frightened by a fox in the porch knocking all the plants over.'

'Oh,' Ian says, 'that's why there is a mess down there and Hebe's bone is sitting on the doorstep.'

Jess comes in. 'That's Tim Penberthy's pet fox, I bet,' she says. 'His dad made him take it up into the woods when it got better, but he says it keeps coming back.'

'Well, I wish it wouldn't,' I say crossly.

'Go to bed, darling, you look tired, I'll bring you up a drink.'

I climb into bed and try to read, but I cannot relax. Ian comes up with a cup of tea and sits on the bed. 'I've put sugar in,' he says, 'because you got a fright.'

He is watching me. He has a torch in his hand which he puts on the floor. 'Anna, you thought it was Hester tonight, didn't you?'

'Yes.'

'Anna, I know Hester very well. If she had found us she would not skulk in the background, I assure you. She would make as big a disruption in our lives as is humanly possible.'

He picks up my hand. 'Hester's behaviour has a pattern, even if she does not act with any logic or forethought. If she had found us, my God, we would know. She would be here, banging on the door, demanding to see me or Jess. Either being terribly polite and seemingly normal or screaming abuse like a mad woman. If she had found us, why would she bother to phone?'

'It's just, how can someone just disappear? How is it that no one knows where she is?'

Ian laughs shortly and gets up off the bed. 'Well, there is no one to miss her, is there? There is no one to care where she is. The only time people care about people like Hester is when they cause trouble.'

It is an awful thought, to have no one to care whether you are alive or dead.

'I'm going to give Hebe her last walk.' Ian picks the torch up off the floor. 'Is it any comfort to know I not only make the rounds of the garden every night, but I go up around the edge of the woods too, every single night? And all I have ever found are two little cartons of children's orange juice. You know as well as I do, children will always trespass up there.'

I smile at him. 'Yes, it is a comfort. Sorry if I'm being stupid.'

'You're not. But that is why I wanted to make sure Alice was in the house with you at night while I am away. You're OK with Alice, aren't you?'

'Of course I am. Go and do your rounds.'

'Go to sleep, darling.'

I turn the light off and make myself think of something comforting. Of Liam and Dan who will be back home for Christmas, filling the house with noise and mess and laughter. Wonderful. I fall asleep making plans.

Chapter 42
Hester

The sun wakes me. It is getting lower in the sky. The mornings are colder now and I ache. Blood red in the sky, it shines through a gap in the trees on to my sleeping bag. There is a funny mist round it.

When I get up I hide my things carefully, deep in the ditch under the leaves where no one will find them. When I leave the wood I always go out at a different place. You can't be too careful. There are eyes everywhere, watching, watching.

My dad used to take me camping. On a bus. Just him and me, not her. Not for nights, just days. We played hide and seek. He was very good at it. We played in huge sand dunes. I don't know where it was.

You have to tuck yourself in, Hester. You have to pick a place where you can see but not be seen. Great hollows and hills. Easy to be found. Easy to hide. Just the luck of the draw, Hester, whether you are found or not.

If he found me too easily he would get cross. 'No good, lovey,' he would say. 'No good at all. You would be in enemy hands by now.'

Sometimes it would take me ages to find him. Sometimes I couldn't find him at all. Then I would cry.

Once, I found him almost buried on the edge of a sand dune deep in the marram grass. He did not hear me. He had his hands over his face. I knew he was weeping. He took his hands away suddenly and he started to rock back and forth, back and

221

forth and sing in a strange funny language I had never heard. A chant. A bit like a hymn. I did not understand. I felt very cold and afraid.

He saw me suddenly and held out his hand. 'It's all right, lovey.'

I took his hand and held it to my cheek. I could not bear his sadness.

'Why are you sad?' I asked.

'Because of the war. Because sometimes, Hester, the bad things we see live on inside us. I escaped. I got to the other side of those gates. My family did not.'

My dad rolled up his sleeve and held out his arm to me and there was a number on it.

'I hid for two months. Moving, always moving. I lived in the woods until the Americans came. But the smell of death has never left me. I survived. That is my guilt.'

He pulled himself out of the sand. 'Come. It was a long time ago.'

As we walked I asked him, 'What was the language you were singing in?'

'Polish,' he said. He looked down at me but he did not see me. 'I say a prayer for a wife and child I left behind.'

I like this time of day, they are still sleeping. The eyes of the house are closed and cannot see me. I make my way down round the house. I have to be careful because the gravel makes a noise and there is a little dog that growls.

I go down the garden, right to the bottom. It is a secret place. Sometimes I turn the hose on a little way and I wash myself. I like it here.

I leave little messages for Jessie, so she knows it is going to be all right. So she knows I am going to save her and take her away.

There are geraniums like my dad used to have in his greenhouse. Some of the pots are too heavy, but I move two little ones near the bench so that there are two pink flowers one side and the white trailing one near the steps is turned towards the pond. It looks much better. I have to be very careful in case she notices. That would give the game away. One morning I saw a fox. It gave me a terrible fright with its beady eyes, but it was not afraid of me. I threw it a biscuit and it ate it, that made me laugh.

I try the door of the shed thing but it is locked. It would be a very nice place to sleep now that it is colder. You would think Jessie or Ian would think about leaving it open for me. I suppose they are afraid she will realize things have to change now that I am well again and back home.

I have to keep away during the day. There are too many people coming and going. It isn't safe. I cannot see them properly. I cannot make a signal. I can't get near enough.

I decide to move. I come down the side of the wood. I find a new place, up from a lake, in a small clump of trees across the drive but facing the house. I can see now. I can just see in lighted windows. It is dryer here because of the huge fir. I am happy. I make a bed amongst the fir needles in a ditch between trees. It is lovely.

One evening I heard the car go out. I was watching but I could not see who was in it. I waited and waited. When a lamp came on upstairs I thought it was my husband and daughter signalling to me. I knew it could be a trick. I was very quiet. I crept round the house, over the gravel towards the front door and I stood still listening. I could not hear anything, no voices, no television, nothing.

Just as I reached out to try the door the fox shot out from under the gap in the porch and knocked a plant over, making a huge crash.

Bloody, bloody fox. I turned and ran, I was frightened suddenly. I reached the dark and crouched near the roses to get my breath back and a car came up the drive, but I could not see who it was. The front door opened and light shone out into the night, then there was a slam and blackness.

I am shut out in the dark. I sit very still. The voices get very loud, they are the wind in the trees. I go back to the fir tree. I

223

dig down among leaves and pine needles. I cover my sleeping bag until I am hidden under the leaves. Hester is gone. Hester is invisible. Hester is no more. Hester is root and dry leaves. Hester is wind and whispers. Hester is shaking.

I am shaking. I am angry. I am very angry. The trees hiss and whisper, hiss and whisper so loudly my head will burst. I crawl further inside my sleeping bag. Down, down. I must get warm. I am tired. I must sleep. I must wait. Can't wait.

Fuck her. Nearly there. They are waiting for me. It's me Ian loves. It is me Ian wants. He likes it, he told me. He always liked it. He used to shake with wanting me. Bloody fucking woman.

Dad did too. He loved. Not her, me. Me.

Dad loved Hester.

Got to get proper food tomorrow. Got to be strong. Tired of leaves. My bones ache. Buried the pills deep, deep in the ground. They think I am stupid. I know what's in them. I hear the owl. It is a signal. I whisper, 'I'm coming. I'm coming.'

Chapter 43
Anna

Myosotis scorpioides. 'Mermaid.' Water
Forget-me-not. Grows in ponds and
shallow water. Small, faded-blue,
forget-me-not flowers in summer.

The tide is coming in and there is a mist hanging over the water in strange swirls which change with the wind, so that when I turn the fog has descended, shutting me in, moving me forward. Ahead St Ives is only visible for seconds at a time, faded colours in the distance appearing like a stage set.

At first it seems I am alone on the wide beach but then tiny figures appear like people in old water colours, fading paintings found in attics. They walk dogs, stand with their trousers rolled up, lift skirts to the waves. But they are not real, they are part of this dream I am in. Part of a painting on the wall of someone's house.

I know I am dreaming but still the excitement of being back home remains. Once more. Just once more back to this place, this life, when happiness soared in my heart like a lark.

I walk the shore line waiting, laughter catches in my throat for I know exactly what I am waiting for. As I wait, the mist descends lower and lower until there is just a circle of beach and light visible where I stand. It happens so quickly, even the sea is disappearing as the tide carries the mist with it closer and closer to me.

I can see no one now and suddenly I am afraid. It is so eerie and complete, so sudden and isolating. All sounds except the surf muffled into endless silence. The sun, and the heat of it obscured. Only the mist rolling relentlessly towards me, swallowing me up and I cry out in sudden terror wanting to wake up. But I cannot and it is like a silent scream.

I stand weeping, looking out to sea where there is no horizon. It is then I see Ben. He appears out of the mist, running along the shallows in his shorts, with Sasha, our golden retriever. He does not see me. I do not think he sees me.

I stand quite still watching him. This is what I have been waiting for. He is beautiful again and unscarred. Still laughing at life, death still one big adventure to come. In my head I hear his voice clearly, that last leave, 'Forgive me, Annie, for all the hurts. You may not believe me but it's an awful long time since I was unfaithful. Life is so good down here with you and the boys. You have always been the only one, whatever you think. The lack was in me, not you, my darling Annie.'

He turns, my beloved, in the shallows of the sea, his lilting voice rolling to me on the mist and stares at me and his face is sadder than I have ever seen it. I cry out and start to run towards him, but he is gone, evaporated into the mist and sea and I am left with only the breath of his voice in my heart, like a soft sigh, 'Annie.'

I turn and little figures emerge again out of the mist as it rises. The moment is gone. Ben is gone. I do not want to wake. I dread to wake as if sleep, this dream, is my life and my life is my nightmare.

I do wake and it is Ian sleeping beside me. I weep and cannot stop. The tears are relentless, soaking the pillow like a sudden, violent monsoon.

I get out of bed and stumble down the stairs in the dark. As I reach the bottom the phone rings out in the hall startling me. I pick it up, muzzy with my dream and it is Liam sounding faint.

'Liam! Where are you? What's happened?'

226

'Mum, nothing's happened, don't worry. We're in Borneo now and we're both fine. I know it's very early with you, but we were near a phone and felt like talking to you. Here's Dan.'

'Mum? Hi, are you all right? In your last letter you sounded sort of low. We were a bit worried so we thought we'd ring you to find out if you were OK.'

'Dan, I'm fine. There's absolutely nothing for you to worry about.'

'Is everything working out with Ian and Jess? Are you happy, Mum?'

I must not hesitate or pause for a second. 'Darling, all is well with me. I'm happy.'

I hear him let out his breath with relief. 'I'll pass you to Liam again.'

'Mum? You really would tell us if there was anything wrong?'

'I promise.'

'Because we've got open tickets. We could come straight back if you need any support. Is Ian being OK to you?'

'Darling, what is all this, suddenly? I'm fine and there is absolutely no reason for you to come home early. Has something happened your end?'

'No, we're still having a great time, we just suddenly felt worried about you. We planned to make our way to Australia in a couple of days, then we'll be home for Christmas.'

'Wonderful, darling! Liam, you are both taking care . . . in all the obvious ways?'

'Sure, sure, Mum.' I hear the smile in his voice. He knows I mean sex and drugs. He is deliberately vague in case I persist. The young always think they are invincible.

'Liam, I'll send you money for this call. Take care of each other. Love you both. We'll have a wonderful Christmas together.'

'It'll be great to see you, Mum. Love you lots. Here's Dan.'

'Tell me,' Dan asks, 'how come you answered the phone on the first ring at four o'clock in the morning?'

I smile, taken back to his little anxious face of childhood. 'I was coming downstairs to make a cup of tea, you know what a bad sleeper I am.'

'Mm,' he says doubtfully and it is odd. As if my strange dream had reached out to touch them too. As if our past had collided in a sudden burst of mutual loss.

'Mum, see you at Christmas. Love you lots.' It is left to me to put the phone down first.

Ian is sitting on the stairs. 'Everything all right, Anna?'

I tell him and he smiles. 'Umbilical cord,' he teases jealously and tweaks my hair.

I move towards him and he folds me to him. I am tempted to tell him of my dream. My treacherous dream, but I cannot.

As if he feels my disturbance he takes me back to bed and makes love to me as tenderly as if I were a child and love and gratitude rise up in me. I suddenly do believe things are going to be all right for the three of us. Ian and I married each other for entirely the wrong reasons. But now I think we have reached a place of understanding. We are growing to love and respect one another.

Despite Hester we are still together and Jessie is growing to be a happier, pretty girl, putting the past behind her as she slips into adulthood.

I must do the same, I must leave my past behind me too.

Ian and I are going to be all right.

I smile and Ian raises his head 'Why are you smiling?'

'Because I think I'm happy?'

He kisses my forehead. 'Me too, Anna, me too.'

He turns and peers at his watch. 'Oh God, I'll have to get up and wake Jess, it's five thirty and I must get going. But you, my darling, can stay warm in bed and go back to sleep.'

I curl in, burrow into the warmth his body has left, switch the radio on low and I fall asleep again as I hear his car purr down the drive taking him and Jessie to Durham.

Chapter 44

Ian

I drive away from the house with a deep feeling of contentment. For once the sun is firmly obscured behind clouds, but it will make driving cooler. Perhaps this strange tropical summer is ending.

Jessie goes straight back to sleep for an hour or so and as I drive along I smile to myself, thinking of Anna curled sleeping in the bed I have just left. Then I think of my mother and how I am going to find her, perhaps this is the end of her ability to live alone. If so I am going to have a tough battle to get her to admit it.

When Jessie wakes I make a stop for coffee and breakfast. She perks up suddenly and eats enormously. Where does it go in that skinny, awkward frame of hers?

When we are on our way again she pushes in the least vile of her tapes and I endure it for half an hour, then switch firmly to Radio Four and she cheerfully plugs in her boogie pack.

Suddenly she takes it off and says, apropos of nothing at all, 'I'm glad you married Anna, Dad,' in a rather embarrassed way. I turn the radio down but not off in case it frightens conversation.

I smile at her. 'I'm glad too. What makes you say that suddenly, Jess?'

'I dunno. I was just thinking . . . When it's time to come

back it's nice to have someone at the other end, you know, there waiting.'

I am touched. It is like being exonerated somehow. I did get it right. I did choose the right person this time. Someone important to Jessie's security and future.

'Especially someone as warm as Anna.'

'Yes,' Jess says firmly. 'And Dad, you are warmer, you are nicer since Anna. Suddenly you are.' She says it in a rush and glances at me quickly in case I am cross or offended.

I laugh. 'How did I seem to you before?'

'Just, you know, like, distant, far away all the time. Busy. I used to feel so lonely.'

'I'm sorry,' I say. 'I'm so sorry you felt lonely.'

'It's OK. You did your best. You know, Dad, sometimes, the time we lived with Mum seems like a bad dream, like we dreamt it, and it didn't really happen . . .'

'Except she is always on the end of a phone, so it did happen.'

'Yeah. It's such a pain. I just hope she goes away again soon, finds something else to obsess on.'

I smile again. My daughter is growing up.

As we approach Durham I try to ring Anna from my car phone but there is no reply. I expect she is down putting her beloved garden to bed for the winter.

Chapter 45
Hester

From the edge of the woods I watch the house. I watch moving shadows in uncurtained, lighted rooms. Soon I will lose the cover of trees, autumn is come and the leaves drift down on the wind like tears. Large and small leaves fall in my hair, cover me as I crouch watching the house, watching at dawn and dusk the people in that house. Leaves are my cloak and cover.

I know now what time they get up, leave for work, sit down to have their supper and go to bed. Now it is colder they sometimes draw the curtains at dusk, shut themselves in, shut me out.

Then I get angry.

I get out of my sleeping bag, make my stiff limbs work and go to the telephone box no one seems to use in this isolated place. I dial 141. Wendy taught me. I ring their number. The woman never answers. It is always my husband or child. Or the fucking answer machine. If Jessie answers, I say gently, 'Hello, Pet. When shall we meet? I've got presents for you.'

There is silence. Then she says, 'Oh, Mum, please leave us alone. I don't want to meet you. I don't want your presents. Wherever you are, just go home, go away.'

I understand. I whisper, 'It's all right, Petal. I know you have to pretend. I'll be in the Market Place at eleven o'clock.'

231

The telephone is banged down. That woman of course. Jessie is never allowed to see me. If my husband picks up the phone I tell him what I think of the woman who stole my husband and baby.

If he puts the phone down I ring again and again. I ring until he yells down the phone, 'Leave us alone! Haven't you done enough damage, ruined enough lives yet?'

The phone is taken off the hook. I throw back my head and laugh. He is guilty as hell and paying for it.

He leaves for work at eight. Jessie is always with him. They do not know I have found their house. Soon I will discover where Jessie's school is, where my husband works and I will surprise them. I always catch up. I always find them.

Today, as I watch from the edge of the woods, under the fir tree, lights go on early. I see my husband and Jessie leave the house. It is only six o'clock in the morning. He puts suitcases in the car, he is going away.

I smile.

The car drives off and I circle the sleeping house. No lights now. I try the front door. I try the windows, all tight shut. I walk round the back. All is firmly bolted against me.

I feel anger rising like a river inside my head.

I am the wife, I should be inside this house. I go back to the front and a glint catches my eye. There is a garage key left in the door. He must have been in a hurry. I lift the door up and over a little way and crawl underneath. In the dim light I see the door to the inside of the house is ajar.

I have waited long for this moment.

I push the door open. I step inside. I place my feet carefully on the beige-carpeted stairs. At the top I pause. Three doors are open. I look. One is a bathroom, one is a large upstairs sitting room. The third is a small dark room at the back of the house with a pear tree practically coming in the window.

Jessie's room. It smells of her. Jessie's dark little prison. I pick up her nightie and press it to my face. Jessie. Something filters through the cobwebs of memory. A baby crying and my body won't move, my mind wants to float away on clouds, away from the voices in my head and the huge bloated faces bent to me, mouthing words I can't understand, wishing me harm.

I fling the nightie away and turn. Now for her. The door which is closed. The bedroom they commit adultery in.

The noise in my head starts again, incessant as a waterfall. I do as I am told. I take what I need out of my bag and turn the handle and go in.

The woman sleeps. Her hair is long and browny gold. She looks smug, cat-like. I watch her. I know suddenly that my husband has just made love to this woman. That is why he was careless. A radio is playing music on the bedside table. This is why she has not heard me. I watch her wake. Anna . . .

Her body goes tense, freezes, as she feels someone in the room. She is afraid to move. She is afraid to turn. Slowly, slowly she turns to face me and her eyes widen in terror as she sees me and what I have in my hand. She sits up with a cry like a startled seabird and the sound echoes round me like a familiar thing I have been waiting for.

Anna cannot move, her fingers shake as she grabs the covers towards her as if they will protect her.

I watch her. I say nothing.

Anna is trembling so much she can hardly speak. 'How . . . did you get in?'

I ignore her and ask, 'Where have my husband and daughter gone?'

'They will be back any minute.'

I smile. They will not.

'Jessie isn't here,' Anna says. Her voice is a little croak. Her teeth are chattering. Her eyes never leave my face. There are shadows under them. She is not as pretty as I

233

thought. 'Please go away. Look, I've never stopped Jessie seeing you, it's her own decision. In fact, I've tried . . .'

'Liar,' I whisper. I run the knife along my fingers to frighten her. She draws a shuddering breath, there is sweat on her top lip. I can smell her smell. I can smell her fear.

Suddenly she tries to smile, she says, 'Look, let me make you a cup of tea. I need one and I'm sure you do.'

I feel anger at her soft cajoling tone. The tone Melanie uses, the tone they all use to tell me I am well again and can go out into a world where everyone is trying to take what is mine. She has taken everything I had. Everything.

I swipe at her with the knife and catch her arm. She screams as blood spills out on to the pretty sheets. I sit on the bed and watch her bleed. 'You stole my husband and child.'

Frantically, she stems the blood with the top of the sheet. Her face is ashen but she no longer trembles. A hopelessness is in her eyes. She speaks to me softly as if I am a child.

'Hester, I met Ian and Jessie a long time after your divorce. You forget. You've been ill. Ian is no longer your husband, but Jessie will always be your daughter. When she's older, she'll understand . . .' She trails off, staring at me. I see pity in her eyes. I turn to the mirror to see what she sees.

Startled, I see a woman with wild grey hair in which tiny leaves are trapped. I see a shapeless figure in a coat done up with the wrong belt. Is this me? I peer at my reflection. I am no longer beautiful. I am no longer slim and young.

When did this happen? From long ago I remember a man swinging me round as if I was as light as a dandelion clock. Kissing me. 'Beautiful,' he cries. 'Beautiful . . .'

From behind me I hear Anna's voice. 'Hester, please let me help you.' I look round. The woman is beautiful and young and she mocks me. The mirror mocks me. I want to be her. I want to be Anna. I want to look like her for my husband and child to love me again.

I watch her hand slowly moving towards the telephone on the bedside table. Her nails are broken and the hand is tiny, like a child's. She reaches the phone but I am quicker. I move, I lift my arm up. Anna too raises her arms, thin as swans' necks, to shield her body. I plunge the knife into her again and again. Anna gives one long shivering cry. It echoes up to the ceiling and floats out of the window into the trees.

Silence. She hardly put up a fight at all.

I wrap her in the sheets, bundle her out of sight like an Egyptian mummy. There is blood everywhere. I clean the knife and put it away.

I go down into the kitchen. I am hungry. I open the fridge and crouch beside it and push things into my mouth. The small dog cowers under the table. It won't come out and talk to me, it growls, so I leave it and go back upstairs to the bathroom to have a bath.

I put her bath oil into the water. I wash my hair and tiny leaves fall out into the red water. I will smell just like her. I will become Anna. I throw my clothes into a corner and put on her pretty underclothes. They are tight, but I do not need to look into the mirror to know how beautiful I look.

I will sleep. I am very, very tired. When I wake, when it is dark, I will get up and pull Anna wrapped in the bedclothes on to the floor. I will pull her down the stairs and out of the front door. I will drag her across the deserted lawn to the edge of the wood.

I will push her down a bank into the darkness and cover her with pine needles and dry rustling leaves. I laugh and laugh. Anna will be the one under the leaves now, I am home in the house with lighted windows.

I must sleep now.

Did I already put Anna under the leaves? I must have done. The bed is empty, Anna is gone, that is good. That is why I am so tired, Anna was heavy. I pull the covers over the blood.

The phone rings and rings but I leave it. I stretch out in the soft bed in an apricot nightdress feeling my slim erotic beauty against the cool sheets. My long gold hair floats across the pillow like thistle down.

In the morning I will wake smiling and put bright scarves in my hair. I will put on my best make-up and lipstick. I will wait. I will wait for my husband to come home to me. I see a trail across the wooden floorboards. Like a snail towards a little door, a red trail. I must sleep. My body is so heavy.

I wake and hear a car rattling, turning fast into the drive. It is making a lot of noise and stops with a screech of brakes. A car door bangs. There is a key in the lock and running footsteps.

I sit up and pat my golden hair 'Anna?' Ian will call in a moment. 'Anna, my love.'

I smile my prettiest smile. He will be so pleased to be back with me, his lovely young wife. So pleased to be home. I wait with my arms outstretched to greet him.

A girl bursts in, her dark hair is flying. Where is Ian? Where is my love?

She is screaming. Why is she screaming? She calls out, 'Anna?' She calls out my name but I do not know her.

'Anna? Oh, my God. Anna? Anna?'

She stares and stares at me. She is frightened. She glances round the room. She sees the blood. She looks along the floor and then at the little door. 'Anna,' she whispers, 'oh, God. Anna?' She moves towards me. 'Please. Let me get help. Anna needs help.'

I laugh. 'Anna is dead. I am Anna now.'

She is moving to the telephone. I pull out my knife from the pillow. Good thing I am careful. Her eyes widen and she backs towards the little door. She is crying. She leans against it. She calls, 'Anna? Anna? You hang on, do you hear me? I'm coming. I'm coming. Don't die. Please . . . Dear God, don't die.'

I can feel the anger. The voices start. 'Anna is dead!' I

shout. 'You stupid bitch, whoever you are. Anna is dead. I am Ian's young wife.'

'No,' she screams. 'Anna is not dead. You are not Anna, you are Hester. You are no longer Ian's wife.'

Whore! Another whore! I lift my knife. I run at her. But she is ready for me, she is strong and young. She throws herself at me, she grabs my arm and pushes me hard and we fall to the ground.

I still have the knife.

She is trying to get it, the bitch is trying to get my knife. I twist it towards her . . .

Whore . . . Ian's whore . . . She is strong . . . Stronger than Anna. She is fighting. Suddenly there is sharp pain. I cry out. I roll away from the pain, see her face white, white as a ghost, mouth open but no scream comes.

She backs away and opens the little door. I hear her moan. She rushes past me and I hear her telephone. It is getting dark now and I am dizzy. It must be night.

Through the open door I see a body lying on the floor. It is very still. The dark girl sits on the floor and she takes the person in her arms and she presses a towel to her stomach and it turns bright red.

She rocks, rocks the body and she is singing, humming a strange long chant. Over and over. Over and over. It makes me sad. A crying song, like another language.

It is peaceful. It is soothing. I raise my head. Pain stabs. Slowly I get up on one arm. I want to see in the mirror. I must look pretty for Ian and Jessie. I reach up to look in the bottom of the wardrobe mirror.

I am not there. There is an old woman covered in blood.

Where is pretty young Hester?

Don't know . . . Tired.

Roll back into the leaves, into the darkness. Into dry rustling leaves. Down, down.

Hester is safely hidden. Hester is dying.

Hester was right. She was frightened of the dark thing

and it got her. They should have kept her safe, away, away from the dark thing. People . . . Everyone . . . taking all, all Hester has ever had.

Hester is hiding with her father beneath the roots of trees, beneath the pine needles. They are safe together beneath the damp-smelling leaves.

Chapter 46

Anna

Cyclamen mirabile. Pale pink flowers
with jagged-tipped petals like small
teeth marks. The mouth of the petal is
a deep-stained purple.

Silence. Water running somewhere. I come up from a dark
place. Piercing pain like birds flying, filling my head with
beating wings. Hard under me a polished floor. I remember.
And terror is back. I crawl slowly, inch by inch towards the
door of my room. Someone is groaning. Must . . . must . . .
reach . . . my room. Pain like fire and I am falling, falling
back into blackness . . .

The sun rising above the creek is glorious this morning. An
orange glow creeps up amongst dark fingers of cloud and
fills the sky, lights up the water below it as if it too will
catch fire and the whole world will be alight, making its
way towards me in this silent room.

I am so cold but I cannot move to put my dressing gown
on because of this sadness, this overwhelming sense of loss.
As if this is the first and last rising of the sun I will see. Is
it the knowledge that my significance, my part in this vast
universe is infinitesimal?

I can make no difference to the sun coming up or going
down or the changing seasons. I care for my garden, I cherish

239

my plants as if they are my children, but I cannot foil frost or disease, virus or slugs. My power and expertise are as nothing against fickle nature. I stand here leaning towards an incandescent sky, shiveringly aware of my tiny part of a frightening and unexplained system.

Out there, somewhere in infinity is my beloved. The spirit of him part of the sun rising and tide turning, the pain of his broken and scarred body, those terrible ugly burns gone. His spirit soaring into a new day. I need to believe this, I need it to be true.

If I were Alice I would know. She would feel the truth like a heartbeat. Guileless, she would not question but feel her way forward with her frightening honesty and she too would weep at the shimmering beauty of this morning.

Autumn is coming. Is my sadness due to this sudden ending of summer? This morning feels like a leave-taking. As if I might raise my hand in farewell, a final salute to a world I love. A world where my garden has become a part of me so that I am border and grass, plant and tree.

If I waved my arms, cold, in my bedroom watching the burst of sun emerge dramatically like a butterfly out of a chrysalis, lightening the day, removing the shadows from the room, it would only be as the branches of some tree moving in the wind. A faded pattern in a vast and unknown fabric. When I cease to exist I will become part of all that is out there. The roots of me lodged in the sweet-smelling earth, having like my plants a season.

I move from the window back into my narrow schoolgirl bed under the mirror full of photos. I cannot get warm. This terrible fear will not leave me.

Someone is lying quite still on the floor next door . . .

I close my eyes. This coldness is like winter when the grass is hard with a coating of early frost and my geraniums, still in the act of flowering, will be caught frozen and drooping like bruised hands.

The mist swallows me. The darkness becomes mist. The

mist separates like fingers and becomes a sound. Pain returns. Someone is pressing something into me. I hurt. I hurt. The sound ebbs and flows like waves. Over and over . . . The spiralling rhythm, a quivering, shivering, tender lament . . . Let me float away . . . Please let me float away.

'No. Anna, no. Please, God. Please don't die, Anna. Anna. Oh God.'

Alice . . . Alice holding me, pulling me back to unbearable pain . . . No, no, darling, let me just float away . . . That's it. That's it.

So much noise and movement. Rushing and shouting. Sirens. Sirens like the long endless sound of whales. Falling. Falling into misty darkness.

My fingers held. My fingers curled around warm hands. I open my eyes for a second. Liam and Dan are here. How good that they are here with me.

All pain starts to fade from me. Joy fills my heart, for suddenly I am running across a beach of golden sand into the blue where mist meets sea.

I am safe now. I am going home where I will be curl of wave and cry of curlew. Where I will live in the echo of my sons' voices, in the scent of flowers and in their memories of my cracked hands and nails full of soil and in my faded postcards on a wall.

In the sound of trees moving in the wind and the cry of a first grandchild.

I will be there in a familiar turn of a head and a song that makes them cry.

In a scent at nightfall and in my love for them, which is as infinite as the space I am running into . . .

'Mum, please. Mum, come on. You can make it. You can. Come on, Mum. You've done so well.'

'Oh, Mum. Christ. Please don't die.'

I am looking down on them. I do not want this joy to fade. I turn back into the waves and Ben is there. He is holding his hands up and out as if I must not go forward. 'Darling Annie, not yet. Not yet.'

I reach down to touch my boys and they shiver. Alice turns her head very slightly as if she catches the fall of my shadow. 'Anna?' she whispers. 'Anna?'

I am in a white bed. My two lanky bookends cannot stop touching me, warming my hands with their own. Alice is crying. I am so glad they are here. So glad they are home.

So glad they are here. So glad they are home.

Chapter 47

Anna

Rosa. 'Remember Me'. Bush Rose.
Gold flowers with abundant and shiny
leaves. Freely borne in summer and in
autumn too.

Ian helps me out of the car and wraps my coat around me
as if I am a child. His face is worried. He did not want me
to come, but I have ghosts to kill.

We leave the car outside the granite gateposts underneath
the huge fir.

I use my sticks because I am still weak but I am willing
myself stronger day by day.

There is a wrought-iron gate between the granite posts
now and a large 'Private' sign, but the gate is not locked.
No one comes here.

I pass through, trying not to look too hard or shake at
the sight of the boarded-up and eyeless house standing, as
if with head bowed, dark among the trees.

I want to see once more and say goodbye to my garden.
Ian takes my arm. He has become so thin and drawn. He
blames himself for what happened, when there is no blame. He
believes it is his fault for leaving me alone here. For thinking
he understood the strange machinations of Hester's mind.

We turn our back on the house and move slowly down the garden. A cold wind blows, bringing with it the smell of the creek.

A gale has blown the water irises and lilies flat, and mossy green pondweed covers the top of the pool. My large urns and pots stand around the steps and garden seat like deserted friends, holding geraniums wilted and dead, stalks hollow and brown like drowned fingers.

The doors of the plastic tunnels bang gently, monotonously, and weeds, huge thistles and dandelions and crouch grass, grow triumphantly up, burying rows of small dried-up plants in polythene pots. The greenhouses stand empty like supermarket shelves at the end of a siege.

My summerhouse is not locked. Ian opens the door and pulls a chair out for me so I can see into the garden. He leaves me to say my private goodbye and wanders down to the creek with his own thoughts.

I watch him move away into the trees. It is hard to watch his pain. He has been living in the middle of a nightmare. Hester is dead. I nearly died. Jessie is in deep shock at the terrible suddenness of it all.

I am relieved they have been with Nick and his warm affectionate family. Where Pud underpins their days with a careful normal routine. They both have so many confusing and conflicting emotions. Hester has dominated their lives for so long.

It is very quiet. I see suddenly that the huge camellia tree has died.

Leaves blow and scuttle across the overgrown grass and I wait for the silence to settle down into a rhythm I can fit into.

When I am bent with my hands in the earth, quite alone, the pulse of the garden will rise up through my fingers in a perfect stillness and peace. Time has no meaning. Primitive joy is complete.

All the small things that make up a private happiness, a perfect whole of smell and feel, sight and sound, are touched with the essence of oneself. Down, down through the fingertips into the sweet-smelling earth . . . It is difficult

244

to know where the wonder and sense of nature ends and man begins.

Already nature is slowly and inexorably claiming my garden back. The wood is encroaching, shrubs and plants will soon disappear in grass and brambles. Vast brambles and wild rose between the tunnels already reach out with long, newly leafed arms to smother and suffocate my years here.

This is how it must be.

The Trevillian estate have bought back the house and land from us. If they had not we would have lost everything, for who would have bought a house and land believed to be cursed with tragedy?

My blood and Hester's stains for ever the wooden floor-boards of the house. Indelible. A reminder of some evil which seems to dog this place.

June's faded cards in my summerhouse have been taken down and lovingly collected by the boys. I get up and go outside once more. It is incredible that Hester lived like a wild animal here in those woods and watched us, unseen, for weeks.

When we chose this place was there something dark and unfinished in Ian and me? A sense of foreboding, of not caring enough where we lived together that drew us to this place?

Yet it was and is so beautiful. I loved it. I made it my own. A place can only reflect evil done by man. It cannot be evil in itself.

Ian has told me Hester was sectioned all those years ago for attacking her mother. He truly believed what he had been told, that it was an isolated incident entirely to do with Hester's difficult relationship with her mother. He never believed her dangerous, so he saw no point in frightening me.

He feels he made a grave misjudgement in not being honest and warning me, and in not being more careful.

But no one, no one, could have anticipated what Hester was capable of.

I look up towards the boarded-up house and shiver. I try to face the memory head on, to lay the ghost of sheer naked terror. A nightmare which came true.

My blood, my life-blood pumped out to stain for ever the timbers of that house.

Hester's life ended there.

A woman Ian once loved. Who was his wife. Jessie's mother.

The Trevillians are pulling it down, although they had to get special planning permission from the authorities. They are laying the ghosts of the manor too. Soon there will be no mansion here and no lodge. All will be razed to the ground. Only the foundations will remain hidden for ever under a relentless undergrowth which will spring up and cover all signs of habitation.

All, all this which was mine and carved out of field and wood, will disappear for ever. No sign that I spent what feels like a lifetime breathing life into neglect.

It has to be so. I am glad now to let it go. I want to be free of it. Free of the constant unease and nebulous fear which coloured my days.

I turn towards the creek where the curlews cry out in the wind and I renounce silently Hester and the ghost of her. I commit her hold on Ian and Jess deep into the ground to be buried for ever.

It is finished.

We are leaving the voices of our past behind tangled and lost for ever among the rhododendrons and camellias that will burst forth among the wilderness.

I refuse to take the sadness of this place or my part in it on with me.

I am leaving it here. I have listened too long to the voices of my past. Ben is gone, but he lives on in his sons and deep inside me. I leave regret and loss under the hard, cold soil to join the endless threnody of this place.

I am alive and I cannot describe the joy of it. I will never, can never, take a moment of my life for granted again. I am alive. I have Liam and Dan. I have Ian and Jess. I have my gentle Alice, who gave me my life back. All of them, Jake and the little boys, have willed me, loved me better, day by long day.

We have bought a huge farm bordered by fields, where the sun can reach into every window, where the sea glitters blue, blue, on the horizon. Alice and Jake are going to renovate and live in one of the cottages. We will spread out into ten acres of valley. Just us.

Liam and Dan are going to spend the winter close to me, helping me and Alice start all over again. Their anger and distrust of Ian will fade as summer comes. It will. Alice will laugh again.

Slowly we will all go on healing, moving carefully forward, leaving the shadows of our past behind us. It will take a long time. It will take years. None of us can ever forget what happened here. This is why we make plans, all the time. To crowd out the horror.

The horror of Hester's death is different for each of us. Yet it is a strangely collective pain that separates us for the time being from the outside world.

Ian comes through the trees towards me. He looks down at me almost as if he is seeing me for the first time. 'You nearly died here. You could have died because of me.'

'Not because of you. Because of Hester.'

We hold on to each other and rock together under the cold leafless trees.

'It's over, Ian.'

'Yes. It's over.' His voice carries over the garden against a rustle of wind.

We link arms and slowly we make our way up the garden. A blackbird starts singing suddenly behind me.

I will try to remember this sound winging out over the trees and not the sound of a phone.

We drive away and we do not look back.

Plantation Lane Time and Tide

Simon Patterson
Arup Associates
British Land

Edited by Paul Brislin

Contents

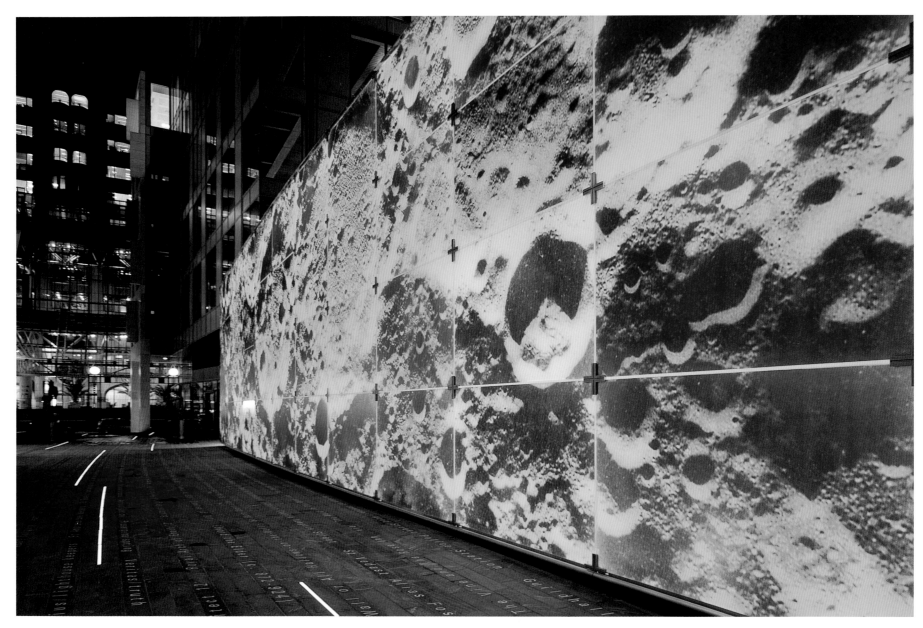

Introduction
John Ritblat

Plantation Place is one of the most important new developments in the City of London of recent years. It is a fine piece of contemporary architecture designed by Arup Associates that sits comfortably in its environment. Its scale reflects that of the surrounding streets: the stone fins of the facades relate elegantly to the more traditional architecture of the City. Yet the glass towers that rise some fourteen floors appear transparent against the sky.

As part of the context of this new development we have created Plantation Lane, a pedestrian walkway between the two buildings of Plantation Place that recreates some of the permeability of the old Plantation House. British Land is committed to developing buildings that improve the environment and benefit the users. We believe that the relationship between art and architecture within the public realm is an essential part of the creation of high quality environments.

At Broadgate, Ludgate and Regent's Place, art forms an integral part of the *genius loci*. We support art in many ways, having sponsored the National Gallery's *Young Gainsborough* exhibition as well as the Wallace Collection's display of Boucher, amongst other events. I am very pleased that Simon Patterson agreed to work with us on the installation in Plantation Lane – his work beautifully encapsulates the City's powerful history as well as our aspirations for the future. It provides an exciting addition to this new City space, which I hope will be enjoyed by all those who work in the surrounding area and those who come to visit it.

John Ritblat is the Chairman of British Land

ROW 2:
Patent Office
Staple Inn
Barnard's Inn
Public Record's Office
City of London Public Buildings West of Guildhall:
Smithfield Market
St Bartholomew's Hospital
Central Criminal Court
City of London School for Boys
College of Arms*
BT Centre
St Paul's Cathedral Choir School
Museum of London
Wood Street Police Station
Guildhall
*Heraldic colours:
Black: Sable/Prudence
White: Argent/Innocence
Blood-red: Sanguine/Fortitude
Blue: Azure/Fidelity
Green: Vert/Love
Yellow: Or/Faith
Purple: Purpure/Temperance
Tawney: Tenney/Joy

ROW 5:
Tyburn
Via
Resurrection gate
Via
St Giles-in-the-Fields
Via
The White Hart Inn
Drury Lane
Via
The Maidenhead Inn
Via
The Owl Bowl Inn Canter's Alley
Via
The Black Bear Inn
Via
The Black Jack Inn
Via
The Black Lamb Inn
Via
The Vine and The Rose Inn
Via
The Maid in The Moon Inn
The Twelve Great City Livery Companies in order
    of precedence:
1) Mercers
2) Grocers
3) Drapers
4) Fishmongers
5) Goldsmiths
6) Merchant Taylors*
7) Skinners
8) Haberdashers
9) Salters
10) Ironmongers
11) Vintners
12) Clothworkers
*Owing to an ancient dispute over precedence the
    Merchant Taylors and Skinners alternate

ROW 8:
City of London Churches West of Guildhall:
St Dunstan-in-the-West
Temple Church
St Bride's
St Andrew Holborn
City Temple
St Bartholomew-the-Great
St Bartholomew-the-Less
St Sepulchre
St Martin Ludgate
St Andrew-by-the-Wardrobe
St Benet Paul's Wharf
St Nicholas Cole Abbey
St Paul's Cathedral
Christ Church Newgate Street
St Vedast Alias Foster
St Botolph Aldersgate
St Anne and St Agnes
Jewin Welsh Church
St Giles Cripplegate
St Alban Wood Street
St Mary-le-Bow
St Mary Aldermary
St James Garlickhithe
St Michael Paternoster Royal
St Lawrence Jewry
St Alphage London Wall
St Mary Somerset+++

ROW 11:
London Churches and Synagogues East of Guildhall:
St Olave Jewry
St Michael Paternoster Royal
St Stephen Wallbrook
St Margaret Lothbury
St Mary Woolnoth
St Mary Abchurch
St Clement Eastcheap
St Edmund the King
St Michael Cornhill
St Peter upon Cornhill
Dutch Church
All Hallows London Wall or All Hallows-on-the-Wall
St Mary Moorfields
St Botolph Bishopsgate
St Ethelberga
St Helen Bishopsgate
St Andrew Undershaft
St Magnus the Martyr
St Dunstan-in-the-East
St Mary-at-Hill
St Margaret Pattens
All Hallows Barking
St Olave Hart Street
All Hallows Staining
St Katharine Cree
Bevis Marks Synagogue
St Botolph Aldgate
St Michael Crooked Lane+++

ROW 14:
Gaius Julius Caesar (102-44 BC)
Cunobelin (c. 5-41 AD)
Tiberius Claudius Nero Germanicus (10 BC-54)
Caratacus (c. 40-52)
Boudicca (d. 61)
Gnaeus Julius Agricola (40-93)
Publius Aelius Hadrianus (76-138)
Lucius Septimius Severus (d. 211)
Magnus Clemens Maximus (d. 388)
Edwin (585-633)
Ethelbald (d. 757)
Alfred The Great (849-899)
Plegmund (d. 923)
Ethelred (d. 911)
Edward the Elder (c. 872-924)
St Dunstan (c. 910-988)
Ethelred II (c. 966-1016)
St. Aelfheah (d. 1012)
Emma of Normandy (d. 1052)
Eadric Streona (d. 1017)
Sweyn Forkbeard (d. 1014)
Canute/Cnut
Harthacnut (son of Emma and Cnut)
Wulfstan, Bishop of London
St Edward the Confessor (1005?-1066)
Harold II (d. 1066)
William the Bastard or the Conqueror (c. 1028-1087)
Maurice of London (d. 1107)
William II Rufus (c. 1060-1100)
Anselm, (1033-1109), Archbishop of Canterbury
    (1093-1109)
Lanfranc of Pavia (c. 1010-1089), Archbishop of
    Canterbury (1070-1089)

ROW 17:
[ ] tered Apprentice 1°
Fellow Craft 2°
Master Mason 3°
Secret Master 4°
Perfect Master 5°
Intimate Secretary 6°
Provost and Judge 7°
The 33° of Freemasonry:
Superintendent of the Building 8°
Master Elect of the Nine 9°
Illustrious Master Elect of Fifteen 10°
Sublime Knight, Chevalier Elect 11°
Grand Master Architect 12°
Royal Arch of Enoch 13°
Scottish Knight of Perfection 14°
Knight of the Sword & of the East 15°
Prince of Jerusalem 16°
Knight of the East & West 17°
Knight of the Eagle & Pelican and Sovereign
    Prince Rose Croix of Heredom 18°
Grand Pontiff 19°
Venerable Grand Master 20°
Patriarch Noachite, Prussian Chevalier 21°
Prince of Libanus, Royal Hatchet 22°
Chief of the Tabernacle 23°
Prince of the Tabernacle 24°
Knight of[ ]

ROW 20:

[ ]enus/love/COPPER
Vulcan/fire
Apollo/light/GOLD
Neptune/sea
Mercury/travellers, thieves/QUICKSILVER
Diana/hunting, fertility/SILVER
Roman gods/deity of/ALCHEMICAL INGREDIENTS:
Pluto/underworld
Aesculapius/healing
Bacchus/wine
Cupid/love/desire
Jupiter/ruler of Gods/TIN
Victoria/victory
Vulturus/east wind
Vesta/hearth, home
Fortuna/fortune
Faunus/herds
Portunus/harbours
Astraea/justice
Proserpina/spring
Veritas/truth
Auster/south wind
Juventas/youth
Mutinus/fecundity
Saturnus/harvest/LEAD
Luna/moon
Carmenta/prophesy
Aquilo/north wind
Bellona/war
Discordia/strife, discord
Flora/spring
Mors/death
Comus/comedy
Minerva/wisdom
Terra/the earth
Selene/moon
Hecate/night, magic
Somnus/sleep

ROW 23:

[ ]/barbers
St Luke/artists
St Crispin/cobblers
St Dorothea/florists
St John Bosco/editors
St Apollonia/dentists
St Lucia/opticians
St Claude/Sculptors
St Margaret/patten makers
St Homobonus/tailors
St Joseph/wine growers
St Sebastian/pin makers
St Venerius/lighthouse keepers
St Ambrose/bee keepers
St Benedict/spelaeologists
St Anthony/gravediggers
St Honoratus/bakers
St Zita/domestic servants
St Matthew/tax collectors
St Gabriel/broadcasters
St Giles/horses
St Brigid/dairymaids
St Fiacre/taxi-drivers
St Jerome/librarians
St Menas, St James/pilgrims
St Cecilia/singers
St Roche/invalids
St Stephen/bricklayers
St Nicholas/children
St Barbara/miners
St George/syphilitics, armourers
St Hubbins/quality footware
St Gabriel/diplomats

ROW 26:

Stonecutter Street
Fetter Lane
Milk Street
Honey Lane
Leather Lane
Wood Street
Cannon Street
Artillery Lane
Pudding Lane
Fournier Street
Butcher Row
Bull Alley
Cow Lane
Pie Corner
Frying Pan Yard
Hind Court
Hart Lane
Oat Lane
Cooper's Row
Hoop Lane
Silver Street
Goldsmith Street
Silk Street
Bread Street
Cordwainer Street
Artizan Street
Apothecary Street
Hosier Lane
Mincing Lane
Vintry
Cole Yard
Carter Lane
Carrier Street
Poultry Lane
Cock Street
Duck Lane
Crane Court
Goose Lane
Fish Street
Friday Street
Cloak Lane
Threadneedle Street
Change Street
Money Bag Alley
Bullion Yard
Hand Court
Harebrain Court

Text Matrix

Complete Plantation Lane floor text as supplied
to stone masons. For layout refer to pages 60–63

[ ] Indicates text hidden beneath building.
+ Indicates spacing instructions to stone mason.
Each cross represents a 125mm module.

ROW 29:
[ ]y of London Underground Stations/etymology etc:
Aldgate/Aelgate
Aldgate East (see Aldgate)
Angel/Angel Inn
Arsenal/Arsenal Football Club
Bank/Bank of England
Barbican/Barbicana (Saxon: burgh kennin)
Bermondsey/Vermundesi c. 712
Bethnal Green/Blithedale
Blackfiars/Black Friars Monastery 13th century
Borough/Old English 'burh-a fortified place'
Cannon Street/Candelwichstrete c. 1180 (from
        Candle and Old English 'wic, a market')
Chancery Lane/Newstrate (New Street)
Farringdon/Farringdon Street
Holborn/Holebourne 951
Liverpool/Lord Liverpool 1829
Moorgate/Moor Gate 1451
St Paul's/St Paul's Cathedral
Temple/The Knights Templars
Tower Hill/Tourhulle 1343
Limehouse/Le Lymhostes 1367+++

ROW 32:
[ ] Martin's le Grand c. 1056 (collegiate church of)
    c) Holy Trinity Priory Aldgate (Augustinian) 1108
    d) St Bartholomew's Hospital 1123
    e) St Bartholomew's Priory (Augustinian) 1123
    f) Hospital of St Mary 1197
    g) St Helen's Priory (Benedictine) c. 1200-15
    h) Greyfriars (Franciscan) 1225
    j) Hospital of St Thomas of Acon 1227-8
    k) Hospital of St Anthony 1243
    l) Priory of St Mary Bethelehem (BedlamHospital) 1247
    m) Austin Friars 1253
    n) Blackfriars (Dominican) 1275
    o) Holy Trinity Abbey, Minories (Order of St Clare) 1298
    p) Crutched Friars (Order of the Holy Cross) 1298
    q) Elsing Spital 1331

ROW 35:
[ ]oman Invasion
    60 Boudicca burns London
    120 A Great Fire
    125-30 Hadrianic Fire
    457 Saxons sack London
    851 London attacked by Vikings
    959 A Great Fire: St Paul's burned
    994 London besieged by Danes
    Invasions and Disasters:
    1016 Third Danish siege
    1066 Norman Conquest
    1290 Expulsion of the Jews
    1348 The Black Death
    1406 The Plague
    1665 The Great Plague
    1666 The Great Fire
    1940 The beginning of The Blitz
    1987 Black Mon[ ]

ROW 38:
[ ]idge
    Chiswick Bridge
    Barnes Bridge
    Hammersmith Bridge
    Putney Bridge
    Wandsworth Bridge
    Battersea Bridge
    Albert Bridge
    Chelsea Bridge
    Vauxhall Bridge
    Lambeth Bridge
    Westminster Bridge
    Thames Crossings:
    Hungerford Foot Bridge
    Waterloo Bridge
    Blackfriars Bridge
    Millennium Bridge
    Southwark Bridge
    London Bridge
    Tower Bridge
    Rotherhithe Tunnel
    Greenwich Foot Tunnel
    Blackwall Tunnel

ROW 41:
+++Wormwood Street
    Camomile Street
    Vine Street
    Grape Street
    Mulberry Gardens
    Ivy Lane
    Grass Church Street
    Rosemary Lane
    Saffron Hill
    Primrose Street
    Dirty Alley
    Dirty Hill
    Dirty Lane
    Addle Street
    Foul Lane
    Deadman's Place
    Gutter Lane
    Dunghill
    Midden Lane
    Laystall Street
    Shiteburn Lane
    Stinking Alley
    St Ercenwald Street
    Costermonger Row
    Limeburner Lane

ROW 44:
[ ]ater noster Row
    Ave Maria Lane
    Creed Court
    Amen Court
    Pilgrim Street
    Trinity Place
    Pope's Head Alley
    Jerusalem Passage
    Idol Lane
    Pardon Churchyard
    Wilderness Row
    Carmelite Street
    Whitefriars Street
    Blackfriars Broadway
    Mitre Street
    Crutched Friars
    The Minories
    Worship Street

ROW 47:
[ ]ch
    Covent Garden
    Plough Court
    Markets and gardens:
    Long Acre
    Moorfields
    Partridge Alley
    Swan Alley
    Haymarket
    Park Lane
    Hog Lane
    Spitalfields
    Smithfields
    Lincoln's Inn Fields
    Springs-Wells:
    Holywell Street
    Sadler's Wells
    Clerkenwell
    Spa Fields
    Monkwell Square

ROW 50:
[ ]es for London:
    Londuniu
    Lundenwic
    Londinium
    Longidinium
    Lundunaborg
    Cockaigne
    Laindon
    Llyn-don
    Trinovantum
    Caer Ludd
    Lundunes
    Lundene
    Lundone
    Lindonion
    Ludenberk
    The Big Smoke
    The Great Wen
    Other London Rivers:
    The Stand
    Queenhithe
    Rotherhithe
    Lea

ROW 53:
+ the Sun, Prince Adept 28°
Knight of Saint Andrew 29°
Grand Elected Knight Kadosh, Knight of the
        Black & White Eagle 30°
33° of Freemasonry:
Grand Inspector Inquisitor Commander 31°
Sublime Prince of the Royal, Secret 32°
Sovereign Grand Inspector General 33°+++

ROW 56:
+++ Seventy King's Heads
Ninety King's Arms
Fifty Queen's Heads
Seventy Crowns
Fifty Roses
Twenty-five Royal Oaks
Thirty Bricklayers Arms
Fifteen Waterman's Arms
Sixteen Black Bulls
Twenty Cocks
Thirty Foxes
Thirty Swans+++

ROW 59:
+++ Bartholomew's Fair Mayfair
Cloth Fair
Southwark Fair
Clare Market
Stocks Market Cheapside
Fairs/Markets:
Coldbath Fields
Rag Fair
Smithfields Market
Penny Fields
Billingsgate
Borough Market
Fleet Market
Petticoat Lane
Field Lane
Leadenhall

ROW 62:
[ ]nd Hidden Rivers West to East:
Stamford Brook
The Wandle
Counter's Creek
The Falcoln
The Westbourne
The Tyburn
The Effra
Fleet
Walbrook
Neckinger
The Earl's Sluice
The Peck
The Ravensbourne

ROW 65:
+++ Sporting Streets:
Knightrider Street
Bear Street
Love Lane
Maid Lane
Addle Street
Cock Lane
Gropecontelane
Giltspur Street
Sweetings Alley
Shaft Alley
Bowling Green Lane+++

ROW 68:
[ ]te Hill
Ludgate Hill
London Hills:
Tothill
Parliament Hill
Tower Hill (White Mound)
Penton Hill/Pentonville
St Hermit's Hill
Cornhill
Snowhill
Dowgate Hill
Peter's Hill

ROW 71:
+++ Plagues:
The Black Death 1348
Plague 1406
The Sweating Sickness 1484
The Great Plague 1665
The Great Stink 1858
Typhus 1905
The Great Smog 1952+++

ROW 74:
[ ]atergate
Newgate
Aldersgate
Ludgate
Moorgate
Cripplegate
Bishopsgate
Aldgate
Albiongate
Billingsgate
St John's Gate
Broadgate

ROW 77:
Glory
Wisdom
Thanksgiving
Honour
Power
Bells of St Stephen, Rochester Row:
Might
Be Unto Our God For Ever And Ever Amen Alleluiah

ROW 80:
+ Bethlehem/Bedlam
Prisons/Madhouses:
Marshalsea
Clink
Newgate
St Mary's Barking

ROW 83:
+ Moll Cut-Purse
Criminals:
Jack Sheppard+

ROW 86:
Mithras
Odin
Gog
Magog
Isis
Hermes+

ROW 89:
[ ]uddledock
Bell Wharf Lane
Cardinal's Wharf

ROW 92:
[ ]ditch
Cattestreet
Houndsditch

ROW 95:
+ Gundulf (?1024-1108)+

ROW 98:
[ ]dward III

Key
[ ] Indicates text hidden beneath building.
+ Indicates spacing instructions to stone mason.
   Each cross represents a 125mm module.

A Space Invader in Mincing Lane
Jay Merrick

The Plantation Lane element of the new Plantation Place development by British Land has an unusual significance. It is a line that has been firmly drawn, physically and metaphorically; an adventurous challenge to the imaginations of those who pass along this fillet of the City of London's public realm. And it injects not just spirit of place, but spirit of *new* place. To achieve that second effect is particularly difficult, which is why Plantation Lane, and the luminous planar artwork that is the focal point of *Time and Tide*, is notable. It has given a literal and metaphysical edge to the overall development by preventing physical compaction along its boundary. It's a breathing space, a modulation, an unexpectedly furnished respite.

There is a relentless inertia to much new construction in the City. But, increasingly, developers are realising the need to provide a great deal more than folds and cubes of architectural wallpaper composed of glass, steel and ferro-concrete. Developed sites are benefiting from unexpected spatial synergies that counter the perception of mere urban familiarity, and substitute a sense of resonant difference. There is an appetite to deliver micro-local distinctness, rather than architectural generalities; and that's an important trend. The challenge is considerable. In any economic conditions the pressure to maximise density is hardly fictional. That, in turn, means that the fictional — the engaging objects and incidents that can fertilise public realm spaces — is rarely part of commercial architecture.

In most cases, and on the majority of difficult sites, developers and their architects cannot be condemned out of hand for their contributions to the architectural *ennui* that may be invoked. But what about those sites where something might be done, where an enlivening and humane fiction could make the difference between yet another development, and something that marks out a place in an interestingly charged way?

Let us set the specific dynamics of the Plantation Lane incursion to one side for a moment, and consider the context from which it springs. Point one: the fusion of public art into architectural projects is often of extreme popular significance and not, after all, just the purview of professional public realm consultants such as Modus Operandi and Art Office. Public art is anything but trivial. Why else did the Al-Jazeera news agency devote website space to Sarah Lucas' bird-limed car sculpture for Trafalgar Square's Fourth Plinth competition? Not, one assumes, simply to advertise the oddity of westerners. Oddity, though, was a factor in the 1970s, when the modern role of artworks in public spaces took root. Public money was fed into projects designed to assuage the cruder results of the brutalist modernism that had invaded inner cities, or wrenched tired old towns into steroidal New Towns that supposedly demonstrated Harold Wilson's 'white heat' of post-war technological culture.

Above
Michael Craig-Martin *Big Fan* (2003)

These 'art provisions' were a new kind of civic do-gooding. And, for a decade or so, they sat on the precipice of condescension. But, by the time of the *Art and Architecture* conference at London's ICA in 1982 and, two years later, *Art Monthly's* still fascinating *Art Within Reach* report, public realm artworks were generally no longer seen as manifestations of inverted cultural elitism. Britain's national post-war spend on such art, first via the Arts Council and then through the handful of agencies funded by the Gulbenkian Foundation, was less than £1 million annually. It was enough: art began to find its way not only into town centres, but factories, corporate headquarters and hospitals. St Thomas's Hospital in London, for example, has possessed as many as 600 works of art.

Today's much beefier bottom line has been underwritten by at least £80 million in Lottery investment since 1996. Double that figure with the required match-funding, add Euro-tranches and other cash conduits, and the funding has clearly been a kind of benign exchequer for architectural and public realm creativity. But what has been achieved in terms of revivifying spirit of place, and particularly in making larger urban developments easier to live with, and work in? And how can we predict whether a public realm intervention is going to succeed? Architecture's spikiest intellectual, Rem Koolhaas, coined the term 'junkspace' in the 1980s to describe the dystopic urban crumple-zones that pass for architecture. The same expression can be applied to much public realm development. Brilliant or banal, a great deal of public art causes significant popular reaction. It is, after all, an appropriation of public space, and is therefore implicitly risky. It messes with people's domains, and with their minds. There is an ominous rider, too: the worst public art interventions can, as the commentator Ben Heywood put it in 2001, 'intentionalise' space by over-ordering it, or by giving it a leaden corporate gravity.

And that's exactly what the artist Simon Patterson, working closely with Arup Associates and British Land, has *not* done. The LED-powered moon screen, the pavement texts of *Time and Tide*, and the subtle meander of Plantation Lane have nothing to do with ostentatious public art, or statement architecture. Plantation Lane is a demonstration of artful restraint and originality in a hotbed of City redevelopment, which needs, quite literally, every break it can get. *Time and Tide* is, in effect, a multi-faceted installation, and it belongs to a humanely provocative club of effective architecture-cum-artworks whose list includes Eduardo Paolozzi's Tottenham Court Road Underground decorations; Bridget Riley's striped Op Art corridors, once displayed in the Royal Liverpool University Hospital; Martin Creed's neon in Linscott Road, Clapton, proclaiming that 'Everything is Going to be Alright'; Michael Craig-Martin's *Big Fan*, at Regent's Place on London's Euston Road; and Mel Gooding's poetry, which meanders along the terrazzo on Bridlington seafront like a beatnik's muttered rant. These interventions work because they amuse, or startle, or mystify in just the right way, or because they happen to fit the local *zeitgeist*.

Above
Martin Creed
Work No. 203: EVERYTHING IS GOING TO BE ALRIGHT
(1999)

In Plantation Lane, we find an artwork that is part of a carefully arranged architectural matrix of new and old – the old being Sir Christopher Wren's 1688 St Margaret Pattens Church at the Rood Lane end, set back from the corner of Eastcheap. Perhaps because of it, Arup Associates and Simon Patterson have evidently followed Henry Moore's measured dictum. 'The setting', said the sculptor in 1955, 'makes a difference to the mood with which one approaches a sculpture, and a good setting is one in which the right conditions are present for a thorough appreciation of its forms.' The screen of *Time and Tide* is 41 metres long and 6 metres high. It is both a stand-alone artwork, and a crucial part of the architectural perspectives in Plantation Lane. Its position means that, from the Mincing Lane end, the key elements of the church's architecture are accentuated: the steeple is unobscured and the angle of the top edge of Patterson's screen leads the eye very precisely to the line of the centuries-old cornice.

Something else is going on, too. The size and position of the screen is part of another important manipulation of the site. The lane is not only *not* perfectly flat, but the long *Pietra del Cardoso* paving setts have been laid in asymmetric arcs; and on them, inlaid in sans serif limestone type, are stream-of-history texts. Two things are achieved: there is a sense of graceful passage, and evidence of the past is trickled into the lane's simultaneously curved and angular physique. Arup Associates' project director, Declan O'Carroll describes these ingredients as 'radical'. But on that site, at one of the world's most historically loaded datum-points of civilisation, radical is almost too tidy a word. Patterson's assertion that *Time and Tide* was designed to be a constant presence in a protean, helter-skelter world is also perhaps idealised, as is Andrea Schlieker's description of the lunar image on Patterson's screen as a reminder of timelessness. The work is, quite clearly, a trigger for free associations.

To me, the significance of Plantation Lane lies in its very lack of conceptual singularity. It is a dynamic space because its meanings are fugitive – shifty, if you like – and because the shards of colour, texture and form bear no symbolic relationship to the greater Plantation Place development. The lane and its contents constitute an artful *roman à clef*, a lacuna, a quirky poem found tucked into the pages of a novel about financial services. And the poem's narrative is not obvious because, ultimately, *Time and Tide* is a completely modern presence whose effect depends on the subtle frictions of its different parts. It's a cut-up of solids and voids, an articulated space invader; a collage that, for all its 'timeless' referential content, suggests change. And does so in a way that doesn't reek of designer glibness, or invoke bathetic drama.

Time and Tide works because its elements, though nominally striking, have been subtly composed. We might wonder what 'The Great Stink of 1858', passing underfoot, has to do with hugely roseate lunar craters. Or with St Margaret Pattens Church at the end of the lane. Ostensibly, nothing at all. Together, though, these

Above
Bridget Riley at The Royal Liverpool
University Hospital

elements nudge us into an engagement based on ruffled perceptions; evidence, if you like, of unusual physical and intellectual activity. Artworked public realm solutions should not come easy. When they do, the result is usually either craven, or yet another conceptual brick in the wall of dumbed-down human and architectural aspirations. The line between essentially ambient public realm solutions and jarring interventions is quite fine. An anodyne installation in a plaza or mall rarely serves any sensible, or sensual, purpose. If public realms are created, then let their design, and the art they may contain, carry the gravity of a humane otherness. The passer-by should be buttonholed by its difference, not harangued by it. The intruder must be an interesting guest.

The contribution of *Time and Tide* to the City of London as a whole is, of course, relatively small. But, in its very particular way, it is potent: it shifts perceptions, takes us out of the quotidian groove so that, for forty or fifty pedestrian seconds, one experiences a break-beat in the urban riff. The invention of Plantation Lane by Arup Associates and Simon Patterson triggers hundreds of reinventions of it every day: ironic reinventions, hilarious reinventions, philosophical reinventions. In the hurly-burly of working life, in particular, public art should remind us that we are – whether fretfully or exultantly – creative individuals. Developers, and their architects, should take every chance, however small or incidental, to invoke this response. And in the City, there are opportunities for such interventions, not least because the Corporation's planning department is broadly in favour of them.

'All things that can give ordinary life a turn for the better', said the water-sculptor, William Pye, 'are useless. Affection, laughter, flowers, song, seas, mountains, play, poetry, art and all. But they are not valueless, and not ineffectual, either. The design of each single thing, however small it may be, is really important. It may redeem a great deal if it's good.' I wonder what Sir Christopher Wren might have made of *Time and Tide*. Inside his church, St Margaret Pattens, there is a plaque set into the north wall. And on it is this grateful inscription, written by the church's rector, St Barbe S. Sladen, MA, in 1929: 'Laus Deo. For my wonderful recovery after a severe operation.'

A few metres away, the effects of a major architectural operation in the heart of the City have been gently and creatively ameliorated by a faith in the public domain, and in the mysterious powers of art. The presence of the greatest Redeemer might well be experienced in the faithful clasp of St Margaret Pattens. But small urban redemptions count, too, even if one is hurrying to catch the 5.12pm train from London Bridge to Oxted and then catches sight of the moon's surface, within touching distance, glowing purple.

Jay Merrick is the Architecture Correspondent for *The Independent*, London.

17

18

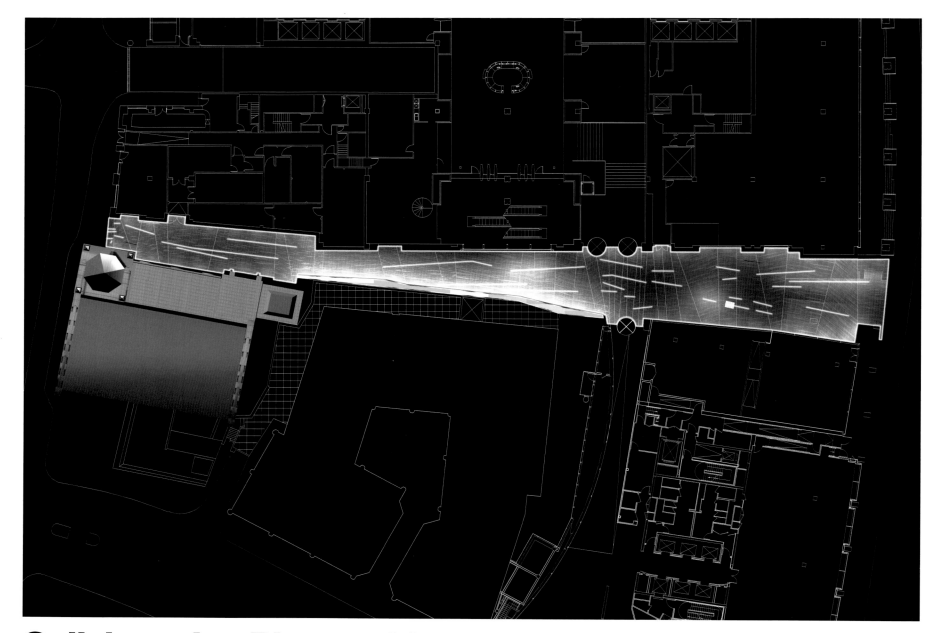

Collaborative Placemaking
Declan O'Carroll

Above
Plantation Place

Opposite page
Arup Associates' original concept sketch
for Plantation Lane

Arup Associates is a design studio interested in the widest obligations imposed by building in cities. Making places is central to our approach – a desire to enhance the greater environment in which our work is sited. Our proposals are in all senses *linked* to their site. We take clues from the context and follow an often speculative and lateral process to find forms and materials rooted in their surroundings. The application of a globalised 'signature language' independent of context and culture is of little interest. Yet we do look to propose radical ideas, expressed in a language that emerges directly and often surprisingly from the context. We believe that even modest and seemingly incidental interventions can enrich the public realm that lies in the heart of our cities.

Arup Associates' Plantation Place sits in the heart of the City of London. It comprises almost an entire city block: an enormous, one hectare site bounded by Fenchurch Street to the north, Mincing Lane to the east, Rood Lane to the west and Eastcheap/Great Tower Street to the south. Christopher Wren's Grade I listed Church of St Margaret Pattens occupies the south-west corner of the site, along with an eighteenth century town house once used as a war office. Another office building, 51 Eastcheap, is adjacent to the church. The Plantation Place development itself – designed for the financial, insurance, legal and trading markets – consists of two buildings: the 15 storey Plantation Place and 10 storey Plantation Place South.

Plantation Lane is the newly formed pedestrian route that separates these buildings. The route cuts east-west through the city block, from Wren's church to Mincing Lane. Plantation Lane provided Arup Associates with an opportunity to establish a visionary public realm, and a unique occasion to understand the city's pre-existing spatial conditions. Twisted alleyways have always been the connective tissue of the city. The alleyways reinforce the organic layout that is a characteristic of this unique London area. Botolph Lane and Botolph Alley; St Dunstans Hill off Great Tower Street; Cullum Street, leading to Leadenhall Market: all exemplify this ancient rhythm. In response, we sought to embed the new buildings into the fabric of the surrounding urban grain through the creation of Plantation Lane, a reflection of the familiar pedestrian passageways of the surrounding area.

From the outset we explored a formal engagement with the adjoining medieval street pattern, particularly the more dominant and heavily used Mincing Lane. An early idea included barrel vaulting the lane, to visually announce the space to pedestrians. Later, a simplification of ideas led us to focus on the essential components that determine the spatial character of Plantation Lane. We questioned the relevance of each item, and sought to charge the elements with a *significance* beyond their functionality. We started with the acceptance that space itself could be constructed by subtle adjustments to the adjacent buildings – Plantation Place to the north, the church to the south, and Plantation Place South to the east.

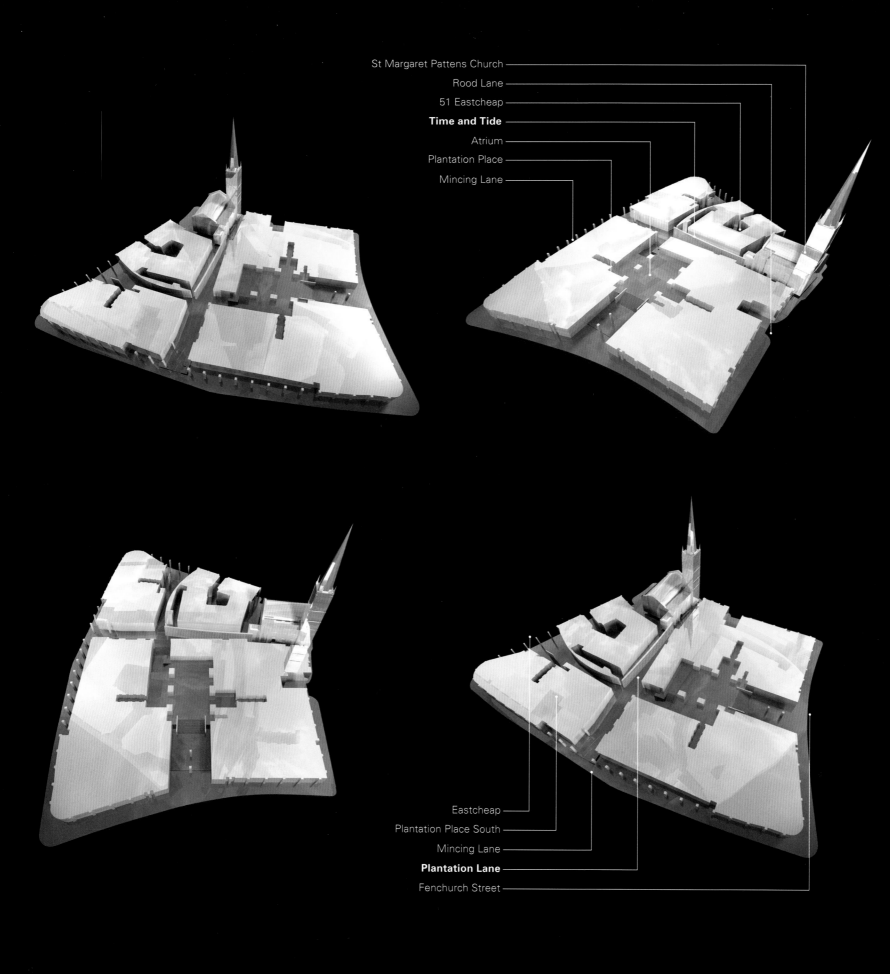

St Margaret Pattens Church

Rood Lane

51 Eastcheap

Time and Tide

Atrium

Plantation Place

Mincing Lane

Eastcheap

Plantation Place South

Mincing Lane

Plantation Lane

Fenchurch Street

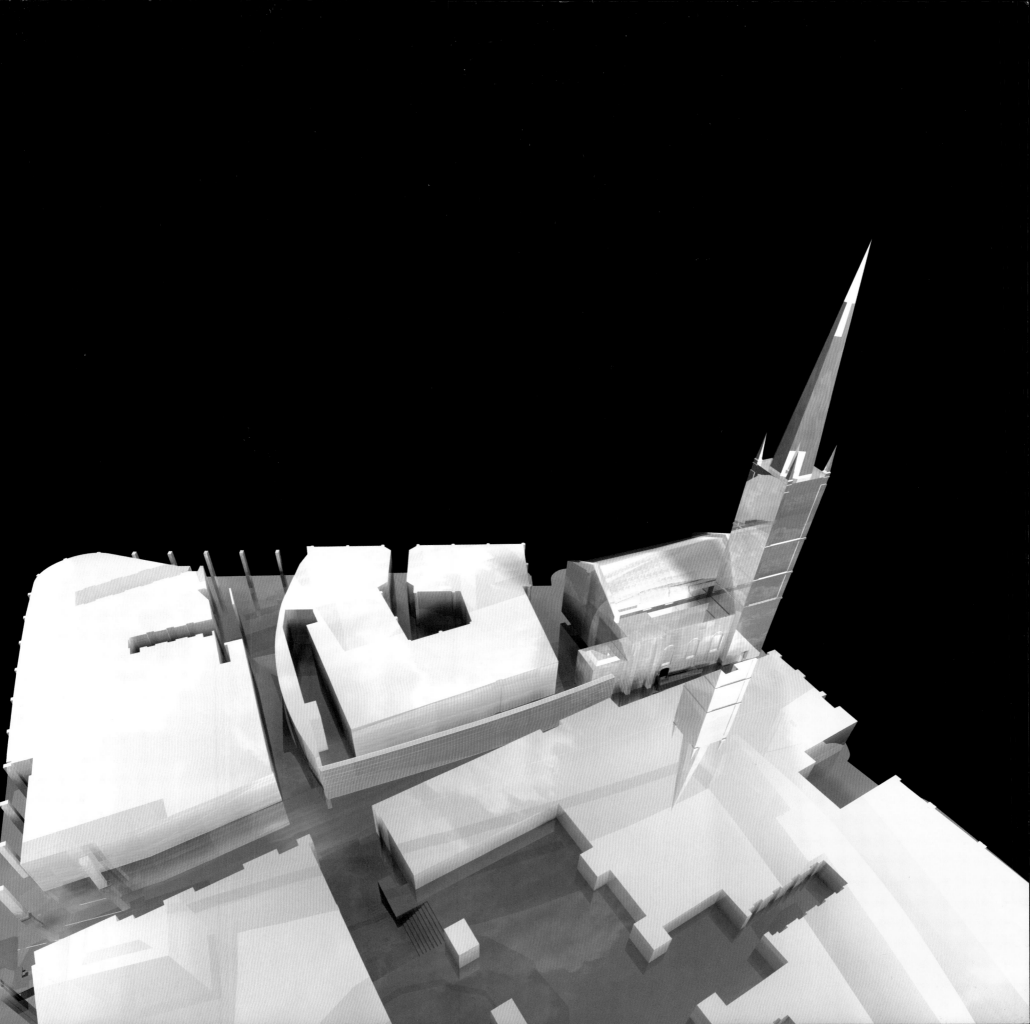

The form and massing of the rear of 51 Eastcheap – of limited architectural merit – was the least convincing element in this composition. Here a major intervention was made: a vertical screen that sharply defined the pedestrian route, and separated an unsightly private service area from the public domain of the Lane. Significantly, this space shaping created an unobstructed vista to St Margaret Pattens Church spire, when viewed from Mincing Lane.

Lateral connections were developed too, to further integrate the new space with its surroundings. Secondary entrances to Plantation Place and Plantation Place South were designed to run into Plantation Lane. These two entrances mark a semi-private route along a north-south axis running right through the site. Here, space flows from the primary building entrance off Fenchurch Street and into the centre of the main atrium; then continues across the Lane, down the gently curving slope into Plantation Place South's double height entrance hall, and on to Great Tower Street. The giant city blocks of Plantation Place were now locked into the weave of the ancient city, to provide a new twenty-first century medieval street.

Plantation Lane is strongly linear. Its scale is relatively humble in plan. Vertically, however, the proportions of the adjoining buildings create a canyon-like space. This 'open' spatial composition embraces the adjoining Rood Lane and Mincing Lane and connects to the infinite city space beyond. The complex edge conditions of the space reflect the disparate historic boundaries, legal ownership and programmes of the individual buildings. The ground plane unites these elements, generating soft undulations of surface underfoot. Inevitably, a site of such diverse historical complexity moved us to question its memory and its meaning. In the creation of this unique place, our ambition was to go beyond the merely functional. Instead, our desire was to explore how the experience of individuals passing through the space could be connected with an experience literally grounded in *this* place: a place with layers of meaning, depth and emotion. The result is a progressive vision, but one distinctly born out of the history and site.

For us, the city is restless: a constantly evolving human creation. Its individual identity is informed by the systematic accretion of generations of historical experience. Great historical places are built upon a lineage of 'modernities' that reflect the ambition of each successive age. Over time the city evolves, growing upon itself, layering over that which was there before. In doing so it acquires an individual voice: as Aldo Rossi suggests, 'a consciousness and memory.' Cities rely on us to understand the past, so as to envision that which is possible in the future. The successful evolution of the city is wholly reliant on this process of sustainable re-invention by each new generation. In this sense we constantly position ourselves on a *threshold*. Looking back, we seek to gain an understanding of the past so as to provide continuity of meaning. Looking ahead, we seek to shape a progressive meaning that is rooted in a specific memory and locality.

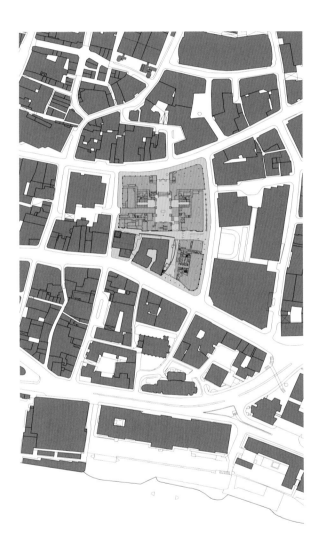

Within our design studio, our experimentation with form and material – the 'sifting' of ideas – is a fluid process. Ideas take time to evolve, and often originate from unlikely sources. Our creative proposals are initiated with certain instinctive responses – themes of enquiry that underpin our work. We run several ideas in parallel, continually revisiting them to challenge their worth. Instinctively we formulate an outline response, and then develop this with a particular vocabulary, language and form. So it was with Plantation Lane, where the composition and content challenge the orthodox boundaries that separate architecture, public art and urban design. Here, an enlightened client was invaluable. British Land was determined to achieve a unique public space in an area of rich and diverse history.

As the spatial characteristics of the Lane developed, the specific *language* of the key physical components was generated simultaneously: the 'light carpet' – a unifying ground plane – and the 'illuminated screen'. It was our desire that these entities should be expressed through a language that was independent of the adjacent buildings. In this way, the Lane that occupies this *in-between* space can exist independently. The search for independence from any pre-established architectural language, and the desire for a place-rooted physical and emotional depth sparked a conceptual theme of text versus image. Both are iconic mediums of communication capable of generating an environment that engages with the senses.

The proposal quickly developed into two distinct areas of exploration: an intentional contrast and interplay between two mediums, or languages. In contemporary European cities the traditional role of written text – of marking territory, of celebrating influential people and important events – has been lost. To re-establish this territorial marking we deliberately set up a duel between the physical and the immaterial: a face-off between an historically rooted text cut into the ground plane, and the twenty first century resonance of the illuminated screen. This confrontation intentionally allowed space for emotional response: a fuzzy edged conceptual and physical *fugue*.

The screen was illuminated as a giant light box, a traditional canvas transformed into a transient painting in light; a medium to explore visual imagery – to 'photo-graph' or draw with light. Lighting the screen and disconnecting it from the ground reinforces its potential 'other-worldliness', and acts as a counterfoil to the perceived traditional craft of the inlaid stone text. The conceptual framework was established. Now we sought to involve artists in the development of the work. As an integrated design studio our collective creative process is centred upon a culture of 'open-mindedness', where orthodox boundaries that separate disciplines are deliberately removed. Good ideas are the only currency of real value. Our intent was to challenge the limitations of traditionally commissioned 'public art', which so often concludes in 'object making': vague formal and formulaic gestures that are independent of context and place.

Above
Original concept visualisation of Plantation
Lane showing inlaid text and light screen

Opposite page
Detail of stainless steel fixing bracket

Artists – as opposed to architects and engineers – generally operate in very different parts of the creative spectrum. The latter are constantly exposed to a process characterised by interaction and driven by stakeholders, planning bodies, and project managers, amongst others. This operation within the public domain sometimes carries with it a limiting sense of responsibility and accountability. Artists, on the other hand, often occupy a more intimate, independent and hermetic creative existence. Such collaborations are essentially journeys into the unknown. They offer neither pre-determined outcome nor guarantee of success: one must be of a certain mindset to allow these creative encounters to flourish. The creation of the vision and the conceptual framework that underpins a project is balanced by the curious idiosyncrasies generated by another point of view. It is essential not to be too precious, but to support the collaborator as they take the proposition in a new direction.

Our initial instinct was to progress with two distinct commissions that would mediate with each other. The first commission considered visual artists to work with the illuminated screen. The second required writers or poets to work on the written text engrained within the ground plane. The search was instantly concluded in our first meeting with Simon Patterson. It became clear in Simon's response to our conceptual framework that he shared our ambition. His body of work reflected an interest in the combination of visual and textual references. He was a natural collaborator for this project.

His – and our – *bricolage* of physical elements, of space, and of conceptual content united to create a particular sense of place. This place is offered as an antidote to universalised commercial public space, with its ubiquitous visual flotsam of randomly competing retail signage, advertising billboards, and ill-considered street furniture. Instead, this is a breathing space, intended not so much to offer answers but to invite questions from those who chance upon it.

It is to the emotional engagement in our lives that we instinctively turn for meaning and value. These characteristics are not easily quantified or calculated. They exist in the realm of the 'immeasurable' and are perhaps all the more valuable for it.

Declan O'Carroll led the conceptual design of Plantation Lane. He is a principal of Arup Associates.

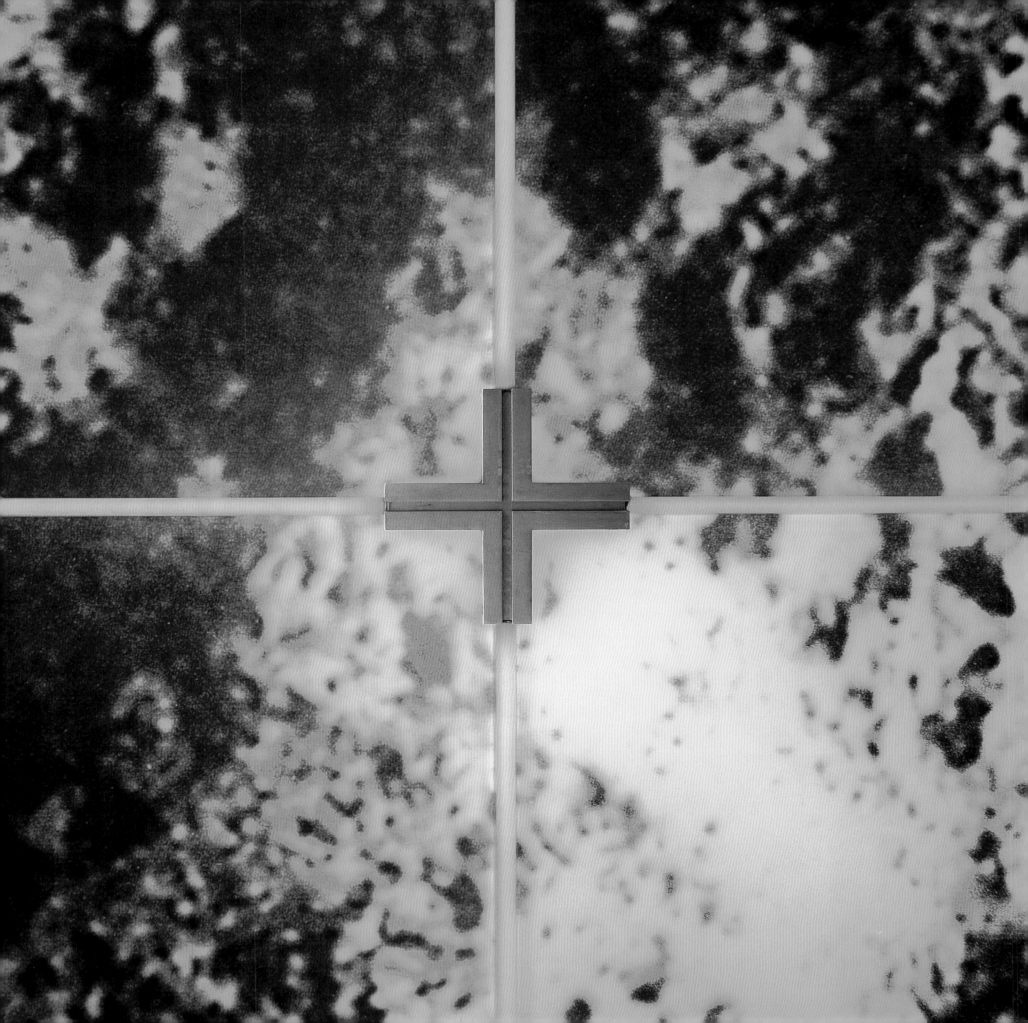

Top
Bed 16, origin of the Jura Limestone
used in the lettering of Plantation Lane

Bottom sequence
Pietra del Cardoso floor slabs; water jet
cutting process; insertion of Jura Limestone
characters; completed text

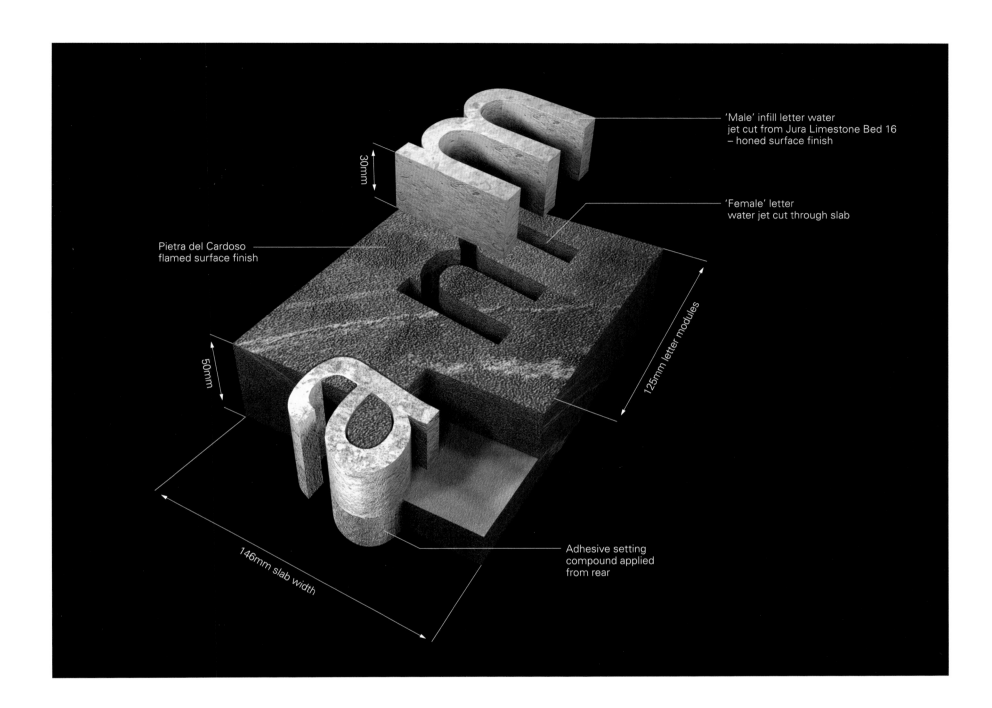

'Male' infill letter water
jet cut from Jura Limestone Bed 16
– honed surface finish

'Female' letter
water jet cut through slab

Pietra del Cardoso
flamed surface finish

30mm

50mm

125mm letter modules

146mm slab width

Adhesive setting
compound applied
from rear

Above
The typeface 'Univers 55 Oblique'
was used for all the characters

Above
Selected images from Simon Patterson's
sketch book

Above
Work in progress December 2003

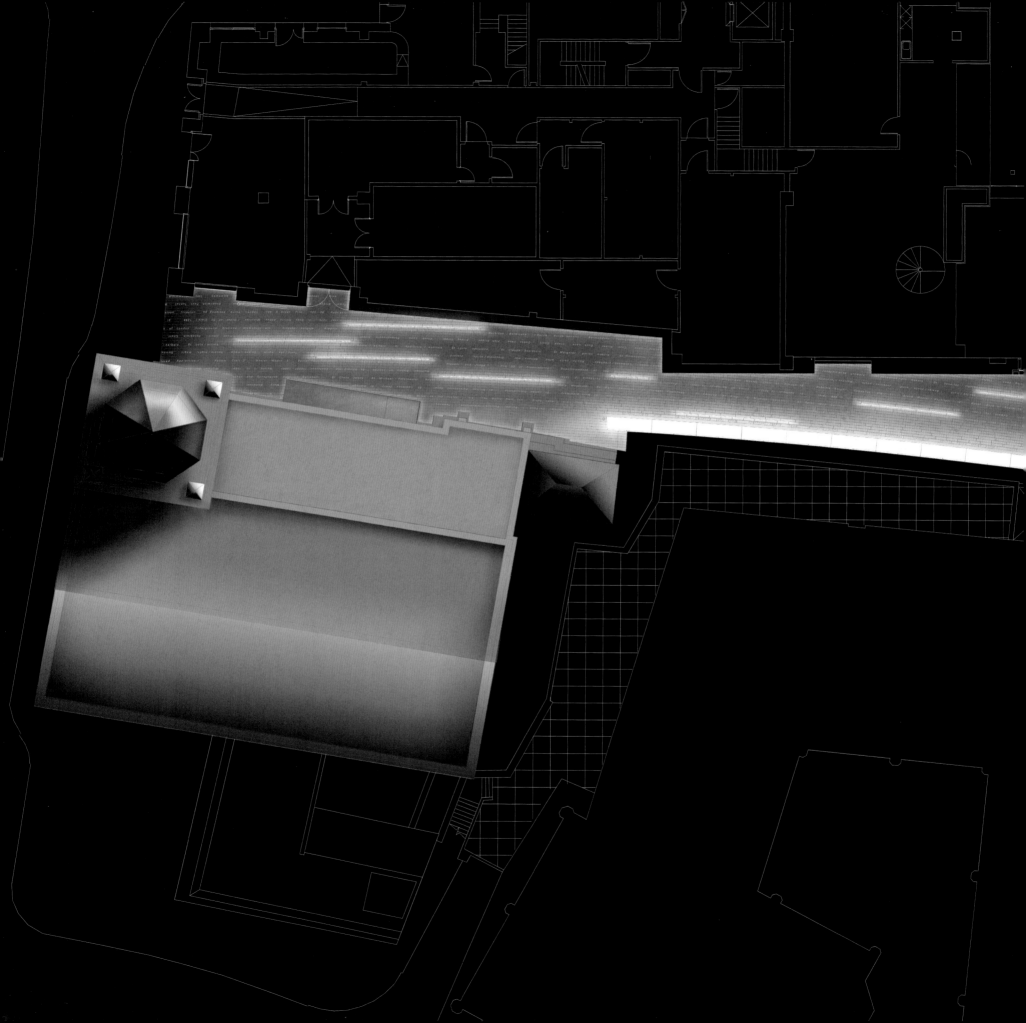

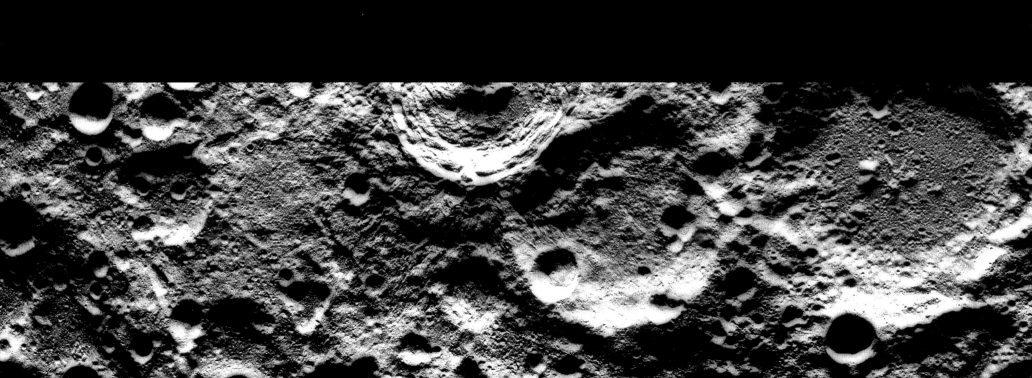

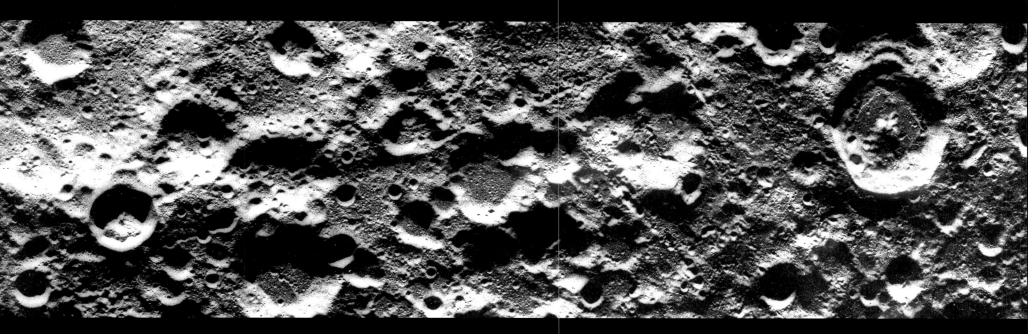

Above

Farside Terra, Moon. Enlarged detail of
re-mastered photograph of the highlands on
the dark side of the moon, originally taken
from a distance of 1600km by the Apollo 16
astronaut Kenneth Mattingly, in April 1972.
The distinctive 76km diameter impact crater
King is partially visible to the upper left.

The image was reproduced by Simon
Patterson from the book *Full Moon* by
Michael Light

Plan

750mm 2400mm 2400mm 2400mm 2400mm 2400mm 2400mm 2400mm 2400mm

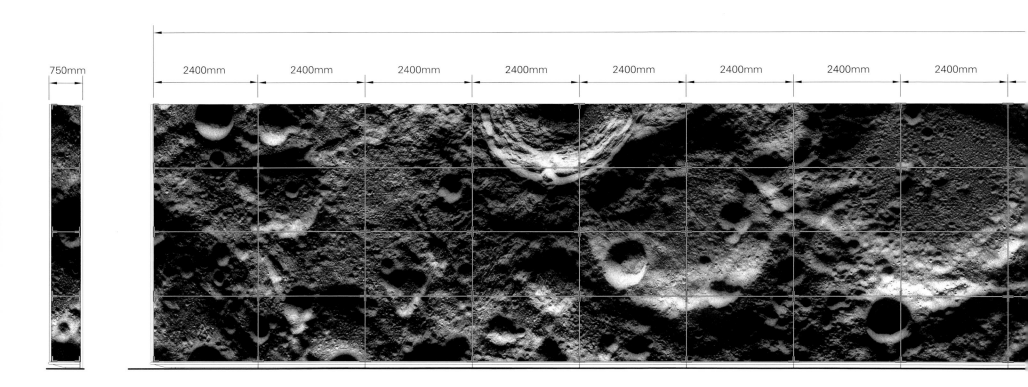

Elevation

40800mm

2400mm 2400mm 2400mm 2400mm 2400mm 2400mm 2400mm 2400mm

750mm

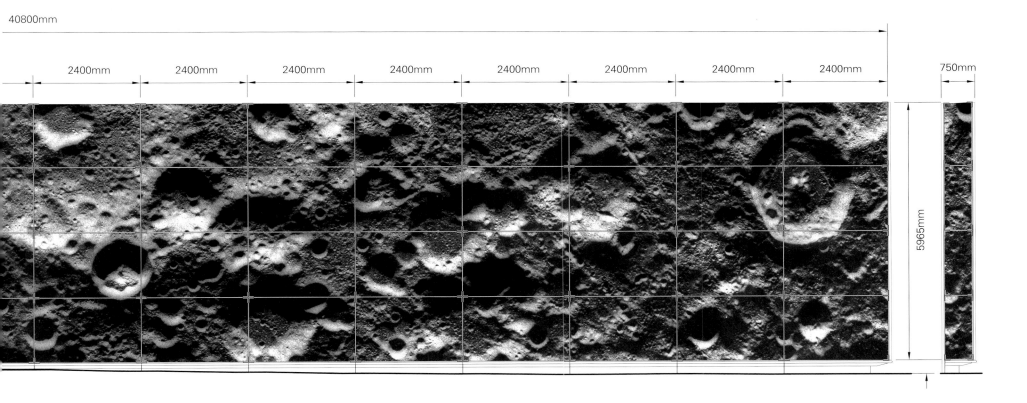

5965mm

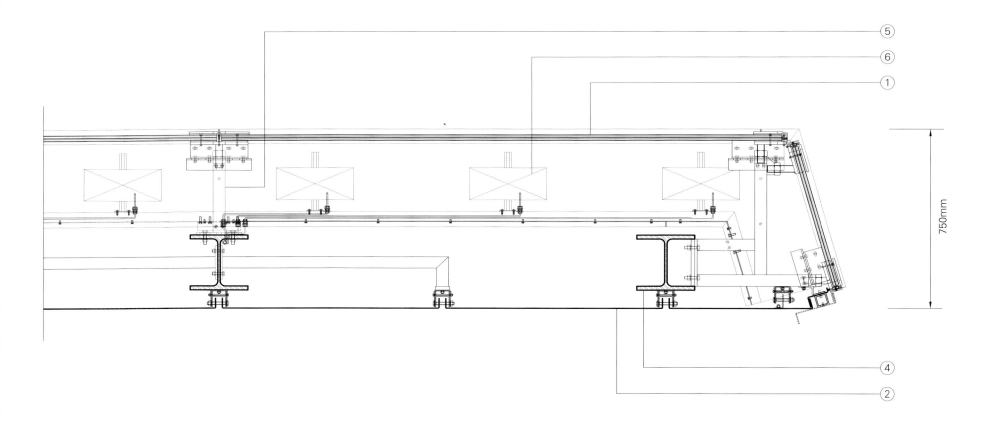

5

6

1

750mm

4

2

Partial plan (detail)

1 Glass
2 Hook–on aluminium panels
3 Stainless steel fixing bracket
4 Structural steel column
5 Steel support tubes & tie rods
6 LED light fittings
7 Stainless steel bull bar
8 Stone floor

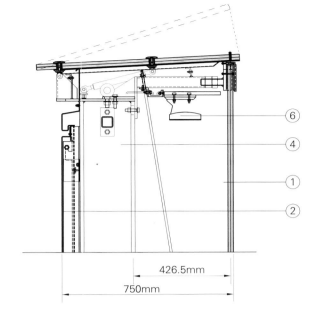

426.5mm

750mm

Accessible lid detail

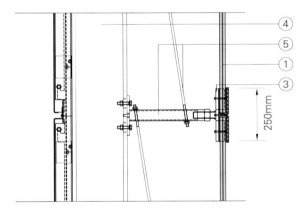

250mm

Fixing bracket detail

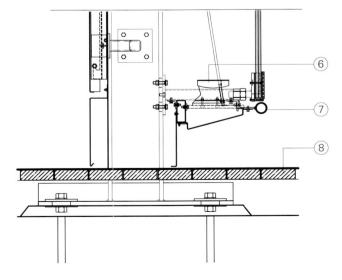

Base detail

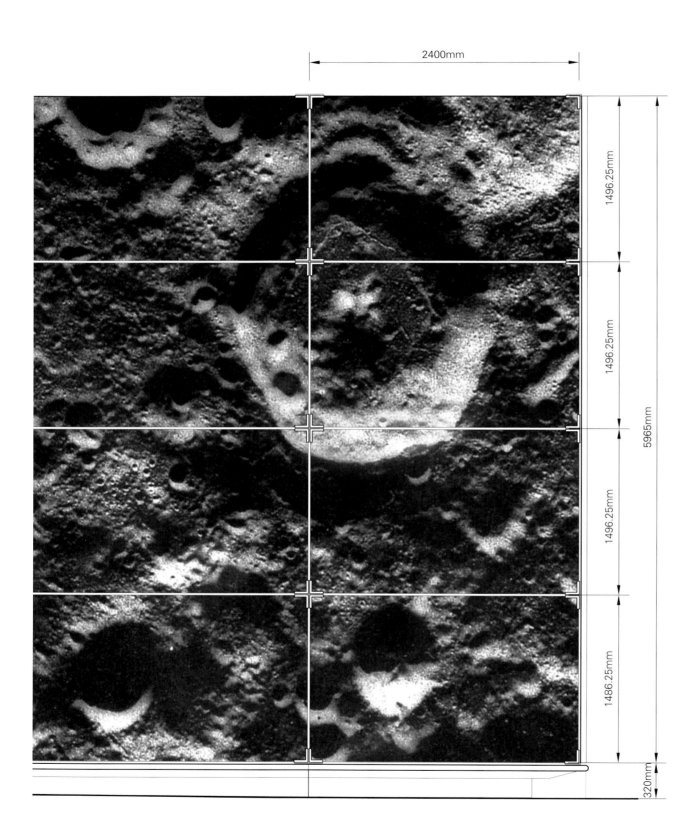

2400mm

1496.25mm

1496.25mm

5965mm

1496.25mm

1486.25mm

320mm

Partial elevation

750mm

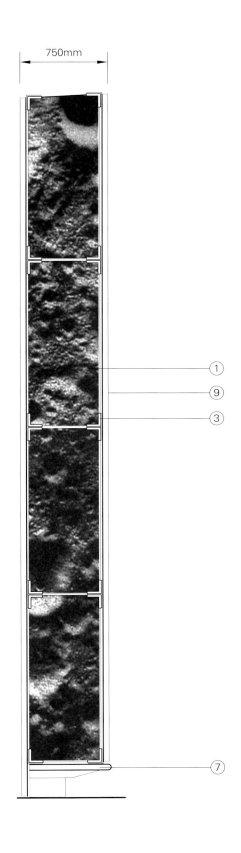

Elevation

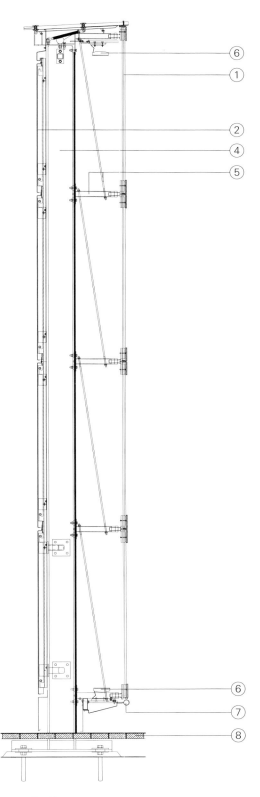

Section

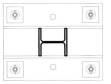

1 Glass
2 Hook–on aluminium panel
3 Stainless steel fixing bracket
4 Structural steel column
5 Steel support tube & tie rod
6 LED light fitting
7 Stainless steel bull bar
8 Stone floor
9 Stainless steel edge frame

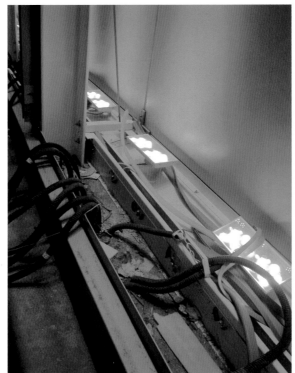

Above
Screen interior

42

Street

Place

Left
Screen interior

Simon Patterson *Time & Tide*
Andrea Schlieker

That orbed maiden, with white fire laden, Whom mortals call the Moon

P.B.Shelley

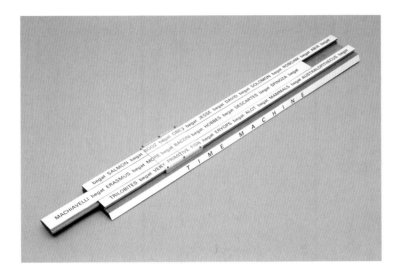

Above
Simon Patterson, *Time Machine* (1993)

Walking down a passageway in the centre of London, we find ourselves stepping on words engraved into the pavement. At the same time we are dazzled by the ethereal, hallucinatory light of the moon. But this moon is not shining from its familiar celestial height, nor in its usual radiance of milky white. This lunar vision has come down to earth, to transport us into its own many-splendoured universe. Simon Patterson's new work, *Time and Tide*, his first permanently sited in a public arena, marks both a departure from and a continuation of his existing œuvre. We encounter his celebrated idiosyncratic use of language and words, his lateral approach to history and naming, his fascination with space travel and the cosmic. But never has Patterson made anything on such a grand scale as this, nor has he before incorporated an actual image in his work.

The site for *Time and Tide*, Plantation Lane, a stone's throw from the Monument to the south and the Tower to the east, is immensely rich in history, situated in one of the oldest parts of London. As every tourist is told on the buses that crisscross this area, the City of London saw the rule of Romans, Saxons and Normans. Here in the Middle Ages the first City Livery Companies grew; later, great trading companies sprang up. Chaucer was born here in medieval times, Edmund Spenser in Tudor times. Inigo Jones lived and worked in this place in the 17th century and William Hogarth in the next. The Plague and the Great Fire ravished the City, and much of the area was destroyed again during the Second World War. Where there has been so much change, it seems fitting that the image Simon Patterson has chosen for the huge screen that runs along this new passageway should be both archetypal and timeless. The upheavals that took place in the City over the centuries find countervailing balance in the image of the moon as a beacon of constancy. As the same hemisphere of the moon always faces earth, people still look up at what men have seen in the night sky throughout all history, from the first settlers in Londinium to today's City bankers.

During Roman times, the moon was worshipped as the Goddess Diana (analogous to the Greek moon Goddesses Artemis and Selene). Christian iconography has identified the Madonna with the moon. The Romans derived their idea of the calendar from the lunar cycles, and today we understand that lunar rhythms were employed widely before the solar rhythms as measures of time. The theme of time, of course, underscores a number of Patterson's works (see *Time Machine*, 1993; or *24 Hours*, 1995), but here he has chosen the moon as perhaps its most poetic and poignant metaphor. Moon iconography finds a particularly rich nexus of associations within the field of pagan and sacred symbolism, as ubiquitous and enduring symbol in legends and myths, as locus for romantic yearning, but also as manifestation of scientific progress in the 20th century, heralding boundless future possibilities. With this image, both mysterious and emblematic, Patterson alludes to all of these different concepts. It is important to add here that the particular image he has used is appropriated, rather than one originated by the artist himself. The author is Michael Light, who in

Previous page
Simon Patterson, *Le Match des couleurs*
(2000)

Opposite page
Simon Patterson, *Manned Flight* (1999–)

his turn made use of original NASA material. With the author's permission, Patterson, in true conceptual fashion, borrowed the image. It is both homage to the master and evidence of a consistent artistic strategy. The cosmic theme had invaded Patterson's work on several occasions before this commission. Large-scale wallpaintings such as *Straits of Sunda* (1996) or *Lagado* of the same year, or his *Cosmic Wallpaper* (2002) demonstrate this ongoing fascination, as does his large itinerant kite sculpture *Manned Flight* (1999–). The last, which could be seen in the streets of Seoul and Birmingham, displays the name of Yuri Gagarin, the Russian cosmonaut and first man in space. But already in 1988 Patterson had paid tribute to the legendary astronauts of the first moon landing of 1969 in his signature series of *Name Paintings* (begun in 1987 and ongoing) with the triptych *Col. Michael Collins/Neil Alden Armstrong/Col. Edwin Eugene Aldrin Jr*. The concept and iconography of space travel and its pioneering technology serve Patterson time and again as a metaphor for utopian longing, and our inexorable desire to probe beyond the realms of the known.

The particular section of the moon Patterson chose for the image is deliberately overwhelming, seeming almost to be to scale, as if part of the moon has been beamed down to earth. Craters and rock formations are clearly discernible, their haunting proximity increasing the awesomeness of this alien landscape. Plantation Lane is long, narrow and darkened by the tall buildings that flank it like a canyon. Hence Patterson's moon turns into a gigantic galactic apparition, reflecting light – a magical conundrum lassoed into the urban fabric. Walking along the monumental panorama of the glass screen towards the elegant spire of St Margaret Pattens, we experience a powerful physical sensation. The pathway tapers here to its narrowest, and we are forced right up to the moon's close-impending surface. Completely ensnared by its mesmeric perspective (not that of the bird's eye but of the astronaut's), we are drawn by its lambent glow; our bodies become seemingly weightless and, momentarily, we drift out of our earthly being into wonder.

To add to this sense of wonder, Patterson and Arup Associates have programmed banks of LEDs behind the screen into a gradual and constantly changing colour spectacle, somewhat analogous to the moon's different phases. Moving through the spectrum, alternately glowing yellow, orange or green, cold and distant matter transforms into a mysterious translucent jewel full of striking chromatic brilliance. Patterson's inclusion of colour in *Time and Tide* is indicative of his long-standing interest in colour and its associations. Works like *Colour Match Screen Saver* (2001) or *Le Match des couleurs* (2000) or in particular, his ephemeral but hugely operatic *mise-en-scène* of green, purple, yellow, red and blue cloud bursts one summer afternoon at Compton Verney (*Landskip*, 2000) testify to this. To heighten the cosmic sense and to allude to a planet-like segment of a sphere, the artist wanted the screen to be slightly curved, a curve then mirrored and extended in the floor.

Left
Simon Patterson, *Landskip* (2000)

The floor text orbits the screen like rings encircling a planet. It seems that the words continue underneath the surrounding buildings, as if they had been there for centuries and that this particular segment had only now been excavated. The typeface 'Univers', a legible sans-serif, is intimate in scale compared to the enormous image of the moon. To reflect the fact that people will be walking on the text in both directions, the arcs of words are alternately reversed, thereby also suggesting a spinning or orbiting motion. An impression of velocity is further enhanced by the integration at various points of LED lights into the curving floor. Like shooting stars, they strengthen the conceptual link between screen and floor, whilst also providing a functional light source. These LEDs are programmed to change colour in synchronisation with the screen. The sense of an orbital geometry is thus articulated on both the screen and the floor.

As an artist, Patterson is best known for his text works, and it was because of these that I suggested him for this commission. *The Great Bear* (1992), his widely acclaimed re-invention of the London Underground map – replacing the names of tube stations with those of Philosophers, Planets, Musicians, Explorers, Footballers, Saints or Sinologues – has become a landmark work of the 1990s. Here King's Cross metamorphoses into Piero della Francesca and Oxford Circus into Titian, Liverpool Street becomes Immanuel Kant, and Gina Lollobrigida finds herself immortalised at Tottenham Court Road. Patterson's recurring heroes, Neil Armstrong and Yuri Gagarin, are given a station on the Explorer Line. Where else can you travel, without changing, from Mao Tse-Tung to Mars? Patterson's ability to fuse the high and the low, the universally familiar with the obscure and personal, his interest in taxonomies, identification and systems that help us order the world, and, in particular, his approach to history as non-hierarchic, associative and anecdotal, seemed above all fitting for a work that was to be specific to a site so saturated with history.

Language, and especially the act of naming, has been central to Patterson's work for the past two decades. His *Name Paintings* (1987 to present) are exactly that and nothing more: a white primed canvas, the name of a (well-known) personality silk-screened centrally. What is important in these 'reduced portraits' is the selection of a name that instantly conjures a store of associations in the viewer's mind. In these paintings, following a simple prompt from the artist, memory and imagination are triggered and narrative unfolds. For an artist preoccupied with codes, diagrams, maps and constellations, it was obvious that Patterson had to create an indexical order from the abundant material this site offered. In *Time and Tide* each slender curve of text therefore represents a different chronological timeline or taxonomy of history or topographical reference. That closest to the moon screen refers to Roman hagiography, naming its gods and goddesses, as well as the metaphysical field of reverence, and, perhaps less predictably, their alchemical ingredient (Venus/love/Copper; Saturnus/harvest/Lead, etc).

Radiating outwards, the arcs list the local Guilds and their patron saints (St Margaret/pattern makers; St Hubbins/quality footwear, etc), the City Churches East of Guildhall (St Olave Jewry; St Clement Eastcheap, etc) or the twelve City Livery Companies in order of precedence, or the different membership degrees of Freemasonry (Intimate Secretary 6°, Knight of the Eagle & Pelican and Sovereign Prince Rose Croix of Heredom 18°, etc). Each name is evocative, like a poem, making us delve deeper into Patterson's enthralling tapestry of historical data and place names. His delightful and occasionally paradoxical system of classification effortlessly straddles fragrant Rosemary Lane, Camomile Street and Primrose Street, and the rather less appetising Foul Lane, Deadman's Place and Stinking Alley. From Markets and Gardens to Sporting Streets, London Hills to Lost and Hidden Rivers, Plagues and Disasters, Invaders and Madhouses, Patterson excavates a network of astonishing taxonomies, sounding a paean to the richness of London's long and layered history.

This 'carpet of words' is almost entirely related to the history of the site, but it also includes some deliberately miscellaneous information, for example the list of names of early British, Roman or medieval leaders, from the well-known (Boudicca) to the obscure but beautifully suggestive (Sweyn Forkbeard). Patterson has a proclivity for the anecdotal and the idiosyncratic, for establishing unexpected connections and relationships. Walking in effect on a book, the visitor can either follow a particular timeline, or choose a more random but equally beguiling route by cross-referencing different timelines. The possibility of this vertical and horizontal reading creates both a logical as well as cryptic sense of history, which is typical of Patterson's strategy.

The artist's intention in the *Name Paintings*, 'to evoke an image of the subjects in the viewer's mind using text alone', still holds for this latest and most epic and immersing work. Patterson acts like a collector, but of names rather than of objects. By arranging and orchestrating them within the rules of his eclectic system, he makes them his own. In his *Time and Tide*, Patterson offers us a sublime breadth of other-worldly experience, visually poetic, poetically visual. We are invited to take a space walk around the moon, which is also a walk through time and abounding allusions to moments in this city's extraordinary history.

Top
Simon Patterson, Name Paintings:
Sadat/Carter/Begin (1988)

Bottom
Simon Patterson, Name Paintings:
Richard Burton/Elizabeth Taylor (1987)

Opposite page
Simon Patterson, detail, *The Great Bear*
(1992)

Andrea Schlieker is curator for British Land's public spaces, as well as for the Fourth Plinth Project in Trafalgar Square, and is co–curator for the British Art Show 2005.

Wormwood ...reet Camomile ... Street ...ine

Greenwich Foot Tunnel ... Bridge

...oman Invasion 60 Boudicca burns London 120 A Great Fire '125 - 30 Hadrianic

... 1298 ... Holy Trinity Abbey, Minories ... Order of St Clare) 1275

...y of London Underground Stations / etymology etc. Aldgate / Aelgate Aldgate ... Barbican / Barbicana (Bacon

... Court ... Hatebrain Court ... Threadneedle Street Close Lane ... Friday Street Fish Street ... Goose Lane

/ barbers St Luke / artists ... Musca / editors St Apollonia / dentists St Lucia opticians ... St Claude / Sculptors

... Hecate / night, Selene / moon Terra / the earth, magic Somnus ... Discordia / strife, war ... discord

...tered Apprentice 1' Fellow Craft 2' Master Mason 3' Secret ... Provost and Judge 7' The 33' of Freemasonry

... William the ... Walfstan Bishop of London ... St Edward the Confessor (1985) Harold II (d. 1066)

...ches and Synagogues Basil of Guildhall ... St Olave Jewry St Michael Paternoster Royal

... Mary Somerset St Lawrence Jewry St Aldmary ... St Michael Paternoster Royal ... tower 15...

... Giles in the Fields via The White Hart Inn Drury L...

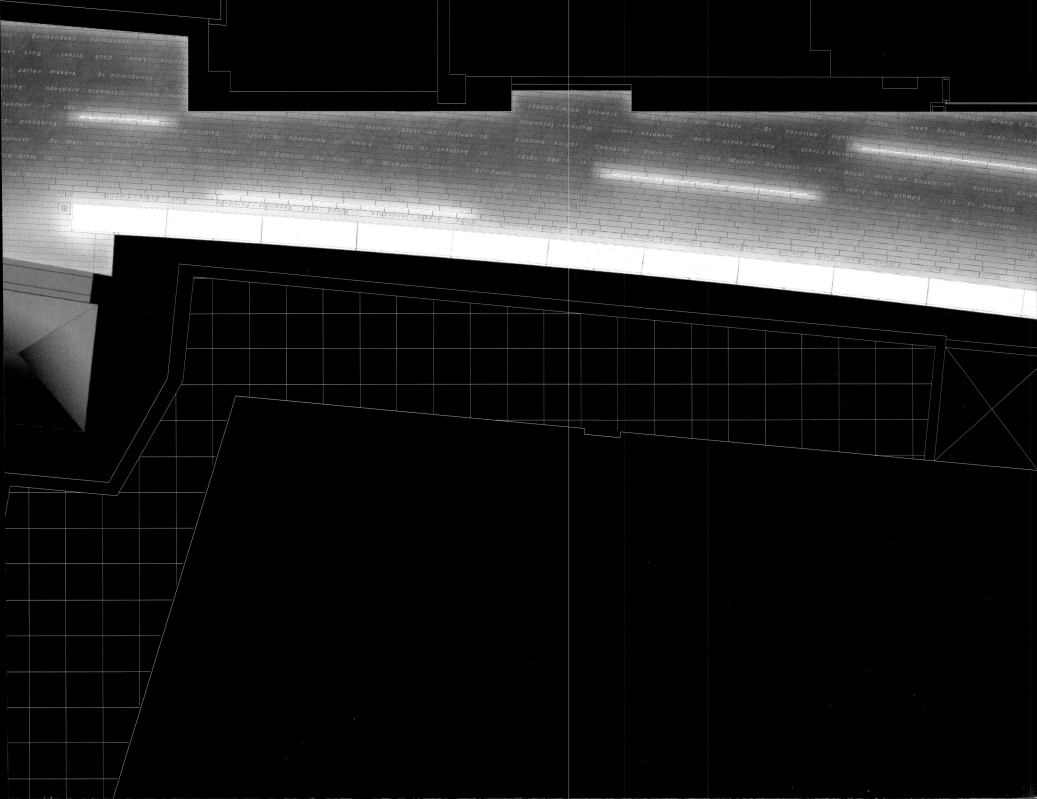

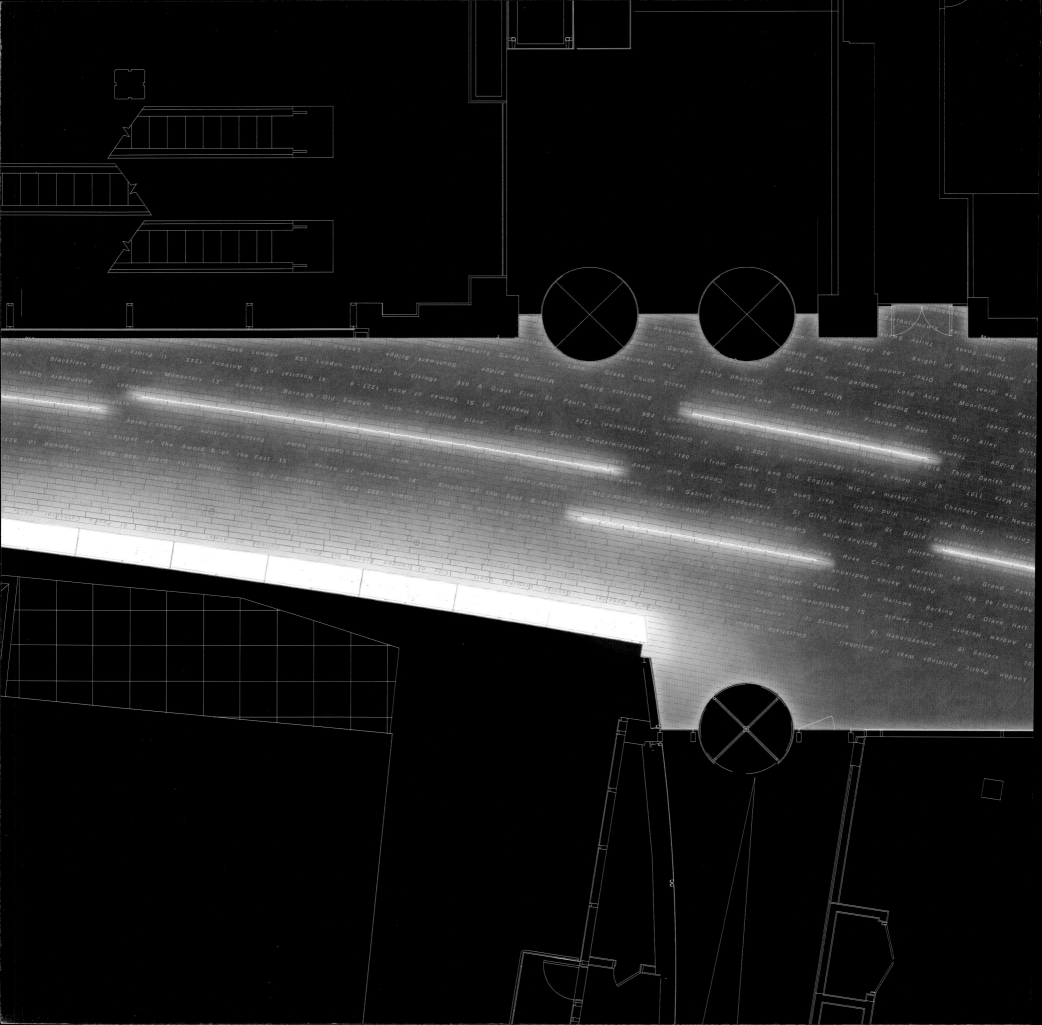

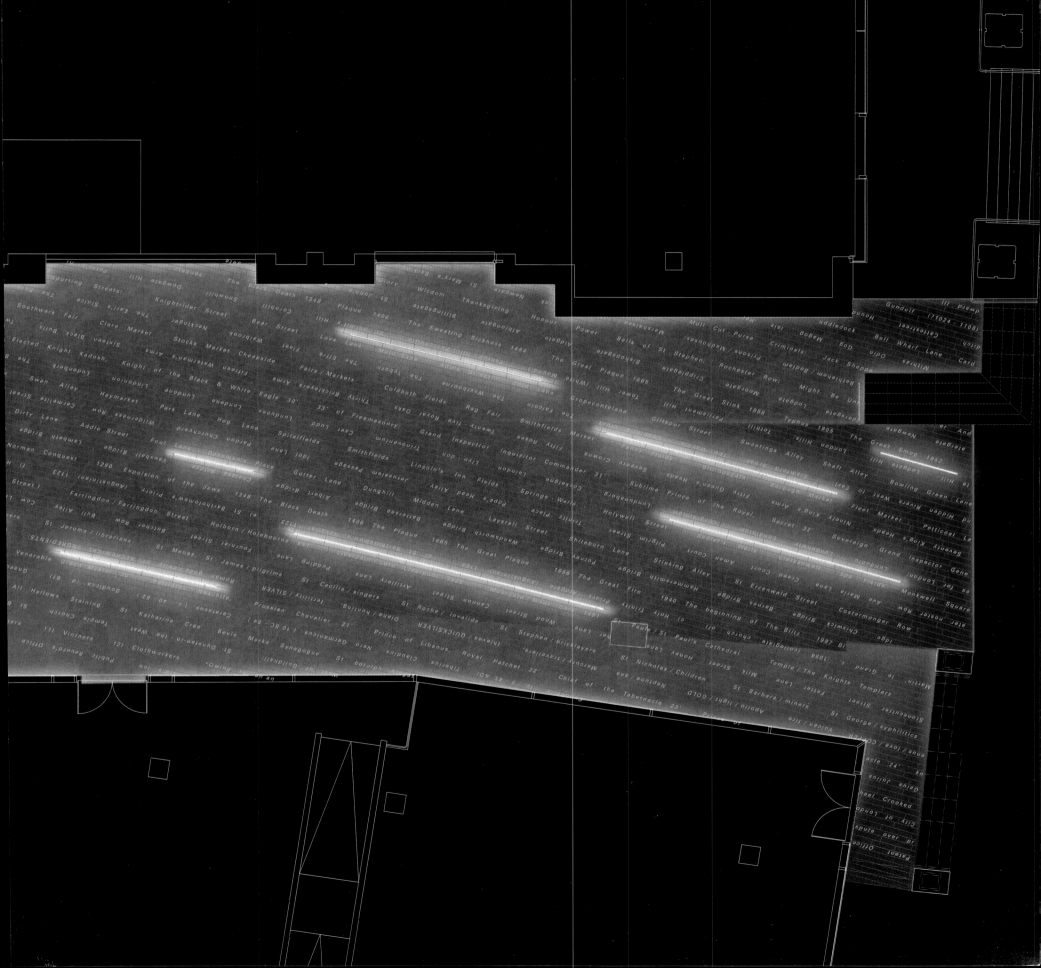

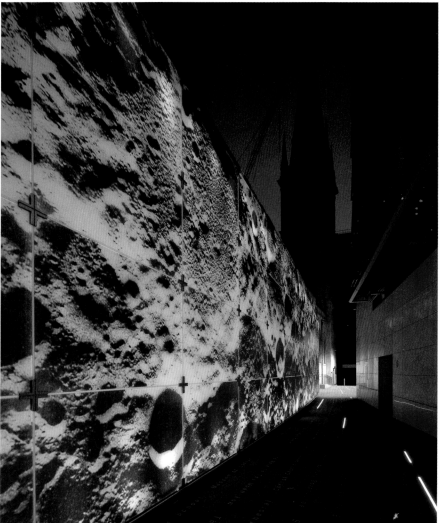

Above and following pages
Time lapse sequences

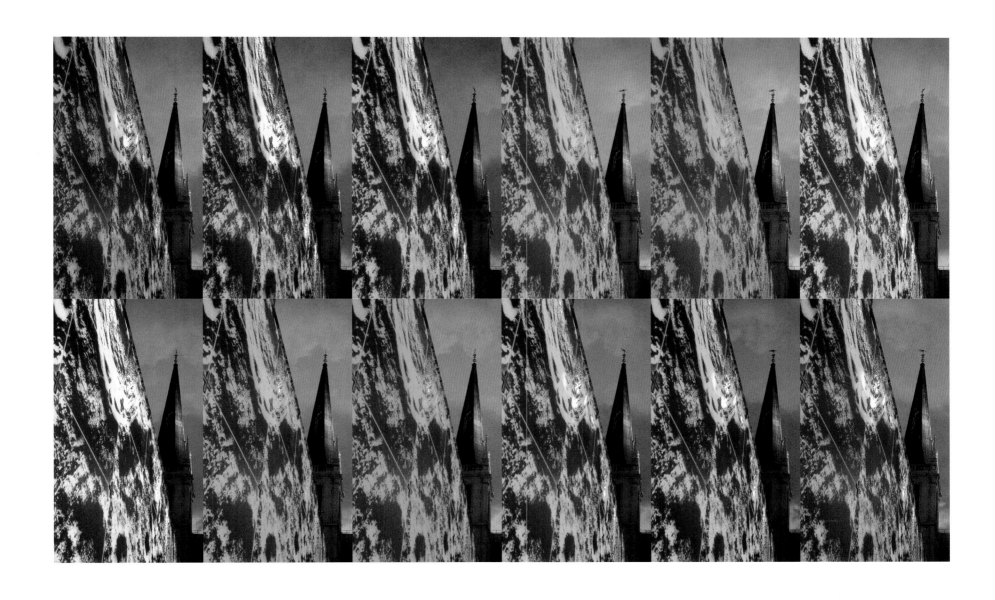

New Moon Waxing Crescent Moon First Quarter Moon Waxing Gibbous Moon Full

Moon Waning Gibbous Moon Last Quarter Moon Waning Crescent Moon New Moon

Biographies

British Land

British Land is one of the largest publicly quoted UK property investment companies. Its opportunistic but risk-averse strategy seeks to achieve long term growth in shareholder value by:

- focusing on prime assets in the office and retail sectors
- creating exceptional long-term investments with strong covenants, long lease profiles and growth potential
- enhancing property returns through active management and development; and
- maximising equity returns through optimal financing and joint ventures.

The company believes that the key to high returns is flexibility, both in terms of business organisation and financing, to take advantage of shifts in the property market.

Arup Associates

Arup Associates is a design studio focussed on the creative integration of architecture, structural engineering, environmental engineering, urban design and product design. Every new project expresses the multi-disciplinary philosophy that is at the heart of the practice. Their aim is pioneering, technologically advanced architecture that is appropriate, economic, and sensitive to environmental and human needs. They believe that design has the power to transform people's lives. They create buildings and places that benefit those who use them, and that demonstrate responsibility to others who are affected by their presence.

The Arup Associates studio forms a focus for holistic design in Arup. The work of the practice is both local and global and is commissioned by clients in the public and private sectors. Projects range across all scales, from urban masterplanning to the development of products and components. As evidenced by Plantation Lane, every project is an individual response to the opportunities presented by the client, the brief and the site.

'Total Architecture' implies that all relevant design decisions have been considered together and have been integrated into a whole by a well organised team. This is an ideal which is well worth striving for, for artistic wholeness depends on it.

Ove Arup

Simon Patterson

Simon Patterson (b. 1967) is one of the new generation of contemporary artists in Britain. He studied at Goldsmiths' in London, and took part in the seminal *Freeze* exhibition in 1988. In 1992 he made his best-known work to date, *The Great Bear*, a reworking of Harry Beck's classic London Underground map. In 1993 he showed a pair of Last Suppers at the Aperto of the Venice Biennale, in which the disciples took the formations of football teams, with Jesus Christ in goal. He was nominated for the *Turner Prize* in 1996.

He has made numerous temporary works and installations and has exhibited in major museums worldwide, including the Museum of Modern Art, New York; Kunsthaus, Zurich; Staatsgalerie, Stuttgart; the Hayward Gallery and Tate Modern, London.

Simon Patterson

Credit List

Client	**The British Land Company PLC**
Artist	**Simon Patterson**
Design	**Arup Associates**
Concept	Declan O'Carroll, Mick Brundle
Project Architect	Lee Hosking
Assistant Architect	Caroline King, Matthew Vaudin
Lighting Design	David Hymas
Structural Engineer	James Bown, John Roberts, Mike King
Project Manager	Paul Dickenson
Screen Visualisation	Will McLardy
Curator	**Andrea Schlieker**
Specialist Consultants	**Arup Facade Engineering**
	Tom Linder, Simon Webster, Roddy Wykes
	Arup Materials Consulting
	Graham Dodd
Artist's Visualisation	**Stephen Kirby**
Development Manager	**M3 Consulting**
	Richard Elliott, Nimitt Karia
Construction Manager	**Bovis Lend Lease**
	Tim Atkinson, Robert Dudley, Jim Uttley
Stone Flooring	**Gabriel Engineering**
	Peter Hyde
Stone Supplier	**Italmarble Pocai** (Pietra del Cardosa)
	Agostino Pocai
	Neumeyer and Brigl (Jura Limestone)
	Hans Neumeyer
Illuminated Screen & Glass Gates	**Josef Gartner**
	Rainer Hoffman, Maximillian Lausenmeyer, Stuart Miller
Printed Interlayer Processing	**Concepta Colourglass**
	Serge Benichou

Glass Supplier	**Eckelt** Klaus Langoth
Stainless Steel Gates	**Kimber Engineering** Geoff Kimber
Architectural Metalwork & Glass Balustrades	**Glazzard** Darren Rowley
Floor Lighting	**Zumtobel** Matt House
Illuminated Screen Lighting	**Lighting Technology Projects** Terry Reeves
Photography	**Christian Richters**
Book Production Design Illustrations Image Researcher	**Arup Associates** Tom Hardy, Nik Browning Sherman Ou, Benny Lee, Suzanne Li Helen Massy-Beresford

Typeset in Univers.

Distributed by:

RIBA Enterprises Ltd
15 Bonhill Street
London
EC2P 2EA

Telephone +44 (0) 20 7256 7222
Facsimile +44 (0) 20 7374 2737
Email sales@ribabooks.com

www.ribabookshops.com

Designed and Produced by:

Arup Associates
38 Fitzroy Square
London
W1T 6EY

Telephone +44 (0) 20 7755 5555
Facsimile +44 (0) 20 7755 2561
Email info@arupassociates.com

www.arupassociates.com

Published by:

Wordsearch
5 Old Street
London
EC1V 9HL

Telephone +44 (0) 20 7549 5400
Facsimile +44 (0) 20 7336 8660
Email studio@wordsearch.co.uk

www.wordsearch.co.uk

Acknowledgements

The Moon image is used with the kind permission of the artist and photographer Michael Light and is taken from his book *Full Moon.* NASA gave Michael Light unprecedented access to the 32,000 pictures from the Apollo missions and allowed him to take 900 of the 'master' negatives and transparencies offsite for electronic scanning, enabling him to produce the sharpest possible images.

Simon Patterson wishes to express his sincerest gratitude to Michael Light for the use of his image.

The editor and contributors also wish to thank Christian Richters for the use of his rich and evocative photographs.

ISBN 1-85946-173-5